Prologue

'Oh, George! She's going down! Save the boy! Take poor little Johnny!' Lady Violet stared agonized into her husband's wild eyes, as the deck tilted crazily, and a great shudder seized the doomed steamer. There was a splintering crash as the foremast toppled, and a final blast of escaping steam from the tall funnel, its jagged hole visible as it slipped towards the waterline. The rails on the port side of the *Venturer* were almost awash, though, strangely, the savage seas which had driven the ship on to the hidden reef were calmer now.

The rain was driving down as fiercely as ever. It reduced visibility to no more than a few yards, thus making it impossible for the wretched souls on board the stricken ship to see how close they were to the long curve of the shore. Lady Violet's black hair hung in long strands either side of her terrified face, was plastered to her shoulders and her breasts, whose outline showed clearly through the thin cambric of her nightgown. Even now, in the midst of this scene of such nightmare horror, Sir George acknowledged his recognition of her beauty.

1

She fell to her knees, began to slide on the wet planking towards the waiting sea, and he clawed desperately, caught hold of the lace hem of her gown, which split in a long tear before he could drag her into his arms. She was clinging on to their six-year-old son, who was paralysed with fear, his head buried in his mama's bosom. The deck reared once more under them, the bows plunging beneath the surface. The crew were leaping overboard, with regard for nothing but their own safety, and Sir George cursed bitterly at their cowardice. The suddenness with which disaster had struck had filled everyone with panic. One minute they had been uncomfortably dozing in the heaving cabin, the next scrambling up on deck with the roar of the sea on the reef, and the ship slewing round to her destruction.

Aware that the ship might founder at any second, Sir George tore at the tangled remains of a hatch cover, snatched at a length of rope and passed it swiftly round his wife's waist, binding her and the infant she was clutching to the wooden frame. There was a splintering sound, and the ship broke in two, the deck opening up fearsomely at his very feet. With one despairing effort, he flung the grating forward, and saw the pale form of his wife and son disappear in a welter of foam.

He had time only for one last cry, her name on his lips, as he fell into the darkness, and his death.

★   ★   ★

Violet felt the blessedly sweet coolness flowing down her throat. She gulped eagerly, some of the water spilling down her chin on to her chest.

'Thank you!' she whispered, startled at the weak croaking in her voice. The giddiness settled, vision came again, and she was aware of the fierce sunlight, its reviving warmth. And also of the solid comfort of the strong arm which was supporting her round the shoulders, holding her up from the ground. She leaned back with a delicious sense of security, yielding to its strength, and dizzily grateful at the realization that she was alive. Then came fresh panic. 'My boy! Johnny!'

'He's well enough. Don't you worry about him!'

She blinked up at the red, bearded face looming over her. She did not recognize it. Which one of the crew could it be? She thought she knew them all. At any other time she would have been alarmed, but now her slowly returning consciousness could only register the fact of their miraculous rescue;

that this rough diamond was her saviour, was ladling this divinely cold water into her, bringing her back to life. She stared up at the tangled growth of black hair, covering most of his visage, the bushy eyebrows, the broad grin as the eyes moved down from her face . . .

The man laughed, and plucked her up from the sand, carrying her easily in his arms. She hung there, too weak to struggle, or even to try to hide herself. She realized all at once that there were others, none of whom she could recognize as being from the *Venturer*, though all were dressed roughly, and looked like common seamen.

'Mama!' She heard Johnny's frightened cry, and turned wildly, her feet kicking helplessly. He was a few yards behind, still wearing his nightshirt, his dark hair standing up, his eyes huge with apprehension.

'It's all right, Johnny!' she called out desperately. 'We're quite safe now. Don't be afraid!' But the deep laugh which she felt rumbling in the barrel chest of the man who was holding her sent a chill of horror through her.

★   ★   ★

'My name is Lady Violet Able. My husband is . . . ' her voice quavered, she bit at her lip

4

to try to stem the threatening tears, 'Sir George Able. We were on our way to Zanzibar. He was on government business. We had letters of introduction to the Sultan. From Her Majesty's Government!'

Violet tried to muster the dignity she felt dissolving, like the pitiful shreds of the ruined nightgown she had managed to drape saronglike round her body, which covered her only from breast to mid-thigh. She could feel the darkly piercing stare of the figure sitting opposite her. She must not give way to the numbing fear she could feel ready to erupt. She cleared her throat, tried to bring back to her voice all the breeding and command her privileged position in society had given her throughout her young life.

'You will be well rewarded, sir, if you deliver my boy and myself safely into British hands. I promise you . . . '

'I will be strung up from the nearest gallows if I go anywhere near the British!' her captor said, with that thin smile of which she was already deeply afraid.

Again, the stifling sensation of being caught in some terrible dream overtook her. All her wealth, her lofty status, meant absolutely nothing here, in this savage land. These men were cut-throats, murderers! Pirates! The very word seemed so absurd, in these modern times, when Britain's power was spread all over the globe. This is 1885! she told herself disbelievingly. The queen had ruled for almost fifty years. Why, her husband's father, Lord Strenshaugh, was a relative of Lord Salisbury, who had just ousted that dreary Mr Gladstone as Prime Minister!

But this God-forsaken little patch of jungle on the East African coast was still existing in the dark ages, it seemed. Surely, though, even these ruffians would value money? She blushed again as she saw the leader's gaze directed so blatantly at her. Tears blurred her eyes, she could no longer hold them back, at the depth of her humiliation, and shame. She studied him covertly. What was he? she wondered. He was undoubtedly foreign, despite his excellent English. The brown skin, the dark, flashing eyes, the hooked nose. Hardly European, she thought. Perhaps Arabian? But then she had so little knowledge of foreign races. Her grief welled once more at the painful memory of the eagerness she had felt at George's posting, her joy on learning that she was to accompany him. And now, he was dead, and her own life, and that of Johnny, too, was in mortal danger. From this creature, who was staring at her so pitilessly, his eyes falling like so many hateful caresses on her tender flesh.

'All you have to do is to let us go free!' she pleaded desperately. 'Show us how we may find someone — anyone — who will help us. Please! There will be money! Much money! My family is wealthy! They . . . '

The pirate leader nodded thoughtfully. His crooked finger rubbed at his lips, which parted yet again in that sinister smile.

'Oh yes, there will be much money, I think.' He laughed, stood up and came towards her. The strength drained from her all at once and she whimpered softly as he scooped her up and carried her over to the narrow trestle-bed standing in the corner of the crudely furnished, filthy room. 'Even though you are not a virgin, there will be much money.'

★   ★   ★

Violet stared up dully at the woven grass of the roof, on which she could hear the rain drumming steadily. If she looked through the opening which served as a window, she would see the grey curtain of water, the shapes of the palm trees ghostly and dim on the other side of the compound. Yet, in a few hours, the rain would cease, and the sun would come out with all its tropic ferocity, to set the jungle steaming, and dry the puddles which lay on the bare earth of this crude township.

Leaden despair settled within her. Already, it seemed a lifetime since she had been captive here, the plaything of the strange, fierce character they called simply, 'Capitano'. She heard his step outside the veranda of the hut, then he came in. He was carrying a large platter, made from the tough banana fibre, on which was a heap of fruit and the flat loaf of bread they baked here. He also had yet another bottle of wine tucked under his elbow. He put the food and drink down on the table. His teeth flashed whitely as he grinned.

'You must keep your strength up.'

As he spoke, he drew the loose shirt up over his head and tossed it aside. It was the only garment he had been wearing. His lean, muscled body was thickly covered with the dark whorls of hair over much of its surface. He flung back the thin sheet and slumped down beside her on the creaking bed. 'Tomorrow we begin the journey.'

The hollowness of her despair fastened its empty coldness on her once more. He had told her it would be soon, but still the shock of it overwhelmed her. She could only pray that Mamma Lucy, the plump, big-breasted Swahili woman with whom Johnny spent almost his entire time now, would continue to be kind, and that the Capitano would keep his word that he would take care of the little boy.

The journey began in the damp greyness of dawn. When she discovered that she was not to be allowed to see her beloved boy again, not have one last chance to kiss him, to say her goodbye, she broke down completely, shrieking dementedly until a blow knocked her off her feet. In a trice, she was bound tightly by wrists and ankles and flung over someone's shoulder, her head hanging down and bouncing crazily a few feet from the rough ground as they set off.

It ended a day later, at a creek well hidden from all approaches save that to seaward. She was dumped unceremoniously on the planking of a makeshift jetty, to which was moored a neat sailing-barque. The Capitano himself carried her nimbly up the gangplank to the deck. At last she was released from the fibre ropes, which had cut deeply into her ankles and wrists. Though she had tried to prepare herself, she stared about her in growing, sick terror. The whole of the space forward of the main hatch was closely packed with glistening, black bodies, of both sexes. They were tethered in lines of six or seven, with planks of wood running along their shoulders, between which their heads emerged, secured to the wood by the stout noose of rope at their necks. This was the slave-ship, pursuing the wicked trade which still flourished in this part of the world, despite the British government's efforts these fifty years and more to suppress it, and the occasional Royal Navy gunboat to reinforce their zeal.

Her knees gave way, she sank on to the scoured deck. The Capitano's words seemed to echo, coming from a long way away as he bent and took hold of her hand, squeezing it tightly.

'Listen. You're a beauty. The prince will value you highly. So long as you please him. You'll have a good life, an easy life. There will be many girls, from all nations. Just remember — you're his. Obey. There can be no escape. You will not leave his palace.'

The cold certainty of his words was colder than the despair clutching at her heart. She reached up for the withdrawing hand. Her eyes were luminous in their appeal.

'Please — spare my Johnny,' she begged. 'See that he is safe. I implore you!'

1

'Look, Bwana Johnny! What you think? I look damn fine, yes? Like *mzungu* — white memsa'ab, yes?' Gukimi held the wide skirts of the gingham gown away from her, showing her feet in the shiny buckled shoes and her slim ankles in the white cotton stockings. She spun round, her teeth flashing in the light-brown face as she laughed merrily.

Johnny Able looked up at her from the depths of the cane chair. His handsome features, as dark as her own with their constant exposure to the African sun, creased in a frown.

'What do you want to look like a *mzungu* for? You're a hundred times better than any of those cold little white fillies! Come here and get those ridiculous rags off!'

She squealed as he reached out and pulled her forward on to his knee. She kicked out and struck at him playfully as his hands swept up the wide hem of the chequered cloth, to expose her limbs clear up to her thighs, which showed an enchanting coffee shade against the rolled white tops of the thin stockings.

'It new century now!' Gukimi protested,

11

struggling in his arms. 'Nineteen Hundred! This place changing. Miriamu said at Pemba everyone wear clothes like this one! Black *and* white folks!'

'Those poxy missionaries putting these stupid ideas in your heads!' Johnny grumbled. He knew he was only echoing the Capitano's words, but he was coming to feel as deeply as the old man about the changes which were taking place almost every day along this beautiful coastline where he had grown up. Gukimi's struggles had become considerably weaker since Johnny's fingers had strayed to the conflux of those shapely thighs, which lay bared to his caresses. He laughed aloud. 'I see you don't bother with the drawers and stays those white bitches wear!'

She squirmed now with a different movement, caused by the emotion his skilful hands were arousing.

'Miriamu no have them things. Miriamu say white memsa'abs no wear them in Zanzibar Town and Mombasa.'

'Faith, I believe you. Still, no red-blooded man would want such cold fish! Not like you Kamba girls, eh?' She stood eagerly astride him, while he undid the flap of his cotton breeches, then sank down, with a soft moan of pleasure. The wide skirts of the gown spread demurely over them as they rocked gently in the creaking chair.

Johnny sighed with contentment. It was true, there was nothing to beat a hot Kamba girl — and he'd sampled plenty, of all shades and persuasions, already in his young life. Twenty, or thereabouts, they reckoned he was. The Capitano was not too sure. 'You were about five or six when we saved you,' he told him.

Johnny had only vague memories of his life before he had been taken in by the Capitano and his men. He could remember the night of the shipwreck, their miraculous washing up on the beach, still tied to the piece of wreckage. His father had bound them to it, thus saving their lives, he guessed. Yet he could remember scarcely anything of him, only a distant, grand personage of whom he had seen very little.

It was different with his mother. He felt vaguely ashamed at the stirring emotion the memory of her beauty caused him, the softness of her body as she clasped him to her, in what must have been the last embrace they had shared. He remembered, too, the nights he had lain awake in this strange place, sobbing for her, yet comforted by the ample bosom of Mamma Lucy, on which he fell asleep, and in whose strong arms he awoke in the morning. She had watched over him as he grew through childhood and youth, comforted him again at the Capitano's brutal words to him.

'Your mama's a fool, Johnny! She's run off and left you here! She'll perish out there in the bush, that's for sure!'

Johnny had clung to the idea that she would one day come back for him. Until, at last, he had accepted the fact that she must have perished, like his papa. Despite her desertion of him, he could not retain his anger against her. He could remember only her beauty as she held him so tightly.

'Anyway, you got a new family now, Johnny!' the Capitano would roar. 'You a *bandido*! A pirate! You're one of us!'

And so he was. He had grown up quickly in this hard school, and learned to look after himself. And it was not such a bad life. Especially with wenches like Gukimi about him, and they had been about ever since he had been an ignorant and curious teenager.

There was no one better than a Kamba girl to teach you what life was all about, Johnny acknowledged happily, as he felt Gukimi's slim thighs move with new vigour as she began to ride him faster and faster. His fingers dug into the smoothness of her hips. She fell forward, pressing her mouth against his searching lips, and they shuddered and whimpered in their shared ecstasy.

⋆ ⋆ ⋆

The first shell falling on the compound came roaring out of the white swirls of dawn mist. Not from seaward, where they would have expected any attack to be mounted, but from the thick bush inland. Johnny was still asleep, with the naked Gukimi at his side. Even as he woke a second shell fell near at hand, and the mushrooming earth rattled down on the grass roof.

There was no real fight, no time even to assemble before the burning compound was full of the khaki-clad soldiers, their bayonets fixed, and jabbing at the slightest show of resistance. Only later did Johnny have time for bitter reflection at the total lack of preparedness for such a catastrophe, in spite of the talk that had gone on for months — nay, years, of just such an event. Ever since Zanzibar had been made a British protectorate, ten years ago, when he was just a boy of ten or eleven, the Capitano had been saying how things would be different, how it spelt doom for them as sea robbers and slavers.

That it hadn't come as soon as expected had made them complacent, made them think that perhaps Her Majesty's government was willing after all to turn a blind eye to these little dens of iniquity tucked away along the coast to the south — and to the dhows and other craft that slipped past up to the Gulf waters with their profitable human cargoes now and then.

Such speculation was of little use now that disaster had struck. They were in chains and aboard the naval sloop before noon. Their own boat had been seized and destroyed at her anchorage even before the troops had attacked the township. Johnny wondered if Gukimi had escaped. He hoped so. The last he'd seen of her had been her little brown hide running off through the smoke towards the native village further inland. Ah well! he thought philosophically, she's well equipped to make her way in life. He would miss her — they had practically grown up together, but now he had more serious things to worry about . . .

As they discovered two days later, when they appeared before the British political agent in Zanzibar. The 'trial' lasted less than a day, the sentence pronounced in minutes.

'For the act of piracy on the high seas, and for the abominable trading of human flesh, to be hanged by the neck until dead.'

'It's all finished anyway, this place,' the grizzled Capitano said that evening, as they lay manacled in the foul-smelling damp of the dungeons beneath the fort. 'Bibles and flags and bloody soldiers everywhere! They've even built the railway to the north of here.'

Later, as they tried to sleep, or pray, he squirmed closer to Johnny, bent his head close.

'Listen, boy. I think I can save you. Those bastards up there today didn't even notice you were white. But I know about your ma and pa — and their kinfolk. I'm going to try to get a word to the governor.' His hand shot out, the chains clinking as he held Johnny's wrist in a grip as fierce as the encircling steel. 'If it works, boy, remember the old Capitano, eh? I've looked after you like a father. You wouldn't have been alive today if it hadn't been for me.'

Next morning, the pirate leader shouted for the guard, and made such a fuss that they dragged him out, with a good many cuffs and blows to assist him. He was away for hours, and when he returned, they called for Johnny to come out into the dimly lit corridor. He had time only to intercept the older man's eloquent glance before he was hustled away, to the long flight of worn stone steps, and the blessed freedom of the spice-laden tropical air.

★ ★ ★

The valet drew back the curtains to let in the blaze of the sun, and opened the double doors that led out to the balcony. He poured the tepid water into the bowl on the washstand, then moved closer to the bed and coughed deferentially. At least the young gentleman lying sprawled as naked as God had made him was sleeping in the bed now, or at least on it, instead of on the woven rug spread on the wooden floor, which was where he had slept for many nights when he had first been brought stinking from the dungeons to be a guest in the residency. He coughed again, a little louder, and was rewarded with a groan. The lean figure turned over.

'Wake up, Mr Able, sir. You're required to see Sir Joseph this morning. I think the last of the papers have come through. They're saying below stairs your passage is booked on the *Afric Star*. You'll be home before the spring's out, sir!'

Surfacing through a wine-induced, throbbing headache, Johnny lay back once more, let his muscles relax into the feathers' softness, the softness he had not been able to bear when he had first been brought here, nearly two months ago now. Day after day, he had waited with growing impatience for the long-winded procedure of verifying his true parentage and his antecedents. And long-winded it had been, in spite of all these modern marvels of technology he had belatedly been learning about since he had been so suddenly thrust into the civilized society he had not known since he was an infant, and of which he had practically no memory.

In spite of his eagerness to have his own affairs settled, he had striven hard on behalf of his condemned comrades, with singular lack of success so far, he had to admit, for the majority of the buccaneers had paid for their crimes with their lives already. He felt guilty now, as he painfully went through the motions of washing and dressing, trying not to mind the attentions of the manservant. He had become acquainted with a group of young naval officers from the sloops on the station, one of which had carried out the attack which had led to the capture of the Capitano's jungle stronghold, and the past two days and nights had been a blur of carousing and wenching. The poor old pirate, languishing in that stinking dungeon with his few remaining men, must think that Johnny had deserted him, for he had not been near him for three days now. Whatever the urgency of his own business affairs, Johnny was determined that first he would go to the fort and speak to the Capitano, to reassure him that somehow he would in turn save the life of the old rogue who had saved his.

He was kept waiting until he was ready to give full vent to his rage. The guards refused to let him enter the noisome prison area, and he paced the corridor outside the commander's office for what felt like hours, before he was eventually admitted to the inner sanctum. A British army captain, whom Johnny had already met at the residency, stood at the swarthy-skinned commander's elbow.

'I'm afraid there's been a rather drastic turn of events, old boy,' the Britisher said, in his suave accent. He paused, gave a little shrug of his shoulders. 'I'm afraid things have moved rather suddenly. Your former associate had fresh charges brought against him. Including kidnap and murder. The sentence was carried out at dawn.'

The commander screamed out, and it took the combined efforts of several of the guards who rushed in to drag Johnny from the British captain, who was sprawling bloody and half-stunned on the rich rug in front of the desk.

'You filthy lying bastards!' Johnny sobbed, pinned down by the soldiers' arms in the high-backed carved chair into which they forced him. 'He saved me, you lying, deceitful swine!'

'Investigations have been made — perhaps your father, certainly your mother, was kidnapped by him and his men — we have evidence that your mother, Lady Violet Able, was taken out into the bush and . . . ' the captain paused, breathing heavily and massaging the red imprints of Johnny's hands at his throat, 'and almost certainly sold into slavery. She was most probably taken into Arabia. We have no way of tracing her — not that she would have survived very long under such conditions, a lady of her background, and sensibilities.'

When Johnny was sufficiently calmed to be released, and when he had left without another word, the captain gazed after him, still rubbing at his bruised neck.

'Young savage!' he muttered. 'God help his poor family. How on earth will they manage to rehabilitate a young outlaw like that into decent society again?'

2

'It's such wonderful news, isn't it, miss?' Kate Addy said. She pushed her white cuffs a little higher up her arms as she knelt by the high, claw-footed bathtub. She picked up the sponge and rubbed gently at the slim shoulders and back. 'Up you get, miss! I expect you're ever so excited. We all are!' As always, Kate experienced that little stab of envy at the sight of Miss Rose's beauty so fully revealed, to be swiftly followed by her shame at her secret jealousy, for Miss Rose was as generous in spirit as she was beautiful in her looks.

She half-turned now, her hand reaching out to Kate's black-gowned shoulder for support. The pressure of the hand increased slightly as Rose Martingale stepped from the tub, and Kate wrapped her in the huge, fluffy white towel. Standing behind her, she patted her dry, her nostrils filled with the fragrant scent from the lovely body whose contours she was tracing beneath the towel. She let the towel fall once more, while Rose stood obediently still as Kate dusted her lightly with the talcum powder. She then held the silk wrap while Rose slipped her arms into its wide sleeves, then tied the sash loosely at her waist.

As she sat at her dressing-table, while Kate stood and brushed out the thick strands of her long dark hair, Rose gazed out over the rich acres of parkland surrounding the eighteenth-century mansion of Strenshaugh Hall, and reflected on the amazing news that had transformed the whole household, and, in particular, her grandfather, Lord Strenshaugh. The discovery that his grandson, John, was alive, that he had not perished at sea off the African coast all those years ago, had brought new life to the stern old man, of whom she had always been in awe.

When he first learnt of his son's drowning, he had become almost reclusive, and that this should be followed nine years later by the death of his only other child, Arabella, in childbirth, when Rose was only thirteen, had been almost too much to bear. Rose herself was lost and tragic. She hated and feared her father — her mother had had several miscarriages, had never carried another child to full term after Rose's birth. Then, one night, Rose had heard her mother's muffled weeping, her father's voice, thick with drink, angry, demanding, behind the closed doors of her mother's room. Later came news of the pregnancy which was to kill her mama.

Apathetic in her misery, Rose had accepted the fact that she was to come and live at Strenshaugh Hall with something of relief. After all, she had no choice, and she did not want to continue living with her father. Apparently, the feeling was mutual. She had seen very little of him in the intervening years: nothing in the last three, since his remarriage.

It had been a lonely if privileged existence for an adolescent girl, for Lord Strenshaugh kept largely to himself, and left her upbringing to the staff, among whom was a number of governesses, who were a poor substitute for the mother and sisters she had longed for. It was hardly strange then that dear Kate here was as close to her as anyone. She glanced up, caught the maid's eye in the mirror, and, smiling fondly, reached up to pat the hand which was resting lightly on her shoulder as the other wielded the hairbrush. She saw the fiery-red hair lower, crested by the tiny white cap, an enchanting blush sweep up the pretty face, highlighting the freckles just beneath the surface, and Rose's smile broadened.

Kate was certainly right. An air of excitement ran through the whole place, for today her cousin John was expected home at long last from distant Africa, and her heart quickened at the thought. She stood impatiently through the tedious procedure of dressing — the light-silk summer vest under all, then the pretty camisole, with its Valenciennes lace and threaded ribbon, the white silk stockings — she slipped a finger under the elastic to ease the pressure of the garters on her thighs after Kate had knelt and carefully rolled them up her calf — then the knee-length drawers, also of spun silk, with the wide lace frills. She braced herself, clinging to the bedpost while Kate laced her into the whalebone stays, tugging until Rose made her laughing protest.

'Hold hard! You're strangling me!'

'You want him to see what a figure you've got, miss!' Kate said archly, and Rose blushed, slapping at her wrist. Last of all she stepped into the pale-ivory day-gown and stood while Kate fastened it. 'There!' The maid stood back, with a critical eye.

'Will I do?' Rose pirouetted charmingly before her, holding out her gown to one side, like a little girl.

'You look lovely, miss!'

The simple force of the declaration was not lost on Rose. Impulsively, she reached out, caught hold of Kate's hands and squeezed them.

'Thank you!' she said.

Kate leaned forward suddenly, and planted a swift kiss on Rose's cheek.

'For luck, miss!' she murmured, her own face flaming up again to match her red hair, and she turned and fled.

★   ★   ★

'And this, my boy, is your cousin, Rose. Your Aunt Arabella's gal. I don't suppose you remember any of us, eh?'

Rose had never seen the lined visage of her grandfather so animated. Then she forgot everything, as those dark, compelling eyes blazed into hers, and took her breath, and all awareness of her surroundings, every thought, away from her. His handsome face was as dark as any farm labourer's, the black hair cropped close to his head. But she scarcely registered these impressions in those first stunning seconds.

When her mind was at last able to struggle with an analysis of her emotions, she still could hardly define the force which had overpowered her. She had a sensation of being trapped, pinned down, by that blazing passion she read there. The colour flooded up from her throat in a hot tide. It was as though, shockingly, he could see right through the layers of her pretty clothing, to the pitiful nakedness beneath. Indeed, her hand made an involuntary jerking movement towards her bosom, as though she would hide the swell of her breasts under the silk and lace which covered them. And there was a responsive impulse from within, deeper, deep down, in the very core of her, a shivery impulse too shocking for her even to contemplate.

'Well, come on, my boy! Don't be shy! Give your cousin a kiss, there's a good fellow!'

Striving to overcome her faintness, and lowering her gaze at last from those magnetic eyes, Rose forced herself to take a step forward, and proffer her hot cheek for a chaste embrace. She was even more astonished when she felt her upper arms seized quite strongly, and her body turned fully to face the lean figure. A hand went round her narrow waist, pulling her in against his smartly dressed form most improperly, and the dark face swooped, to plant a warm and smacking kiss full on her lips, which were still slightly parted in amazement.

'By God! There's a sight for sore eyes and no mistake! A beautiful wench to welcome me! I wish I'd come home sooner! Hello, cousin!'

There was a repressed but audible gasp from the long line of assembled domestics behind her, and Lord Strenshaugh har-rumphed loudly, to cover the excruciating embarrassment. As for Rose, she was struck dumb, her head spinning, her lovely mouth still agape. No man had kissed her full on the lips since she was a little girl. And certainly no handsome stranger, only two years older than herself!

There were to be many such embarrass-ments, though not perhaps as extreme for Rose herself, during the long first day of Johnny's return. His manners and speech were so rough that she could feel her grandfather wince every time his grandson opened his mouth. 'Like the commonest of seamen!' his lordship confided to her, when, after a lengthy lunch during which the young man had imbibed a prodigious amount of wine, he had retired to his room to 'sleep off the effects of the journey'.

'And that's just what he has been!' Lord Strenshaugh mused, in extenuation of Johnny's unconventional behaviour. 'After all, he was condemned to death for piracy. It was only that rogue of a leader speaking out that saved him, otherwise he might have ended his days on the gallows!'

Johnny had already told them, in language which had made Rose blush yet again, and for which he tardily apologized when admonished by his lordship, of his rage and sorrow at failing after all to secure the Capitano's life.

'Those poxy British bastards strung him up while I was still interceding for him!'

'He kidnapped you,' his grandfather answered gravely. 'He brought you up to a life of infamy. He was most certainly responsible for the death of your poor mother.'

Johnny nodded, frowned deeply, and reached for his wine-glass again.

'He wasn't such a bad old f — rogue! To me!'

In truth, he had struggled long and hard with the conflicting tumult of his emotions, both on the island, then on the long, idle days and nights of the voyage home. He had eventually been given copies of the documented evidence, the statements of some of his fellow pirates, and native servants and those around the illicit township, and they indicated that, far from her running off and deserting him, his mother had been taken forcibly and sold to some Arab slaver, to disappear for ever into the seraglio of some prince, or desert sheikh. All subsequent trace of her had vanished, and certainly there was never a hope of discovering her whereabouts now. Most people assumed, most probably rightly, that she was dead. In a way, Johnny hoped that this was true. The thought of all that soft and tender beauty, broken and doubtless long gone, walled-up still in the living tomb of some remote harem, was too painful to dwell upon, and he strove not to.

That evening, when Johnny, reanimated, his face aflush with more drink and excitement, held forth among the blue swirling clouds of cigar-smoke from her grandfather and the other noisy male guests, Rose took the chance, when the ladies had been excused and the port had been brought out, to slip away. She deduced that the menfolk would hardly notice her absence.

Upstairs, Kate was waiting to undress her.

'He's a very striking young man, isn't he, miss?' the red-haired maid said carefully, easing the silk gown off Rose's shoulders, and down, so that her mistress could step out of the pool of rippling material.

'Oh, Kate!' Rose cried. 'I'm afraid he just doesn't know the way a gentleman should behave. We must help him all we can. He has suffered so much, had such a terribly hard life out there.'

She stood while Kate slipped down the stiff petticoat, then struggled with the tight laces of her stays. Rose sighed with relief, gently massaging her ribs and the underside of her breasts when the narrow, rigid band was removed. The maid's practised fingers were untying the strings of the spun silk drawers when all at once the bedroom door swung open, and there stood her cousin, his face split into a knowing grin and in his hands a bottle of wine and two fluted glasses.

Rose gave a muffled little scream and put her hand to her throat as he advanced on tiptoe across the room, and gave a lewd wink at the dumbfounded girls.

'Kate, isn't it? It's all right, my dear. I'll take over your duties from here on. Time I got to know my pretty coz a damned sight better!'

3

Kate reached out and tenderly brushed a stray lock of hair from the lovely face nestled on the pillow. Once again, she remembered how proud she had felt; how, as a mere slip of a girl just past her sixteenth birthday, she had been giddy with success at her promotion to upstairsmaid. Her brother Michael might sneer at her 'running around wiping the backsides of the gentry', as he, with his typical crudity, had put it, but going into service had meant a great opportunity for her — and a vast improvement on sleeping three to a bed in a tumbledown cottage with no indoor plumbing, and a pit dug into the garden for sanitation.

And she'd done pretty well for herself, too, thank you! Personal maid to Miss Rose herself at twenty years of age wasn't bad for any girl. A smile formed, in spite of herself, at the final chapter in what had proved to be such an eventful day. She blushed a little, too, for sympathy with her distraught young mistress, but really no lasting harm had been done. Even if Master John *had* caught more than a passing glimpse of Miss Rose in naught but her cami and drawers!

The poor girl had shrieked so loud and dived on to the bed, trying to grab the counterpane and hide herself in it, while Kate had struggled with the drunken figure, and actually managed to steer him back through the door. Only her quick thinking had diverted a bigger scandal, for Norman Gooding, one of the footmen, had arrived, his eyes big as saucers as he stared over their shoulders at the weeping figure stretched out on the bed.

'Master John has lost his way, that's all!' Kate declared firmly, giving the grinning Johnny a surreptitious shove towards the servant. 'There you go, sir. Gooding'll see you to your room, eh? You'll soon get used to the place. 'Night, sir! Sleep well!'

It had taken a considerable while to calm her mistress down enough to get her out of her underthings and into her nightgown.

'We'll not bother with your hair tonight, miss!' Kate said, swiftly pinning up the raven locks and fitting them under the lacy nightcap. It would take some brushing out in the morning, but that would be another day. She had held the weeping girl to her breast, soothing her before drawing back the sheets and easing her into the wide bed. 'Tell you what, miss. I'll lock your door, shall I, when I go, just to be on the safe side?'

Those great brown eyes had fixed on her so tragically that Kate had wanted to smother her in kisses.

'Oh, Kate! What shall I do?'

Kate had knelt by the side of the bed, holding the delicate hands in her own.

'Well, he was mortal drunk, miss, wasn't he? Everything's so new for him. Like another world. He won't remember a thing about it in the morning, I'm sure.' She had seen the immediate relief which had sparked across the young features. 'No one'll know anything of it, miss. Best not to refer to it again.'

'If you say so, Kate. But — but . . . ' the lace-frilled cap shook in inadequacy, and Kate again felt that flow of tender compassion, while she watched her mistress gradually relax towards slumber.

These poor society girls! Rich, pampered, yet totally ignorant as to what life was really about. Then paraded like cattle to be auctioned off to the highest bidder. She recalled the previous season, Miss Rose's 'coming out', and the hectic round of balls and supper parties, where countless streams of young eligibles pawed her waist on the dancefloor, and held her gloved hand in their sweaty palms. While Kate dozed in the cramped little cubicle of a dressing-room in the town apartment, and woke at dawn, to bathe Miss Rose's poor little red and aching feet.

Not even more than a snatched peck or two on the cheek in the gloom of a conservatory — at least, certainly not in Miss Rose's case, she was sure of that — then the next thing arrangements were made, and the poor, sweet, ignorant things were climbing into the marriage-bed in their pretty lace nightgowns with not the least idea of what lay in store for them between those perfumed sheets.

Her own dear Rose was on the brink of such an undertaking, though nothing official had been announced yet. The Honourable Edward Lovatt, Esq., of the wealthy shipping family, had been an increasingly frequent visitor to Strenshaugh Hall, along with that obnoxious bag of a mother, ever since last summer, and everyone below stairs was certain an engagement would be forthcoming very soon. New money to ally with the old nobility — a perfect match, Mr Reece, the butler, told them.

Poor Rose! Kate reached out, for a last feather-light caress of the cheek before she moved silently towards the door. They were close — much closer than she had ever thought a mistress and her maid could be. It had stemmed from those early days when Kate had proved instrumental in helping the shy young girl through what was becoming a very real and painful crisis for her — her emergence into the society of fashionable London, after the years of conventlike seclusion at Strenshaugh Hall.

Even now, the thinness of that patina of sophistication her young charge had acquired was amply demonstrated by her drastic reaction to her cousin's uncouth, blundering entrance into her bedroom. An embarrassing enough *faux pas*, Kate readily acknowledged, but one which, in retrospect, still made the corners of Kate's mouth twitch in an involuntary smile. The handsome young devil! He was going to prove something of a handful, and no mistake. But what a gale of blustering freshness after the effete and mannered posturings of Mr Edward Lovatt and his ilk, not to mention that calculating old biddy of a mother of his!

★　★　★

'God's teeth! You're as stiff as those damned whalebone corsets you wear!' Johnny's face darkened with angry frustration. He turned away abruptly at Rose's smothered cry of distress. She had risen, moving to distance

36

herself from him, across the uneven flag-stones of the rose arbour. Her face was flushed, she could still feel the sensation of his warm breath, his lips almost alighting on the bareness of her neck, his hard fingers digging into her shoulders before she twisted to escape.

'Please, John! Will you not try — '

'Johnny, for God's sake! I've told you! My name's Johnny.'

'Very well then! Johnny, if you insist.' Her voice was still unsteady, but she made a great effort to control it. 'Will you please — please try to — to — treat me properly? As a gentleman should. You've been here more than a week now — '

'And I've told you, you're a damned fine-looking girl, Rose! We're cousins, damn it! I've a right — '

'You've no right to — to paw me like a — common — a common . . . ' she could not say the word which sprang to mind, and she ended in an inarticulate mew of indignation. Again, she fought to overcome her sense of shock and outrage, and her brown eyes filled with tears as she studied the brooding figure who had stood also now, and had his back to her as he stared across the stretch of parkland, which was beginning to have a slightly parched look in the steady heat of high summer. Another week or two, and harvesting would begin on the farms of the vast estate.

'I know we're cousins,' she resumed, her voice soft with reason and compassion. 'I want us to be close. As close as brother and sister. I've never had anyone, since mama died . . . ' Already, she noted that impatient jerk of the close-cropped head once more. She struggled on. 'We all of us want to help you to settle back into your life here. Grandfather, everyone. I know it can't be easy — '

'Easy?' His voice rang with mocking laughter. 'Jesus!' She winced at his crude blasphemy, and he laughed again as he noted her reaction. 'It's like you're all dead from the waist down! Don't you feel — '

But she was already squealing in horror at the shocking depravity of his words, the colour flooding her face and neck in a rich crimson tide.

'Oh, I can't talk to you at all when you — you insist on being so — so — lewd! Excuse me — please!' She fought against the threatening spill of tears. She nodded swiftly and picked up the frothy sweep of her wide organdie skirts, from which her white-stockinged ankles peeped above the light summer slippers. She almost ran from the terrace.

Johnny resumed his contemplation of the shimmering landscape. He compared the rolling, rich greenery, the ordered shape of the dark woods ahead, the distant, hedged neatness of the estate's farm fields, with the fierce wildness of the African bush, the burn of the tropical sun. And now he contrasted his cousin's slim, innocent, unattainable sweetness with the fiery beauty of Gukimi's lovely brown flesh, bared so readily for his pleasure. His heart ached with sharp regret, even as his manhood throbbed against the tight restraints of his clothing.

'Oh! I'm sorry, sir! I thought Miss Rose was here.'

He turned, as startled as Kate was. He watched with amusement the colour mount up the pretty face, to match the red curls he could see perched under the white lace of her cap. He smiled ironically.

'She was, until a minute ago. She left in rather a hurry. Seems I put my clodhopping foot in it again! No! Don't go, please!' he added quickly, as Kate was already turning to leave. 'Surely somebody in this miserable place can talk to me for more than a minute without being offended by my oafishness?'

'Why, yes, sir,' she murmured, with her

practised little bob of obeisance. She kept her eyes down, the pink still evident on her cheeks.

'You don't find me all that offensive, do you, Kate? Or are you maids all as prim and prissy as your starchy mistresses?'

The grey eyes lifted at once, challengingly, though her colour heightened.

'Miss Rose is a young lady, sir! She's not used to . . . ' her voice tailed away.

'To such ungentlemanly behaviour, eh?' he finished for her, with a bitter little laugh. 'Well, you're quite right, of course. I'm not a gentleman, and never likely to be one!'

'You'll be Lord Strenshaugh one day, sir,' she said quietly, gazing directly at him, and he saw something of the warmth and sympathy she felt for him in his new existence. He recalled how discreet she had been about his drunken blunder that first night, and how, he was sure, it was she who had persuaded Rose to say nothing about it, or even to refer to it again.

'Ye Gods!' he answered feelingly now. 'Don't remind me of it! I don't think I'll fit into their stiff-necked aristocratic ways here!'

'You will, sir. Of course you will! Just give it time!' She stepped forward involuntarily, her voice ringing with conviction, then she blushed once again as she realized the strength of feeling she had betrayed.

He had picked up on it, too, and he stepped even closer. He reached out and took her right hand, held onto it as she tried feebly to withdraw it.

'There's an honest hand. A hand that does real work, and doesn't have someone to fetch and carry for it all day! You know, Kate, you're the only ray of sunshine in this god-forsaken place, I swear it! You've got the prettiest smile . . . ' he raised her hand to his lips as he spoke, and kissed it gently.

She snatched it away quickly, with a gasp.

'Don't, sir! Please! I'm only a serving-girl. I — '

'You're worth ten of the whole poxy crew!' His eyes blazed out at her, she felt the overwhelming male strength of him, and her own giddy weakness, the imprint of his lips burning like a brand on the back of her hand.

She found it hard to summon enough breath to speak.

'You mustn't talk like that, sir. I'm a good girl — '

'I know you are! And I can see you've got some life about you, some red-blooded feeling in your veins, not the miserable ice-water that these prim and proper little virgins carry — '

'*I'm* a virgin!' she squealed indignantly,

then flamed again at the import of her words, and at the broad mischief of his grin, which she was almost tempted to share as she realized how ridiculous her reply sounded. How beautiful his mouth was, curved in that smile. She felt her breasts heaving, her eyes misted with sudden tears, her own lips pouting. 'Like I said, sir, I'm a good girl.'

She thought of Ben Hindwell, the grooms-man, his hot hands clutching at her leg under her skirts, moving up her thigh, until she fought and twisted away, thrusting him from her, escaping from that searching mouth at her neck.

And afterwards, the hot tears and shame at his wicked behaviour. And her innocent fear that she would lose her newly won place at Strenshaugh because she had not let him have his way with her, until an older girl, more worldly-wise, had shown her how to tease and appease the menfolk, holding out promise, allowing them some liberties which would not land her in the ultimate and all too common trouble which so frequently befell girls in her position.

But this was different. This riot of sensation Mr Johnny's dark gaze caused inside her, the blaze of passion, frightened her. She felt helpless under the compelling intensity of his scrutiny. 'I have to go,' she whispered beseechingly. He moved close, and she was utterly helpless to move away, her body quivering. His left hand circled her slim waist, the crooked forefinger of his right hand lifted her chin, as he stooped and kissed her, softly but fully, on her lips.

★ ★ ★

'Why, Master Johnny!' Kate felt the hot colour mounting. Somehow, she realized she was not really surprised, even though she had jumped with shock at the sudden appearance of the light, hooded cart. She squinted up at his dark silhouette against the morning sun, then he had leapt lightly down to the grass beside her and was taking her arm.

'Come on! Up you get! I'll give you a lift. I know you're going to Coultsby. It'll save you a long walk and maybe a long wait for a wagon.'

Helpless to refuse, she allowed him to steady her around the waist, to hold her hand firmly as she lifted her skirt to place her foot in the iron step and hoist herself into the curve of the narrow leather bench seat of the cabriolet. Then he was up beside her, his hand descended, again shockingly, but with firm, unambiguous friendliness, on her knee, before he picked up the reins and flicked the whip lightly over the twitching flanks of the horse to set it moving again. The sprung cart swayed over the grassy track, and their shoulders rubbed intimately.

'You shouldn't, sir. It's not right.'

He chuckled, letting his body bump against hers.

'You know me, Kate! I never do the right thing, do I? I knew this was your day off. And I knew you'd be going to Coultsby. So I took Jubilee and put her between the shafts. She'll love our little jaunt, won't you, girl?' He reached forward, tickled the horse's ears with the end of the whip.

'You can't go on like this, sir!' Kate protested. 'If anyone should see us — there'll be a scandal! You can't be talking to the likes of me, sir. Like I said, it's not right.'

'It's right for *me*, Kate!' He spoke so fiercely her protest died on her lips. 'I don't give a fig for their snooty ways! For two pins I'd leave 'em all tomorrow and head back for the Afric coast! Christ, Kate, there's red-blooded maids there, aye, and men, too, for all their savage ways!'

Kate's head swam. His words were too wildly beyond anything in her experience for her even to be shocked as she listened to his vivid talk of his former life out in the African wilderness. She had no idea how much later it

44

was when she glanced round and saw that they were far from the track, deep in the quiet woodland surrounding the estate, and that Jubilee had been pulled up beside a crude wooden hut, one of those which the gamekeepers used for storing equipment, and for rearing young pheasant chicks for the season.

'Oh, please! No, Master Johnny!' she whispered pleadingly, yet making no effort to resist him as he reached up and took her by the waist. He lifted her down bodily, held her for a moment pressed against him, her toes touching the leafy ground, her hands resting on his shoulders. She felt the lean, hard length of him against her, felt her helpless excitement, trapped by those darkly blazing eyes, watched his mouth come slowly, possessively, down to claim hers, and hold it in a timeless, thrilling kiss until the earth spun itself crazily all about her.

4

Johnny was lying back on the rug, his hands cradled behind his head, but now he stretched out his left hand and very gently let his fingers trace feather-lightly over the curved ridges of Kate's spine as she sat hunched forward, her knees drawn up, her arms crossing with instinctive modesty to shield her bare breasts from the strange caress of the warm sunlight. She shivered, felt again the faint stirring pulse of her excitement. The power of his touch on her renewed that sense of helplessness she felt each time she was intimately alone with him like this.

Just as she had that first day — so long ago it seemed now, though it was still only a matter of days distant — in the quiet of the gamekeeper's hut, when she had first surrendered to him on the pile of musty sacking he had tossed on the dusty floor. She had shed tears, pleaded with him, but without true conviction, as she admitted to herself later. She had no real will to fight the desire firing through her limbs, no real resistance to his determined advances, even though she had lain on the sacking, stiff with fright.

Until, all at once, his kisses, the sure but gentle touch of his hands on her trembling body, sent that wonderful lassitude of passion stealing over every nerve. Even when he had progressed far beyond what was proper, had unlaced her boots and eased them off, unbuttoned her serge skirt and drawn it off her bunched legs, then her calico petticoat to follow it. His gentleness, the tender warmth of his kisses, that compelling gaze, held her completely in thrall.

He pulled down the garters, rolled her black worsted stockings from her feet, eased off the last plain undergarment, and still, in spite of the tears, all she knew was that she wanted him to go on, to do what no one had ever done to her before. Then all was gone but flowing physical sensation at the magical caresses of his lips, his hands, playing on every part of her melting, blazing flesh until her body arched up in desperate hunger, in search of the final possession she had never known. When at last it came, the pain and pleasure were fused inescapably, and she shook with transformed joy even as she sacrificed herself to his burning manhood.

He knew her body intimately now, traced with sure propriety every plane and curve of her supple figure. She was so far gone already in her infatuation that the two of them lay coiled like Adam and Eve in this Eden he had created, up among the chimney-pots, hidden behind the mock battlements of Strenshaugh Hall's rooftops. The unaccustomed feel of the sunlight on her bare skin was almost as erotically stirring as the touch of his hands and mouth. She shivered once more, and searched for the scattered items of her underclothing.

'Please, Master Johnny! I'll have to go! Miss Rose'll be back from the village by teatime. And she might want me early. Specially with Mr Lovatt arriving tomorrow.'

'What's he like, then, Master Ned Lovatt? They reckon down in the *Fox* that he's really keen on her. That there's matchmaking afoot between the two of them. Don't tell me she really fancies the fellow! Surely our milksop Rosie doesn't harbour any real passion beneath that modest little bosom of hers? Or anywhere else where no man's hands or eyes have strayed these past nineteen years!' As he spoke he slid his hand suggestively around Kate's smooth flank, and she gasped and grabbed at his wrist.

'Stoppit, sir! I don't know about that. But I reckon she's all set to do whatever his lordship wants of her. If he wants her to wed, she'll do it. Unless . . . ' As so often these past few days, whenever she thought of her mistress, Kate's mind was beset by a whirl of conflicting emotions. Tormented by a genuine and painful guilt, she had listened to Rose's private musings over her new-found cousin, knew that, in spite of his ability to shock her constantly with his outrageous conduct and manner, Rose found him far more fascinating than she was prepared to admit, even to herself. And she had seen that hungry look in Master Johnny's eyes, too, despite his mocking denigration of her narrow morality. It was even more painful then for Kate to reflect on what she had allowed to happen between Master Johnny and herself, and it disturbed her even more to discover how painfully jealous such ideas could make her, how distressing was the thought that he had claimed the maid as conquest because he could not have the mistress.

'Unless what?' he pursued, picking up on her hesitation.

It hurt her, but she went on compulsively, 'The talk below stairs is that it's you and Miss Rose who'll be matched together. That that's what his lordship really wants!'

He sat up abruptly, pulled her round to face him. His eyes narrowed. He stared at her with that mocking smile.

'Eh? Me and my milksop cousin? Hah!' The dark head was flung back, he laughed loudly. 'Can you see that, Kate? By God, you'd have to prepare her long and well for the marriage bed, eh? Still, you'd do well by it, Kate. You'd be a lady's maid then, and no mistake! And I'd still have your warm little arms to run to when the ice-water Rosie had turned me cold!'

To her horror, Kate burst into tears. Belatedly, his arms came across to caress her shoulders, and she shrugged him off angrily.

'Come now, Kate! I meant no harm! Besides, do you think a virtuous maiden like Rosie would have a scallywag like me for a husband? No, she's better off with her namby-pamby Mr Ned Lovatt and his lah-di-dah cronies!'

His contemptuous words did little to ease Kate's private distress. She had already shed bitter tears, away from him, at her weakness in succumbing to his power. Her guilt was all the more painful because she felt she was betraying her beloved mistress, as well as her own code of morality with this madness. How could she, after guarding her virtue for so long and with such care, abandon herself like this to what could be nothing more than wicked and perverse lust? Yet all her tormented self-flagellation vanished hopelessly at one look from those captivating eyes. Her body trembled, and beat with fierce need to slake its thirst for him. It was useless to upbraid herself, to argue how depraved it was for a servant-girl like herself to be in love with the heir to Strenshaugh Hall and all its wealth.

His very next words drove home this cruel truth like a well-aimed bullet.

'Tell you what! Why don't you and me run off together, Kate, my darling? I'll take you far away from here, show you the African territories, we'll make our fortune together! Come now, give us a kiss!'

'No, you shouldn't — Master Johnny — '

He stopped her further protests by planting his mouth firmly over hers. The tearful recriminations were forgotten, the freckled form soon stretched out once more in languorous abandon as she opened herself to the melting caress of the high sun on her eager body, and the even fiercer blaze of their relighted passion.

★   ★   ★

The antipathy between the two young men was evident from the start, though Ned Lovatt, with his polished gentleman's manners, was better at disguising it, or at least wrapping his dislike in the urbane wit which stayed within the bounds of polite behaviour.

It showed up Johnny's boorishness even more plainly, and earned him his harshest rebuke yet from his untypically patient grandfather.

'Curb your tongue, sir!' his lordship hissed, at the dinner-table that first evening of the visit. 'You're a gentleman, Johnny, whether you like it or not, and you'll behave like one at my table! Apologize, now!'

Rose was blushing as deeply as Johnny himself. For a second, it seemed as though he might refuse, and storm out, but he swallowed hard. The atmosphere was electric, then all at once the tension seemed to flow out of him, his taut form relaxed visibly, and he smiled broadly across at Ned, while the dark eyes lost nothing of their glittering mockery.

'Of course, Ned. I'm sorry. I apologize most humbly. You mustn't mind me, or my rough pirate's ways. No harm done, eh?'

Ned smoothly waved aside the apology, while Johnny studied with concealed resentment the effete good looks, almost too classically perfect, the luxuriant but perfectly groomed blond waves of neatly parted hair, the precisely clipped, fair moustache, modest in proportions, not hiding the sensual quality of the lip beneath, which belied the patrician languor of the pale-blue eyes. Eyes which came to life only when they rested on the beauty of Rose's features, and which fanned the flames of Johnny's animosity to a degree which surprised even Johnny himself.

Ned was accompanied on this visit by an elder married sister, and it soon became evident to Johnny that they were here to cement an alliance between the families. A spirit of quite fierce competition developed between the two young men, which Johnny seemed helpless to prevent, even though he quickly realized that he was being made to appear more and more outlandish and ill-equipped for his role in society by the contest. Riding, shooting, cards, drawing-room entertainments — Ned displayed all the attributes required of a young gentleman to a far higher degree of skill than Johnny could ever aspire to — even if he had not felt them to be a waste of time in the first place.

His grandfather summoned him late one night, after the Lovatts had been staying about a week. Johnny went along the carpeted corridor to the old man's dressing room and bedroom with truculent nervousness. He was wondering what misdemeanour he was about to be ticked off for this time. Once again, he felt that restless urge to get away, to escape from this privileged life altogether, and his thoughts strayed yet again to those happy, precarious days of his growing-up in that distant environment which now seemed so attractive.

Lord Strenshaugh was sitting up, wearing his corded-silk smoking-jacket and tasselled cap. He pushed the box of cigars and the bottle of brandy towards Johnny, and nodded towards the comfortable leather chair opposite. Johnny sighed with relief, poured himself a noggin, and slowly lit up before sinking back attentively.

'You know why young Lovatt and his family are here, don't you?' his lordship began, without preamble, and Johnny nodded.

'He's keen on Rose, sir. Anyone can see that.'

'And your cousin? How do you think she feels about him?'

Johnny shrugged, affected an air of careless disregard. 'I wouldn't presume even to guess what Rose is thinking,' he answered gruffly. 'These young society girls — '

'You ought to know, damn it!' Lord Strenshaugh cut in. 'The two of you — you should be so close! Family!'

'I know.' Johnny spoke with a hint of weariness. 'Like brother and sister. We should — '

'No! Not like that!' The force with which his grandfather said the words startled

Johnny. 'It doesn't have to be like that at all! She's a lovely-looking gel, isn't she. Don't you feel fond of her, my boy? If only you'd pay her some proper attention. Start behaving like any normal young man — you're a likeable enough rogue!' He grimaced. 'I'm sure she'd get to like you if you set yourself to woo her a bit!'

Johnny was staring at him, all attention now. He recalled the words Kate had murmured in the privacy of the rooftop a week ago.

'Nothing would make me happier than to see you and Rose wed!' the old man went on emotionally. 'I don't trust these new bankers and merchant fellers like Lovatt. At least we know the stock would be true, eh, Johnny? What do you say? Wouldn't you like your pretty little cousin as a wife?'

5

'Please, Johnny! I've asked you — so many times! Please don't — don't maul me, as though I were some — some common bargirl!' Twin spots of colour stood out on Rose's exquisitely pale face, their vividness visible even in the dimness of the light that spilled into the conservatory from the corridor. She stood, twisted away from his embrace, her gloved hands pushing at his shoulders, her head turning as her long neck swayed to avoid his searching lips.

'I wish you were! I'd know what to do with you if you were!'

She drew in her breath, still amazed at his ability to shock and hurt her with his words. But she was learning. She was no longer quite so easily reduced to helpless squeals of outrage and gushing tears.

'I'm sure you would!' she answered roundly now, her cheeks still flaming. 'But, unfortunately for you, I am not. And I still expect to be treated with the decency you ought to show to anyone of my sex and position!'

He did not attempt to come near her again, though she stood eyeing him warily.

'Good God, Rosie! Don't you have any red blood in your veins?'

'Hah! Are we back to the old cry again? I'm the ice-maiden once more, am I, because I don't fall swooning in your arms, ready to surrender my virtue for a kiss?'

'I suppose you prefer your simpering Neddy boy, with his sighs and groans and tender little love songs round the piano, eh?'

The blush that spread so readily over her lovely features told him his words had hit home, and he felt a mean satisfaction.

'At least Ned knows how to behave in front of a lady!' she retorted coldly.

Another crude reply sprang at once to mind, but Johnny smothered it. He thought of his grandfather's words of the other night, and of Ned Lovatt's subsequent stiff-necked departure, clearly out of joint because he had not received the encouragement he had hoped for from his lordship in paying court to Rose. Johnny wondered if the old man had said anything of his own plans to Rose herself, and wondered even more how she had taken it if he had.

Of course, Johnny found the prospect of being married to his cousin exciting. Who wouldn't want a beauty like hers in his possession? He had from his first sight of her been passionately attracted. His body wanted her every time he clapped eyes on her, even now. Even her annoyingly prissy innocence began to seem perversely attractive, too, when he thought of her being handed over to him in marriage. But it was so hard to keep his feelings for her in check, to play the part of the proper suitor, when her looks were so damnably tempting.

And there was more. He was becoming more and more confused as to what his feelings for her actually were. He wanted her physically, that was clear enough, but somehow, there was something else, something different about his wanting her, that he could not properly understand himself. When he looked back over the few relationships he had enjoyed with women over the brief span of his life so far, they seemed to have been so joyfully simple. Because, he could recognize well enough, they had been concerned only with satisfying his sexual needs. In some way he could not analyse, his feelings for Rose were far more complex. And that both scared and, at times, infuriated him. Perhaps it was that in his innermost being he acknowledged that he would never be truly worthy of her. He would never be able to live up to her expectations, her standards of goodness, of purity.

Such reflections as these made him blurt out angrily:

'You should take a leaf from your maid's book! There's life enough in red-headed Kate, I'll warrant!'

He saw again the expression of shock, then the dawning of suspicion in the beautiful face, and he cursed his own foolishness.

'What on earth do you mean? What has my maid got to do with anything? You don't mean — you haven't — '

'All I mean,' he blundered desperately, 'is that she's got a sparkle in her eye and looks like there's a bit of fun about her! Not like her frosty-faced mistress, who daren't even allow a kiss on the lips from her own cousin!'

'It's not — just a kiss, though. It's not as — as innocent as that, is it?' She stammered a little, and blushed, but she looked him directly in the eyes.

'How the hell would you know *what* it is?' he snarled, guilt and frustration welling up inside him. 'How would you know anything?' He gestured, in pent-up rage. 'What's the use? I'm going down to the village. To the *Fox*. Where the low, common people gather. I feel more at home there, as I'm sure you'd agree! Good night, coz!'

That night, as Kate undressed her, Rose was unusually silent. She had a brooding, abstracted air, and, when the red-haired girl had fitted the fine summer nightgown over her head, and was standing behind her brushing out the black locks, letting the long tresses slide over her splayed fingers, Rose glanced at the reflection of the trim, black-uniformed figure hovering dimly in the glass.

'Kate! Has Master John ever — done anything — said anything — behaved improperly towards you?'

Kate's heart hammered. She felt the colour flood up her neck and face, bent her head at a slightly sharper angle to conceal her shame. Her hands moved more agitatedly as she wielded the long-handled, tortoiseshell brush. She could not keep the breathy tremor from her voice when she murmured softly:

'No, miss. Nothing. Why do you say that? Has someone been gossiping — about me?'

'No, no!' Now Rose's face, too, was tinged with embarrassment. Kate could see, from where she stood over her mistress, the white bosom moving beneath the thin piping of lace and the delicate silk which hugged its modest contours. 'It's just — something — a remark he made.' She half-turned, to glance up at Kate. She raised her hand to her shoulder, lightly brushed Kate's fingers as they busied themselves with the thick strands of hair.

'Don't be afraid — to tell me, if there *is* anything. You mustn't feel ashamed — we're both friends, you and I, aren't we, Kate?'

Friends? The word echoed mockingly in Kate's brain. The fear Rose's innocent enquiry had caused, the riot of confused thoughts at her question, caused an uncharacteristic bitterness to spring up in Kate's mind. How can we be friends, you and me, when I'm stood here, brushing at your hair, getting you out of your clothes, doing every blessed thing for you? She jerked at the tresses, and with the other hand pulled the brush through the locks with such force that Rose's head titled back involuntarily.

''Course I'd tell you, miss, you know I would. There's nothing, honest! I swear it! You know Master Johnny — John!' She corrected herself hastily, but she saw from the fleeting expression which passed over Rose's face that the use of the familiar diminutive had registered with her. 'He's always larking on. Always joking with the girls! The serving girls, I mean. Like me, miss.'

Later still, up in the attic room she shared with two of the other maids, Kate lay in the darkness of her narrow iron bed and thought over her mistress's words. Did she suspect? Had she seen from Kate's behaviour the guilt which the red-haired girl had felt was branded all over her face? Rose's words rang again in her disturbed mind. *We're friends, you and I.* How could a mistress and her servant girl ever be such a thing? For a second, the blazing anger returned, and jealousy of the lovely girl whose every want she attended to. The girl who, if the growing gossip which was spreading throughout the large household was to be believed, would one day share the bed, and the life, of the only man Kate had given herself to. The man for whom she had yielded her decency and every moral precept she had subscribed to. And the thought of whom even now made her twist and turn, her young body in the clinging cotton of the cheap shift damp and feverish with hunger to feel his consuming touch once more.

She swore she would not meet in their secret trysting-place on the roof again. She was furious, as well as chewed over with anxiety, that he should have been so careless of her good name as to allow Miss Rose to become suspicious. But, some fifteen hours later, under the heavy, humid sky, which was darkly bruised with the threat of rain, she lay in his arms again, and shivered with that same hunger for his body she could no longer deny.

Only when it was abated, and she lay

replete in his embrace, was she able to admonish him, while the tears came swiftly to replace those of her earlier release.

'You'll ruin me! If Miss Rose ever thought . . . ' she looked down at her sprawled limbs, exposed to the tops of her thighs by the turned-back black skirt of her gown, and the simple lace hem of her petticoat, and shook her tumbling red hair in despair. 'You mustn't!' she wept. 'I don't care if you *are* going to marry her — I don't want to be sent away from here!'

He cradled her gently, held the vivid head to his chest, and pressed his lips against it.

'And you won't be, my sweetheart, I promise! I just told her I wished she had just a spark of the life you've got in you, my love! That's all!'

'Oh my God!' She sat up, staring at him, her grey eyes round with shock, her mouth open with wonder. 'You didn't!' Her voice was a whisper of delicious outrage, and, all at once, she let out a snorting, unmistakable giggle.

Relieved, and encouraged by her change of mood, he nodded happily.

'I did! And I meant it, too!' he went on strongly. 'Of course you can't leave her, Kate. I'm counting on you! To teach her how to be a real woman one day. Just give her half the spirit you've got in this divine body, Kate, and I'll be a happier man by far, I swear to God I will!'

'Oh, sir!' Kate protested, scandalized, but too giddily delighted by his ardent praise to be truly offended at the improper nature of his suggestion.

★　★　★

A week later, both cousins were summoned before Lord Strenshaugh. If Rose had any inkling of what was on his lordship's mind, she had given no sign of it. Nor did she appear ready to swoon when he made his views known, though she lived up to her name by the enchanting colour which mounted to her face and the little that could be seen of her neck above the high blouse, with its ruffled collar and the mother-of-pearl brooch at her throat.

'I think I could die a happy man if I could see you two young people wed to each other and the Strenshaugh line secure with another male heir. You make a handsome couple. You're so like your father, my George,' he said emotionally, then turned to the blushing girl. 'And you're so like my Arabella. Will you consent to the engagement?'

The long lashes brushed her cheek.

'Perhaps my cousin does not wish it. There is very little we agree on. I fear he finds me a very cold fish, Grandfather.'

'Nonsense! He's a rough diamond still, aren't you, Johnny?' He guffawed encouragingly. 'But he thinks the world of you, I know he does. Even if he doesn't always show it!' he added, with a significant glance at his grandson.

'Yes,' Johnny put in awkwardly. 'I mean — you know I think you're damn — well, I like you well enough. Of course I do! And in time — '

'Could we wait, grandfather? For a few months at least? Before any formal announcement — I'm not sure — we both need some time to adjust to the idea — of marriage. John has not settled in yet. There's so much . . . '

His lordship frowned, taken aback by her clear reluctance.

'You're not taken up with that Lovatt feller, are you?' he barked, and she shook her head at once, murmuring her denial. 'Johnny will do right by you, I'll see that he does! You'll behave yourself, my boy! And that's an order!'

He stood dismissively. 'I want this thing settled, you hear? Before your twentieth birthday, Rose. I want to announce it then, in October. So you've got two months — to *adjust to the idea!*' He echoed her words sarcastically, and she flushed. 'Then the wedding by spring. We'll have to give 'em six months to avoid any scandal!'

Rose tried to suppress her gasp at her grandfather's indelicate outspokenness. She could almost feel the smile forming on her cousin's handsome face. As they left, he placed his arm solicitously on her elbow, steering her out of the library. His head bent low towards her, his lips almost brushed her ear as he whispered: 'Can I come a-courting at your door tonight, my love? Perhaps you'll welcome me with open arms this time, and not squeal with fright like a stuck pig because I catch a glimpse of you in your smalls!'

6

Now that the betrothal of the cousins was acknowledged, if only unofficially for the next two months or so, the relationship between Johnny and Rose became more prickly than ever. The innocent warmth of friendship, which Rose had at first extended to Johnny as a long-lost and welcome member of the close family, had already been drastically tempered by the disappointed girl, when she experienced what seemed to her his quite improper and coarse familiarity towards her. She became even more coolly polite and icily correct in her manner. She avoided being alone with him if it were at all possible, as it generally was, and, indeed, shunned his company altogether whenever she could do so.

'I don't think Rosie sees me as suitable husband material,' he confessed moodily to his lordship one evening, when they were alone with the port at the dinner-table.

His grandfather grunted.

'Give her time, Johnny. She's a delicate creature. Led a sheltered life, you know. Like most gels of her station. You've got to treat 'em gentle, me boy. Coax 'em along a bit.' He stared thoughtfully at the younger man. 'P'raps you ought to distance yourself from her for a while. Give her some room to get used to the idea.' He stroked his flowing whiskers; a sardonic glint appeared in his eye. 'Maybe a good time for you to cut loose, too. Sow a few wild oats, eh? I've kept you cooped up here for too long.' He gave a short bark of laughter, to match the expression in his gaze. 'To tell the truth, I've been afraid of what you might get up to in town on your own. But I can see you're champing at the bit. And the village girls could do with a rest, I dare say! Time you were seen around up in London for a week or two. Plenty of young bloods to keep you company — and get you into mischief, I'll be bound!'

Johnny was only too eager to obey. Since the intended betrothal had become common knowledge around Strenshaugh and its environs, even his illicit relationship with Kate had become fraught with difficulties. Not least because of Kate's tempestuous emotional seesawing. 'I can't go on like this!' she wept, one afternoon when the bursting thunderstorm, which had been threatening for days and added to the air of sultry tension, had driven them from their hideout on the roof to a dusty corner of one of the

68

attic storerooms full of old furniture and nursery toys.

A pile of discarded mattresses had made an effective love-couch, and, despite her genuine distress, Kate's longings had matched his in their intensity, so that she had shed her clothing as feverishly, if not as quickly, as her lover, who was ready, as always, to assist her in removing the last of her intimate garments before he swooped on her eagerly. The physical storm his loving created, and then dispelled in that magical way, was as powerful as ever, which largely accounted for Kate's bitter tears, penitent, but too late, which came after he had slowly eased his sated body from hers.

'We're doing no one any harm,' Johnny sighed, striving to disguise the hint of weariness he felt at the prospect of yet more moral twists and turns from his lovely partner. He reached out to stroke her pointed breast, whose small, pale nipple was still engorged, the flesh around this desirable peak still rosily pocked with the dusting of freckles which came enchantingly on her white skin after they had made love. She flinched away from him, and he smothered a spark of irritation. Stretched out naked beside him, she was not in a position to indulge in such belated displays of modesty and temperance, he reflected.

'We're doing a great deal of harm!' she said accusingly, her voice catching on a sob. 'We're committing a mortal sin for one thing! And for another — you're going to be wed to my mistress! You're as good as engaged already and here we are — doing all this, day after day!' she ended, somewhat inadequately.

A smile tugged at the corners of his mouth at her nice reluctance to put a name to what they had both just enjoyed, but the violence of her sobbing smote his conscience, and, overcoming her struggles, which subsided as he held her firmly against her resistance, he gathered her gently to his warm body. His kiss, too, was gentle, and she soon yielded her soft lips to his.

'Maybe you're right, Kate. But you're such a damned beautiful girl!' He let his cupped palm fall with firm appreciation on the jut of her hip as she lay half-turned towards him, then traced the smooth roundness of her upper thigh. 'I don't know how I'll ever be able to keep my hands off you. Not to mention other parts of me that just refuse to behave themselves whenever you're around!'

He glanced down so plainly to his lap that she blushed and smiled even in the midst of her tears. 'In any case,' he went on, so casually that it smote at her heart, 'I'm going away a while. Grandpa thinks I ought to leave Strenshaugh for a few weeks. Give your mistress a rest from my clearly obnoxious presence. He thinks London might do me some good. Give me a chance to kick over the traces before our nuptials are announced!'

Kate thought of the hectic round of balls and supper parties Rose had attended at her coming-out season the previous year. She also thought of the other, unmentionable pleasures a young gentleman might get up to in London, a world very different from that in which his female counterpart lived, one which genteel ladies like Miss Rose had probably never heard of. And never would.

She stiffened, moved out of his arms and knelt up, trying to hide her breasts as she reached for her underclothing and dragged it on, reflecting bitterly as she did so how plain and ugly her garments were, compared with the frills and silks her mistress wore. Garments which those wonderful hands lying so near her would one day toy with, and remove from that beautiful, fragrant body, just as he had . . . the tears blinded her again as she banished the disturbing image from her mind.

'You'll soon find girls enough up there to make you forget all about me!' she muttered pathetically. She sat with her back to him, and

71

rolled on the black stockings, slipping the thin elastic garters over them. How she hated dressing like this in front of him! How shameful it felt to haul on her clothes again, so painfully aware of his gaze on her all the while!

'No, Kate!' She wriggled away from his grasp as she stood and fumblingly tied the strings of her drawers. 'I swear to God I won't look at another woman the whole time I'm there! It won't be worth it. I know they won't be a patch on my red-haired Kate!'

She knew full well he was lying, and her heart was torn at the thought. But it was no more painful than the image of what would happen in the spring, not with some unknown city drab, but with her own beloved Miss Rose. Not only that. Kate would have to share in all the excitement, all the wild anticipation of the great event, all the weeks of preparation, and days of celebration. Worse still, she would have to be Rose's confidante, share the intimacies of the trousseau, the frills and lace and satin that were meant to transform the ignorant, innocent virgin bride into the enchantress of her avid mate's dreams.

Already, Master Johnny had told Kate of her role in initiating Miss Rose into the 'mysteries of the boudoir', as he had phrased it, with that deep, coarse laugh of his. Tearfully, Kate had wondered how he could be so insensitive, or worse — and she feared this was really the case — so cruel, only moments after he had enjoyed to the full the pleasure he took from possessing her eager body. Pleasure they both took, Kate bitterly acknowledged, though her admission made her feel flayed with shame. It was not as though she were wanton. Or maybe she was. She was uncertain of everything now. Her world had been turned upside down, had tumbled into chaos since that hot afternoon in the dusty little hut.

He was so tender with her, so gentle, so solicitous of her being able to share that wonderful, consuming passion which blazed through both of them. Was it simply that her nature was so corrupt, her blood or flesh so charged with that abandoned force? Had he somehow known this? Was it something that men like him could instinctively recognize? But if it was so, why then had she not felt it long before now? Why had she not lost her maidenhood long ago, under a hedge outside the village, as had a good many of her acquaintance? She had been so full of moral condemnation, of righteous contempt. And at Strenshaugh, she knew how many among the staff enjoyed such illicit relationships, and all the risks that ran with them. Well, she was no better than any of them now — except that she had aimed so much higher — so high it frightened her to think what must happen to her if she could not break the spell he had put her under.

She tried to tell herself that this temporary separation would be the start of that recovery, that not seeing him every day would help her to build the necessary resistance to his power over her. She would be strong enough not to succumb to his charm or his urgings when he returned. That was what her head told her, but it was her own urgings, of heart and blood, that cast doubt on her resolve, as she stood beside her mistress, seeing him off into the carriage which would take him to the railway station.

Lord Strenshaugh was there, too, and displaying a surprisingly visible emotion as he hugged him to his breast. Under his watchful eye, Rose inclined her head, turning it to the side to offer her unblemished cheek for a chaste kiss. To Kate's relief, and no doubt to Rose's, too, he placed his mouth on the proffered spot with admirable decorum. But then his dark eyes danced as they lighted on Kate's face, and she prayed fervently that the blush she could feel rising from her very toes would be interpreted as nothing more than her shy maidenliness.

'Goodbye, Kate. Take care of my darling coz for me. I leave her in your capable hands till I return!'

* * *

'Well well! If my little coz could only see us now, eh, Ned?' Johnny gazed down with a beneficent, drunken smile on the reddened features, the tousled blond hair, the pale neck and V of chest showing through the unbuttoned, collarless shirt. Ned Lovatt blinked up owlishly around the plump bare arm of the girl who was sprawled across his knee. She was wearing some kind of fancy, lace-encrusted camisole, and extremely short, loose knickers, whose embroidered lace legs were gathered high on her shapely thighs. The pale flesh was revealed in the gap between this abbreviated garment and the tops of her black stockings, held in place by the long suspender ribbons stretching from the new, naughtily fashionable corsets of stiffened satin tightly laced round her waist. She was giving a generous display of her lower limbs as she lay back in Ned's arms. Her feet, waving in the air, were encased in a pair of light evening slippers of the same exotic, dark crimson hue as her underwear.

Johnny guffawed loudly.

'Your face is as red as your doxy's drawers! Don't worry, Ned! I won't give your guilty secret away!'

Ned recovered swiftly.

'That sort of remark is totally unnecessary from one *gentleman* to another.' The implied insult in the emphasis was clear.

Johnny's grin remained infuriatingly broad.

'Well, you know me, Ned. What would I know about the ways of gentlemen, eh?' He nodded at the scantily clad female in Ned's arms. 'Enjoy yourself. It's good to see you here, Ned, I declare. It's comforting to see that such a paragon of virtue is human after all!'

Mrs Moss's was one of the most expensive and opulent brothels in all of London. More like an exclusive gentlemen's club, really, where the most famous faces and names could rely on discretion, and satisfaction, no matter how extreme or bizarre their tastes. As well as the services the beautiful girls provided for their distinguished clients, there was a luxurious bar and several gaming-rooms on the ground floor. In addition, a number of private banqueting chambers could be hired, where private parties were catered for. It was towards one of these Johnny's partner, a diminutive girl with

white-blond hair, was tugging him possessively.

The family name had proved to have an
'open-sesame' magic, as far as his entry into
the capital's society was concerned, while his
own romantically exciting background was an
added bonus which made everyone eager to
meet him. One such was Sir Charles
Forsythe, a forty-two-year-old with a youthful
zest for high and loose living, who claimed to
have been a friend of Johnny's father.

'Of course, George was a couple of years
ahead of me at school. Damn fine fellow,
though. I remember the wedding. Such a
beautiful gel, your mama.'

Johnny had been invited to one of Sir
Charles's private entertainments at Mrs
Moss's. The festivities were well under way. A
small stage had been erected at one end of
the room, on which the bright, theatrical arc
lights were trained. Johnny was stirred by a
powerful memory as he heard the throbbing
of drums, then he felt his blood racing, his
whole body tightened like a bowstring as his
eyes fell with rapt attention on the figure
which was the centre of this diversion.

An African girl of stunning beauty was
performing some kind of swaying dance. Her
colour was of deepest brown, burnt-chocolate
hue, much darker than the Kamba and

Swahili peoples with whom Johnny was most familiar. Her tall slenderness, her fine features, were very different from the Bantu tribes, and reminded Johnny of the fierce, nomadic cattle-owning tribes from the vast plains of the interior, whom he had come across from time to time. Fierce, proud, and afraid of no one, white, brown or black.

The room had grown hushed as the performance continued. When it ended there was a collective, gusting sigh, before the cheers and applause rang out.

'That's Lucy,' a neighbour in the crowd told him, as he continued to stare at the tall figure now gathering a long, dark cloak about her scantily clad form and leaving the stage. 'No good setting your sights on her, old boy. She's spoken for.'

'Is that so?' Johnny murmured softly. The white-blonde gave an impatient little tug at his arm.

'Here, Johnny! You said we . . . '

His gaze still following the retreating figure of the African, he dug in his pocket and pulled out a bank note.

'Take this, my love. And go and lose yourself!'

7

Rose gazed speculatively at the silent figure of Kate, who was folding up Rose's discarded clothing, and tidying prior to leaving her for the night. It was just after eight o'clock, but Rose had excused herself from the dining-table and left her grandfather and his three friends to their brandy and cigars, then the billiards and the cards which would occupy them, probably until the early hours. She had put on her warm quilted housecoat over her night things. A fire burned in the grate, against the sudden autumnal chill of the evening and the gloom of the spattering rain-showers that had persisted all day. Her black hair hung luxuriantly down her back, and she shook it out, enjoying the sensation of unbound freedom.

'Will there be anything else, miss? You sure you don't want me to come back later and pin your hair up?'

'I think I can manage to tuck it into my nightcap.' Rose smiled. She hesitated, embarrassed to speak out, yet feeling she must say something. For the last few days, Kate had been so withdrawn, so unlike her usual bubbly self that Rose was certain something was wrong. She wondered if there were troubles at home, and waited for Kate to confide in her. She had felt disappointed and dismayed when no confidences were forthcoming. Goodness knows life was quiet enough at Strenshaugh Hall these days. It irked her to have to admit it, but there was a kind of deadness about the place since her cousin's departure more than two weeks ago. Her own sense of restlessness troubled her, for this feeling, almost as though she were waiting for his return to feel fully alive again, was quite new, and one whose strength startled her. Everything seemed muted somehow, in suspension. At times, Rose felt almost tearfully angry with herself, for surely she should have been glad of the respite Johnny's absence provided? After all, he did nothing but provoke her when he was present. Why should she miss him so?

The staff clearly missed him, too. Fancifully, Rose had thought that maybe it was his absence that was causing her maid to be so untypically quiet, but then she dismissed such trivial nonsense. Clearly, Kate was despondent about something, and maid and mistress were so close that Rose felt she had to speak, in spite of her natural diffidence.

'Kate — don't go for a minute. Is there

anything wrong? I mean — are you well? It's just — you seem a little out of sorts. You've been very quiet these past few days. Is there anything the matter?'

Rose had pinked a little herself at initiating her enquiry, but now she saw the redheaded girl's features suffused with colour.

'Wrong? No, miss. Why should there be anything wrong?'

The sharpness of her answer, and the tension which accompanied it, disconcerted Rose further.

'No problems at home? The family are all well?'

'Yes — thank you, miss. All fine.'

The awkward atmosphere was still there, and in an effort to alleviate it, Rose smiled.

'P'raps you're missing Mr John. Things are certainly quieter without him.'

Kate turned her back, began squaring the objects off on the dressing-table. She did not answer.

'He's too busy maffiking to even write home!' Rose's light-heartedness sounded forced. She used the popular new term for wild celebration, which had come into vogue recently because of the war in South Africa — even on that topic Johnny had managed to anger her, with his shocking lack of patriotism, and mockery of the young men who were eager to join the fray. *If I fought for anyone, it would be on the side of the Boers!* he had said flippantly. *Time someone taught Britannia she doesn't quite rule the world!* As usual, he was impervious to all her argument, and left her speechless with exasperation.

Still Kate had her back to her, and said nothing.

'Grandfather hasn't had a word from him. And of course, I don't need to tell *you* that I've received nothing. Not even a postcard. Even though there is supposed to be an understanding between us!' She could not keep the bitterness out of her tone. However, she was shocked at the baldness of Kate's reply.

'That won't bother *him*, miss! Will that be all? I'll be off then, miss. 'Night.' Rose stood blinking at the retreating figure, who left the room without even waiting for the permission that fluttered like a withered leaf against the already closing door. Rose remained for several seconds staring after her. She felt the sudden sting of tears, and a welling of loneliness. She swallowed hard. What on earth had got into Kate? She racked her brains to think of how she had offended her in some way, and could find no answer. No! It must have been something Johnny had done. In some way, he had hurt Kate, upset her deeply. The import of her words, as bitter as anything Rose could have come up with, registered disturbingly.

Her cheeks grew hot again as she examined the idea. Unworldly as she was, she knew just what her maid had meant by her accusation. She remembered all at once Johnny's insulting comparison between her and Kate, his cutting references to her own ice-water lifelessness. *You should take a leaf out of your maid's book*, he had told her. Naturally, she had assumed that he had spoken merely out of spite, his malicious desire to upset her, especially when she had questioned Kate about his conduct. But perhaps he *had* after all behaved badly towards the poor girl, even though she had been at pains to deny it. An even more mortifying thought occurred to her now. Maybe all the staff knew far more than their mistress. Maybe they were well aware of Johnny's rakishness, and maybe they felt sorry for her naïve ignorance of the ways of the world.

She had intended to write letters before settling down with her book, but now she sat uneasily on the edge of the chesterfield, staring into the fire, stretching her limbs towards the glowing coal, comforted by the heat on her bare ankles. She was deeply troubled. Once more, she felt the prick of tears, and could not dispel them. They gathered on her lashes, hung there, and impatiently she dashed them away. It was unfair that girls should be put in this position. Ignorant, defenceless, and then pitched literally overnight from unschooled virgin to wife — and, inevitably, she supposed, mother.

The tears came faster. She remembered her own mama, scarcely free from the illness which had been an inescapable adjunct of her confinements almost all the way through Rose's childhood. Then, on the very threshold of adolescence, just when Rose needed the love, the understanding, the knowledge that a mother alone could fully give, she had been taken so swiftly, so cruelly, from her.

She was glad that she did not have to endure the louring hostility of her father for long. The thirteen-year-old girl found herself both hating and fearing men. But her grandfather, a distant and awe-inspiring figure, was different. Their paths in the great old house hardly crossed. Her life was directed by a series of maids and governesses, some of whom were less severe than others, with none of whom she could form any close relationship. It was only since Kate had been promoted to be her lady's maid that she had felt anything approaching the closeness of ties she had often as a lonely girl longed for. That was why she had been so excited when the news came about her long-lost cousin. At last there would be someone of her own age or thereabouts, someone really close, with whom she could forge a bond of lasting friendship.

How cruelly had her fond illusion been shattered. And the irony was that, in another six or seven months, she was to become his wife. Share his bed, and his life. Bear his children!

She had eased off her slippers, and now she stretched out her bare feet towards the fire's heat, studied their narrowness, their daintiness. How girlish they looked still, and the delicate ankles. She felt the inner warmth stealing up as she contemplated the marital intimacies she would be forced to endure with Johnny. Forced? She felt the quickening pulse deep inside that made her wonder at the appropriateness of that word. In truth, the fluttering beat she could feel, the tremor of her flesh, could not be ascribed to fear alone.

He might not know about bearing children, but begetting them would hold little mystery for him. It surprised her how painful this conjecture was to her. Again, the unfairness of the conventions of sexuality struck her: the unwritten law that allowed a young man to discard inconvenient morality and gain the knowledge deemed necessary for the marriage-bed, while a bride who came to that bed with the self-same knowledge would be branded a slut, little or no better than a harlot.

Was that why Grandfather had sent him away? She shivered with revulsion at the thought, yet she could not deny her conviction that Johnny no longer had need of any such instruction. The wildness of his life among the cut-throats he had been brought up with had ensured that.

Meanwhile, to whom could Rose turn to discuss such intimate secrets? There was only dear Kate. In spite of her ingrained reluctance to do so, Rose felt that she must speak with the red-haired girl soon, though of course Kate would have no first-hand knowledge of such things, any more than she had. But the vibrant, gossipy life below stairs was a better school for such things than the schoolrooms and drawing-rooms of aristo-cratic society, especially such an old-fashioned, formal bastion of masculinity as Strenshaugh Hall.

★ ★ ★

Kate came out of the maids' water-closet at the end of the corridor. She pinched her cheeks to restore a bit of colour, and hoped no one had remarked on the hasty way she had left the communal table, when the big platters of curling bacon, fat sausages, and the glistening fried eggs had been placed on the scrubbed wooden surface. The pungent richness of their aroma had overwhelmed her, sending her stomach churning, even though when she was locked in the sanctuary of the roughly plastered little compartment she had hung over the bowl retching ineffectually. Ironically, she now felt positively ravenous, but there was no longer time for eating, for Miss Rose had already rung down for her morning cup of tea. Then there would be her bath to see to, and the dressing. Kate would have to wait until Rose herself went down to breakfast, then she would have time to take her own food in the kitchen. That was, if she was prepared to face the quizzing the cook, Mrs Fielding, would give her.

What she really wanted to do was to run, as fast and as far as possible, from everyone around her. She had been in blind panic for days now, so afraid that she could not think clearly. She had wept and prayed, the corner of the sheet stuffed into her mouth to muffle her weeping from the two other occupants of the servants' bedroom. The truth was too awful to contemplate. She was late, just late, that was all! Things would return to normal.

She tried to will the discomfort and the griping pain to begin, and each day the nightmare continued.

The worst part of it was the inevitability of it all. She had imagined all the terror, a hundred times, ever since she had allowed Master Johnny to have his way with her. And it *was* a wicked way, however trite that might sound. So many times, she had vowed not to give way to him again, and so many times she had failed. And at the very time when she needed him, desperately, to help her from this nightmare, he had vanished altogether. There was no one to tell her where he was, how she could get in touch. Surely he must have known that this must sooner or later be the consequence of their illicit passion? After all, *she* had! And still had failed to do anything about it, she reminded herself bitterly.

She would have to speak to Miss Rose. There was no one else she could turn to. Even as she thought of this solution, part of her mind dismissed it at once as out of the question. She could imagine all too well what the innocent girl's reaction to the thunderbolt would be. Disgrace would fall on all of them, for Rose would want nothing further to do with a man who could behave as abominably as he had. And that meant in turn that his lordship would find out, and then all hell would break loose.

Well, as far as she was concerned, hell was already here. The longer she kept quiet, the greater the ultimate disaster would be. Yet she was terribly frightened of approaching anyone, even those who would be knowledgeable about avoiding such things, and there were such, both here at the hall and down in the village.

Miss Rose's bell jangled again, and Kate picked up the tray, with the china cup and saucer on it, and the tea-things. She could feel the tremble of her hands, as she set off, pushing through the doors with her hip, and heading up the narrow staircase from the kitchens. You have to tell her! Tell her! Do it now! She'll help you, even though it'll break her poor heart! Tell her!

Kate came out on to the wider, carpeted corridor on the first floor, expertly balanced the tray while she tapped on the heavy panelled door before she called out, and entered. Rose was already up, standing by the window. She had pulled back the heavy curtains, to let the morning light through. There was a sweet freshness after the day and night of rain, and the sun poured in. Kate could see the dark shadow of Miss Rose's slim form through the whiteness of the fine linen.

Rose turned, and gave her a beautiful smile.

'Good morning, Kate. Isn't it lovely? How are you feeling this morning?'

'Morning, miss. Yes, it's a grand day. I'm fine, thank you, miss.'

8

Rose was checking on the tall vases of cut flowers, which stood in the entrance hall, and at the foot of the wide staircase, when Gooding approached her, smiling deferentially. Her grandfather's newspaper, carefully ironed, had already been taken in to him in the library, and Gooding was carrying several letters on the small, round tray of polished silver.

'There's one for you, miss.'

He held out the tray, and Rose took the proffered envelope. Her name and the address were printed, in heavy, square capitals, which did not help to identify the writer. Rose's heart beat a little faster with excitement. A letter addressed to her was an unusual enough event. Normally, her post consisted of trade catalogues, embroidery patterns, and the like. She was buoyed up by her anticipation that it might be a missive at last from her errant cousin.

'Thank you, Gooding.'

Her heart beat faster still, as she saw the London stamp. She realized she had absolutely no idea what Johnny's handwriting was like, and she felt a sympathetic twinge of shame for him at the untutored coarseness of the heavy, square printing. Of course, it was obvious even from his spoken language and the uncouth accent in which he spoke, as well as his lamentable ignorance of the civilized world and its ways, that he was virtually uneducated. Grandfather had already engaged a tutor to help put that right. Rose smiled involuntarily at the difficulty Johnny found with the idea of being seated at a desk in study, even for a couple of hours a day. Rose had fondly imagined herself eagerly fulfilling just such an instructional role, until her cousin's conduct, or, rather, *mis*conduct, whenever they found themselves alone together, had swiftly disabused her of the idea.

She moved quickly up the staircase, feeling the hobbling, unaccustomed stiffness of the dark, narrow skirt, after the lighter, freer material of the summer dresses she had been wearing for so long. The September day was once again sombre, the heavy banks of billowing grey cloud threatening the rain which would surely come if the stiff breeze stirring the distant trees should drop a little. One of the young upstairs maids was kneeling at the grate of Rose's room, clearing the ashes before laying the new fire. Rose saw the ugly, upturned soles of her boots, the metal tips nailed at the toes and heels. Like a horse's shoes, Rose thought inconsequentially.

The girl sniffed, and glanced up worriedly. She drew the back of a thin wrist, whose hand was blackened with coal dust, across her dewy nose, transferring a little more grime on to the pinched features, where dark streaks already marred the brow and one cheek, under the voluminous mob-cap.

'Sorry, miss. Won't be a minute, miss. Didn't know you'd be back so soon, miss.' The apology came out in a monotonous whine, almost like an automaton, and Rose hastened to reassure the youngster.

'Best get on with it, then, and stop your jawing, eh?' Kate appeared, from the small, adjoining dressing closet, which was used as an extra wardrobe for Rose's things.

The tone was harsh, and Rose felt sorry for the cowed figure kneeling at the hearth, and for the further mumbled apology, and the more frantic clattering of the fire-irons. *Don't be such a martinet, Kate!* Rose wanted to say, but she kept silent. She knew that the hierarchy of rank was just as rigid below stairs as it was above, and Kate would not welcome such a chiding of her authority. Besides, Kate's unaccustomed, moody reticence was deeper than ever, in spite of all Rose's efforts to ascertain what was wrong.

She tried again now to lighten the atmosphere, and held up the letter.

'Look! I wonder who it's from? A London postmark!' Kate stood motionless, staring at her, and Rose was disconcerted by the intensity of the grey eyes, the pallor of the face, and its stillness. She turned away, uneasy all at once, and moved to her writing-bureau close to the window, to make the best of the light. She sat, and dug the embossed knife into the corner of the envelope, acknowledging the thrill of antici-pation which passed through her.

Her eyes passed disbelievingly over the contents of the single sheet, which quivered in her unsteady hand. It was written in the same, ugly, square print as the address, which seemed somehow to blazon the revolting words on her brain. It told briefly but graphically of Johnny's whoring in London, and, in particular, of his blatant association with an African woman, known as 'Lucy', and his affection for her. *He brags of moving into your bed soon. You'll have to get your maid to black up your face my dear if you want to get the best out of him*, the letter ended. It was unsigned.

Kate saw the drained look on her mistress's face, the stunned expression in her eyes. She snapped at the girl crouching at the fireplace.

94

'Leave that! Now! I'll finish it off later.' The girl gathered up the materials she had brought in her large wooden box, and clutched it to her chest, where a rough piece of sacking hung down to protect her uniform. She bobbed a curtsy and hurried out.

Kate's heart was thumping with apprehension. Clearly, the news must be from, or of, Master Johnny. What had happened?

'What is it?' Her fear made her brusque, but Rose was far too upset to notice. She tried to speak, and felt her throat close. Wordlessly, she handed the sheet of paper over, and Kate skimmed over the contents, the fear now transformed to a fierce, white-hot rage.

'You're not to breathe a word of this to anyone, you hear?' Rose whispered, and was rewarded with what, at any other time, she would have recognized as a glance full of scorn.

'The swine! The wicked, filthy swine!' Kate's hissed words reverberated in the quiet of the room.

Rose's eyebrows curved steeply. Distressed as she was, the vehemence of the maid's tone shocked her. Without thinking she reprimanded her.

'Kate! You mustn't speak like that of Mr John.'

'Well! It's true, miss. That's what he is! A lying, whoring — '

'Be quiet!' Rose had jumped up, crying out shrilly, her cheeks glowing. 'You forget yourself!'

'Well, what do you think of him, then?' Kate's face was equally flushed, her eyes flashed as she faced the startled Rose like an adversary. 'You think it's all right him sleeping with every harlot in London town, do you? You'll welcome him into your bed, will you — after this?' She flourished the letter in Rose's face, then flung it down on the desktop.

Rose's mouth opened and closed before she could find her words.

'Perhaps . . . it's wicked slander. Someone who holds a grudge against him — wants to tarnish him. Hurt him.' Her voice was faint, her protest punctuated by Kate's bark of scornful laughter.

'Do you really believe that? Take my word for it, that filthy letter's true, and if you can't see that, you're even more innocent and gormless than I took you for!'

Rose's bosom heaved. Again, she seemed to fight to get the breathless reprimand out. 'How — how dare you? You can't — I won't be spoken to — you'd better leave me!'

'It's time you had your eyes opened about

Master Johnny, miss! Like — others have! I just wish he'd never come here! He should have stayed back in that jungle of his, with the other beasts!'

Rose had a sensation of the whole world tilting, spinning crazily, as she stood there and the door clashed to after the departing maid. For long seconds, she was paralysed, her mind whirling confusedly, then, all at once, she was swamped with a misery so deep it was like a physical pain. She moved blindly to the freshly made bed, and fell across it, face down, her frame shook with the violence of her grief, and the counterpane was soon soaked beneath her cheek with her tears.

★   ★   ★

Rose's face was paper-white, as pale as the small handkerchief she twisted in her fingers as she faced her grandfather, in front of the crackling fire, in his favourite room, the library. The curtains were already drawn against the darkness. They had dined alone, but with the formal business of the meal, the servants bustling back and forth, and Gooding and Mr Reece's silent presence in the background, Rose could not bring herself to broach the subject which had occupied her tortured thoughts all day.

The one person she had believed she could rely on in the crisis had behaved so uncharacteristically towards her that Rose could not comprehend what had happened to her. It was all part of the fearful, looming shadow Johnny seemed to be casting over her life. She was almost afraid to explore Kate's defection, for the girl would never have behaved so rudely unless she, too, were deeply distressed by the news, which, Rose painfully reminded herself, was not news at all to the red-haired girl, who had accepted it as proven fact at once.

Rose was not surprised that at five o' clock, when Kate normally came to see her mistress changed for dinner, there was a hesitant tap at the door, and Helen, one of the upstairs maids, appeared.

'Kate's taken bad, Miss Rose. An awful headache. Mr Reece told me to come along and wait on you, miss.'

Rose, her eyes still reddened and swollen, in spite of the liberal amount of bathing in the scented water, was close to tears yet again at this evidence of desertion. In all her lonely life, she thought, she had never felt lonelier.

Her grandfather was in his plum smoking-jacket, that strange oriental-looking red cap perched on his grizzled head. He sat in his usual armchair, the footstool in position, brandy-bottle, glass, and cigars at the small table beside him. He waved expansively to the chair on the other side of the wide hearth.

'Brandy?' His hand was already moving towards the small bell next to the bottle, and Rose hastily declined his offer. Her heart was racing. She felt faint. It had taken all her courage to reach this point, and she knew she had to speak now, before her resolve melted.

'Grandfather!' Her voice was shrill, it sounded girlish to her ears. She swallowed the great lump in her throat. 'Why is John in London?' His lordship's creased brow wrinkled further, his ruddy nose lifted, scenting trouble. Before he could answer, Rose rushed on. 'I'm not a child! I have some idea what kind of life he prefers. Why he has not been in touch since he left. I really cannot allow — '

'Tittle-tattle, girl!' Rose flinched at the volume of his interruption. 'Idle, wicked gossip! You should be ashamed of yourself for listening to such scurrilous nonsense, spread about by muckrakers who have nothing better to do with their time! Who's been filling your head with this nonsense? The servant girls, is it? That maid of yours?'

She was on the point of blurting out the truth about the anonymous letter, but even acknowledging its presence was somehow tainting. Besides, she realized miserably, her grandfather's virulent condemnation might well be applied with equal force to its contents. Except for the fact of Kate's shocking outburst, which undeniably had the ring of cruel truth about it. But already Rose could feel her resolution wavering.

'Please,' she said weakly, struggling against the tears she could feel close to the surface. 'John and I — you know he's not taken. Can't we wait a little longer? Say, a year or so? Then, perhaps — '

'No, Rose! I've waited long enough. All summer, confound it! I told you we'd announce the engagement on your birthday, and that's what we'll do!' All at once, he heaved himself upright, and came over to her. His gruff voice gentled a little. 'Listen, my dear, you know what a wild one he's been. And who wouldn't, having lived the dreadful life the poor boy was forced into since his infancy? So he's perhaps been kicking over the traces a little up in town!' He chuckled encouragingly. 'He's a young spark still! Never had the chance to cut up before, sow some wild oats! A few drunken parties — where's the harm? Young men are different, Rose. He'll be all the better for it, believe me.'

His wrinkled hand fell on her shoulder, pressed heavily, digging into the fragility of bone beneath the silk gown. 'He'll soon settle down. He needs to. Needs you to help him do it. After all, he's his father's boy. The best of the blood's in both of you. Come now, Rose. I'm relying on you, my girl. All these years — it's my dream come true. You know your duty, my girl, as Johnny knows his!'

9

'I'm sorry, miss, but I'm afraid I shall have to give notice. There's some things have come up. Problems at home. My folks are going to need me for quite a while. I'll have to go, miss. I'm sorry.' Kate had steeled herself not to cry, but she almost broke her promise to herself at the sight of utter dismay on Rose's lovely face.

'Oh, but surely . . . isn't there some way I can help? I mean, without you having to leave? There must be something — '

'No, miss! There isn't! I've got to go!' Kate's own distress made her words come out more harshly, and her conscience was stabbed with sorrow at their blunt effect on her mistress. 'I'll stay on two weeks, miss. Train Helen up, to fill in. She'll be good, miss. Though of course you can advertise in the meantime, if you wish.'

'But — couldn't you just take some time off? Some leave? Then you could come back to me, when things are settled. If there's anything at all I can do, help in any way . . . ' her voice sank lower. 'You know you only have to ask, Kate. I don't want to lose you. Not now!'

The last two words pierced Kate's heart, for she knew exactly what Rose meant; how lost and lonely the poor girl was feeling, with her grandfather insisting the engagement must go ahead, and the wedding next spring. Kate knew well enough, despite all her protests, that Rose felt a great deal more for her wayward cousin than she would ever admit to. And why not? she thought bitterly. *She* had fallen for his charm herself, and it was to be the ruination of her. All her hopes, all her dreams, all her achievements shattered now, through the recklessness of her passion. And yet, even now, she could not bring herself to drag him down, to denounce him as her seducer. It would be the finish for Miss Rose, she had no doubt of that. She was too delicate a flower to take any more such news about Master Johnny, and who knew? He might yet settle down, his intended partner might yet be able to tame that wildness in him, though, in her inmost heart, Kate doubted it. But perhaps the sweetly innocent Rose might learn to live with it, to adapt herself and become a little wiser to the world and its wicked ways.

In her weaker moments Kate was tempted to see herself as innocent, too; the victim of the wily philanderer, yet she could not escape the truth. He might have taken her innocence, but she had been willing, *more* than willing, for him to do so. She had never believed, even in all her girlhood dreams, that love could be so consuming in its passion. A passion that came from within herself, not just him, and one which, even now, when nemesis was about to fall, and bring disgrace upon her, she could not deny, or regret. All she could regret was its issue, growing inescapably inside her, and that the father, her lover, was placed by society's rigid code so far apart from her that any kind of further union between them was impossible. At least she could do the right thing, and make sure no more harm would come, either to Johnny or to Rose.

But it was her mistress who was almost breaking Kate's compassionate heart now, as Rose made no effort to hide her misery, the big teardrops tracing their path down her cheeks. She stepped close, took Kate's hands in hers.

'I've no one. You're more than — I thought we were close, Kate. Friends! Don't desert me! I'm so afraid!'

The tears were starting now, blurring the red-haired girl's vision. She snatched her hands away, there was a desperation in her voice.

'You don't understand! I've *got* to go! There's no choice!' Rose's lips were parted, her features stamped with pain. 'You'll be all right, miss, I'm sure you will!' Kate looked as though she were about to say more, then she pulled away, her mouth compressed. 'I'll have a word with Mr Reece, miss. Helen can start tomorrow morning. I'll bring her with me for the bath, the laying out of your clothes, hair and all that.'

Rose sank down wearily on the sofa after Kate had gone. She sniffed, searched for her handkerchief to wipe the wetness from her face. She seemed to have done nothing but weep for hours. Along with her loneliness, came a great sense of her own weakness, her inadequacy. No wonder Kate had flared up so contemptuously against her last night! Her toes inside the soft, silk-embroidered slippers curled with scalding shame as she heard again the feeble bleat of her own voice. *Don't desert me! I've no one!* How on earth could she expect Kate to share her troubles with someone so vapid, so useless? The hot tears stung her eyes once more. Why, she couldn't even dress herself, or draw her own bath, keep herself clean!

And now her brooding thoughts turned to the cause of that painful altercation between her and Kate. It was the maid's words she now heard ringing in her head. *It's time you had your eyes opened . . . like others have!* Kate had been quite certain that the contents of that scurrilous letter were true. Was Rose herself really so gullible that she was the only one who could not see her cousin for what he really was? Yet that was not true, either. The truth was, that in her own little, sheltered, virginal world, such wickedness as his was not to be contemplated, or imagined.

Her grandfather had known all right. She recalled that lifting look, that wary anticipation, when she had first questioned his lordship last night about Johnny in London. She was smitten all at once by a wave of self-pity. He knew, and yet he was prepared, nay, determined, that she should become Johnny's wife, bear him children. As in all those nursery fairy tales, she was to be the virgin sacrifice. She remembered the sounds of that far-off, yet unforgotten night. Her father's thick voice, muffled by distance, and by drink, rising, as did her mother's pleas . . . then the sound of that soft, hopeless weeping, which the lonely twelve-year-old had shut out by pressing her hands tightly to her ears.

Was that what she was to be condemned to, unfitted as she was for the mysteries of new life, and death, behind the closed, sacrosanct bedroom doors?

Johnny chased the serving-man away brusquely, and carried on packing his travelling-trunk in the chaos of the bedroom in the town apartment.

'That's not how a gentleman should behave, Johnny!' The exotic figure sprawling at ease among the tumbled sheets of the bed chuckled with amusement. 'What will we poor humble serving-folk do if you take our living away from us?'

Lucy was lying back, propped against the massed pillows. The lace négligé of deep ivory was open, displaying her dark flesh to full advantage. Johnny glanced up, grinning, and saw the long legs slightly parted, the coppery, silken tones of the inner thighs. The distraction proved too much. He cast aside the garment he was holding and flung himself forward upon her.

A considerable while later, they lay still once more, his head resting across her small, conical breasts, while her long, thin fingers stroked through the thickness of his black hair.

'My God! I'll miss you, Johnny! You've ruined me for this game!'

'You don't have to go back to Mrs Moss's.'

'What would you have me do? Become a

lady's maid? You could put in a word for me with your betrothed!'

He felt her mocking laughter transmit itself to his reclining head.

'You know damn well what I mean, you minx! I'll set you up in a place of your own. Keep you in luxury.'

'No, I've seen that caper far too often. A girl sets up with one man, next thing he reckons he owns her, starts keeping her chained up, like a dog on a leash! No, thank you! I've had enough of that in my time!'

He knew what she meant. She had told him something of her colourful history. She had shrugged when he had asked her where she was from. There was none of the African flattening of vowels in her English, which sounded to his untutored ear as polished as that of any native speaker.

'I do not remember,' she had said. 'As a little girl I was brought up on the Barbary Coast, in the house of a Levantine merchant. He had bought me from my mother when I was a baby. But I do not remember her. He sold me on to an Arab. It was terrible there. Beaten every day, sleeping with the animals. I met a seaman, ran away with him, his captain brought me to Europe. He sold me to another, who brought me to Paris. I worked in a brothel, but I got into some trouble. An

Englishman brought me over here. I stayed with him a while, but he was not kind. Then someone told me of Mrs Moss's — and here I am. And here I'll stay. As long as you belong to everyone, you belong to no one!' she had observed enigmatically.

'If you get word to me, I'll always be available for you,' she smiled now, while Johnny reluctantly moved, and resumed the task of packing once more. 'But I think I will not see you for quite a while. You'll be too busy with your pretty little bride! Surely you're not going to make her wait until her wedding-night for the pleasures you have in store for her?'

Johnny gave a bark of sarcastic laughter.

'You certainly don't know anything about my little coz! Never mind *before* the wedding-night! I'll be lucky if she's surrendered by the end of the honeymoon!'

'Oh, you poor darling! Hurry up with that packing, then. You'll need all the comfort you can get before you leave.' Lucy sat up, and rearranged the pillows, tying the thin négligé loosely about her. The thin face suddenly assumed a serious expression. 'There's one thing you should know. That friend of yours. Ned Lovatt. I was listening to him last night, in his cups. You should be careful of him, Johnny. He's a jealous man, for all his show of comradeship. He'd make trouble if he could, I'm sure. Sir Charles told me Mr Lovatt had hopes himself of marrying your cousin, before you showed up.'

'Not a chance, my love! Even if I hadn't washed up on these shores! I don't think there's a man on earth who could warm the ice-water that flows through Rose's virtuous veins.' He grinned wickedly. 'It's a good job the same can't be said for her red-headed little maid. I don't know what I'd have done buried down in the country without her to turn to!'

★   ★   ★

'What do you mean, gone?' Johnny fired the word at her, and Rose noted the sharpness of the look he gave her.

'Finished! Left my service! Perhaps if you hadn't stayed away so long she might have been persuaded to stay. She had some problems at home that made it necessary for her to quit.' A growing sense of unease assailed her at his evident concern. Old suspicions began to eat at her thoughts again. 'But why are you so concerned about the staff? Helen is coping quite well now. I think I'll keep her on.'

'But you and Kate — you were quite close!

Did something happen between you? Did you dismiss her for some reason?'

'No, of course not! Why should I do that? What reason could there be?' She saw just a flicker of something behind those eyes, something that disturbed her even more. 'Do *you* know something about it? Something more than I do?'

'No, no. It's just — like I said. You two seemed so close.'

He seemed distracted, and she felt that gripping anxiety growing inside her, without properly understanding its cause.

'I'm surprised to see you so upset,' she said coolly. 'I didn't think our problems at the hall bothered you. You've been away more than a month. It's only the birthday — engagement party,' she corrected herself, 'that's brought you back. Reluctantly, I'm sure.'

She expected a sarcastic rejoinder, and was startled when he dismissed her accusation with a hasty gesture of his hand.

'Where is she? Have you enquired at her home? Do you know where she lives?'

She felt herself colouring, floundering, as though she were the guilty one.

'Well, her family lives over at Garrowby. She has a brother who works on one of the estate farms, I think.' Her feeling of indignation began to reassert itself once more. 'I tried! I asked her to tell me what was troubling her. Practically begged her. I offered to give her leave, as long as she wanted. Asked her if she would come back, but she was adamant.'

'I'll talk to stuffy old Reece. Or Mrs Fielding. Somebody must know what's happened to her, where she is.'

Her face was crimson with anger and with this unaccountable guilt he was making her feel.

'She won't want to hear from *you*! Of all people! I'm sorry to have to tell you, but she doesn't think much of you — or of what you've been up to this past month and more!' She felt a mean-spirited triumph at the clear look of surprise on his face. For once she had got through his insufferable imperturbability.

He recovered quickly.

'Oh! I expect she got that from you. St Peter himself probably won't measure up to your standards when you reach those pearly gates, coz!'

10

'I'm sure you all know just how happy this wonderful day has made me!' Lord Strenshaugh announced, his gravelly voice unsteady with emotion. There was a burst of enthusiastic applause from the glittering assembly gathered at the foot of the grand staircase as his lordship held Rose and Johnny by the hand either side of him and drew them forward to present them to the guests. The ballroom rang with the good wishes cried out to the young couple whose engagement had just been formally announced.

Their grandfather released them and stepped back. Johnny moved in close and slipped his arm round Rose's narrow waist. His fingers pressed with surreptitious intimacy into the shiny satin. He felt her stiffness, the unyielding rigidity of her whaleboned slimness, the instinctive little flinch of withdrawal, which she tried to disguise as she blushingly smiled at the upturned faces fixed upon them. His hold tightened, dragging her in even closer, and now she could no longer resist without making her reluctance apparent. His hip bumped lightly against hers, crushing the frothy flounces of organdie layering the skirt of her evening gown.

He made a short, modest speech accepting the congratulations, declaring 'our mutual happiness, and eagerness for the great day when we can be truly joined in the sight of God and man as husband and wife'. He held her pinned to his side all the while, his audience indulging in fond chuckles at his evident desire to keep her so close.

'Let me go, Johnny!' she whispered, her chin lifting as she continued to smile. Her gloved hand rested lightly on his at her waist. 'You're crushing me half to death!'

'What a charming gown!' he murmured in reply, in no jot relinquishing the pressure of his grip. 'Such an appropriate colour, too! Ice blue, isn't it?' He sensed rather than heard her gasp of impatience, and his smile broadened.

'Lead us in the dance!' someone called, and the orchestra overhead struck up a romantic waltz. The young couple faced each other and stepped out, though Johnny called out laughingly:

'I'm a damned sight better at jigs and hornpipes than I am at this caper!'

'Oh, surely you've had plenty of opportunity to practise such skills while you've been

114

up in town?' Rose smiled at him with barbed politeness. Her fingers rested feather-lightly on his shoulder. 'I've heard you gained quite a reputation as a lady's man in London.'

His eyes narrowed as he gazed at her. He saw the rising tide of pinkness, which did not owe its existence to the energy they were expending on the dance-floor. He had been all too aware of Rose's increased hostility towards him since his tardy return, and goodness knows it had been severe enough before he had left. His grandfather had warned him of her questions about what Johnny was up to in London.

'Someone's been making mischief, gossiping to her. Maybe that maid of hers she's just got rid of. Anyway, I read her the riot act, told her not to be such a damn fool, talked to her about her duty. Well, now I'm doing the same to you, boy! No more fooling about, not till she's safely wedded and bedded, and with foal, you hear?'

For a moment, when he first heard of Kate's decampment and faced Rose's newly increased antagonism towards him, he had feared that somehow his cousin must have found out the truth about him and the red-haired maid. But then, he told himself, Rose would have been too scandalized to keep it to herself. *And* she was too honest to do so, he had to admit. No, Kate must have acted on her conscience, poor girl. He knew how badly her conscience troubled her, in spite of the passion they had shared. Doubtless, she had somehow found the strength, when he was away from her, to take this drastic step and make the clean break, in order that she should not go on betraying her mistress. Damn ice-water Rosie! he thought yet again. If she wasn't so nice with her virtue maybe he wouldn't have to be such a lecher and spoil the chances of good girls like Kate. The two girls had been close, never mind the mistress and maid separation, and his own conscience felt bad about his splitting them up.

On the other hand, it was probably for the best. The nearer he got to wedding Rose, the more intolerable the situation would have become. But still and all, he felt bad about Kate's disappearance, and was freshly determined to seek her out, as he had threatened, and see if he could somehow make things up to her. Money? The fiery red-head might well fling it back at him. But maybe he could help find her a position in another household (though Rose had already told him how she had offered to give a glowing testimonial) to try to find her a place as lady's maid, and Kate had been evasive as to her future plans.

116

Whatever happened, he would make the effort, once these celebrations were over, to seek out the girl. It was the least he could do.

The party went on until dawn. Because she was the principal on two counts, both as celebrant of her twentieth birthday and as Johnny's fiancée, Rose was unable to make her escape until almost the last. Johnny was ensconced in the billiard room, along with others of similar inclinations. Rose's feet ached from countless dances, as did her jaw from the incessant smiling and her murmured thank yous for the congratulations heaped upon her.

When the last of the guests had retired, except for the noisy group in the blue fug of the games room, a sense of obligation drove her to put her head round the door and bid them goodnight, with weary brightness. Johnny leapt up at once. His eyes shone, he looked as vibrantly alive as ever.

'I'll see you to your door!' he insisted gallantly. She turned crimson at the deep guffaws which followed his remark, and fled, with him in close pursuit.

'There's no need!' she muttered through clenched teeth, still smarting with embarrassment. All at once, she felt tears behind her eyes. 'Go back to your friends, please!' She was almost begging him, but he seized her hand roughly, held it tightly all the way up the staircase's wide sweep, where the footmen and other servants were clearing up. She stopped a few yards from her bedroom door, in the dim lighting of the corridor. She found she could not meet his gaze. 'Thank you,' she whispered, her lips quivering. 'Good-night. Sleep well.'

'Is that the best I get from my beloved?' His deep voice shook with taunting laughter. 'We're engaged now, my love. I can claim a few favours, at least!'

Before she could protest, he slid an arm about her waist, pulled her in to him, and thrust his mouth roughly over hers. She felt it, searching, demanding, with shocking directness. She tried to escape, heart pounding, against his smothering embrace, but now both arms were around her, like iron bands, holding her against him, crushing her against his hard body. She tried to cry out, to gasp for breath, and suddenly her mouth was open against his, and her head swam as his tongue slid shockingly and possessively inside her. Her strength fled, she felt her own tongue touching his, and all at once her body was shaking with a throbbing excitement, both powerful and draining her of will. She would have fallen if he had not held her so close.

When at last he released her, she clung to the doorpost, her shoulders heaving. The tears shone in her eyes as she stared helplessly up at him.

'There's life somewhere under all that starch and whalebone!' He smiled. She continued to stare at him, her eyes huge and luminously dark with her tears. Then she gave a great, shuddering sob and turned blindly, fumbled through the door and slammed it closed behind her.

Helen, still in white cap and apron over her black dress, had been dozing on the chesterfield, by the dying embers of the fire. But she had heard the approaching footsteps, then the long interval of silence. She stood, staring in helpless dismay, as she watched her mistress throw herself with a low cry face down across her bed, saw the shapely, white-stockinged ankles kicking in her agitation until the light dance-slippers flew from the dainty feet, and the slim back and shoulders heaved with the violence of the weeping fit which shook her.

★ ★ ★

Rose was leading her horse by the bridle, through the narrow, treacherous muddiness of the woodland path. New pale and russet

119

leaves were added to the black mush of the mould as they fluttered in a steady drift from the trees stirring and sighing in the strong October breeze. The greyness of the day added to the gloom of the woods. Rose's polished riding-boots were thickly stained up to the ankles with the glutinous mud. She saw the indistinct, segmented shape of a mounted rider slowly approaching through the tall trunks and the clumps of undergrowth, then recognized Johnny, as he called out to her, and swung himself out of the saddle.

'Hello there. I came back to look for you.' They faced one another on the narrow path, and their mounts snorted, softly steaming, and nuzzled.

'You shouldn't have bothered. I always lag behind on these outings. End up miles behind, and missing everything. I'm no Diana. I'm terrified of the lowest hedges. I always stop and look for the gates!'

He made a dismissive sound, held on to the tossing head of his beast.

'I'm no better! Give me a rolling deck in the roughest of seas and I'm as agile as a monkey, but these four-legged creatures!' He chucked at the bobbing animal affectionately. 'I can't imagine me ever being master of the hunt, can you?'

'You go on,' Rose urged him. 'I'll be all

right. I'll probably make my way back through Coultsby. I'll see you back at the hall.'

He shook his head. 'I've no mind to see another poor little Reynard ripped to bits. Let me keep you company a while, Rose. I'll behave myself. I promise.'

His last words, and the quiet sincerity with which he said them, startled her. She nodded.

'If you're sure. Let's tie the horses and walk up through that way, to the top of the hill.' He hobbled the animals, and they moved off. He offered his arm to her, and she slipped her hand into the crook of his elbow. She had an urge to smile at the conventionality of the gesture.

'About last night,' he began, and at once she felt the hot flood of colour, knowing at once that he was referring to that wild kiss outside her door, and her toes squirmed in her boots with shame. She experienced a keen disappointment, for she had hoped he would at least play the gentleman and not mention it again. But she was astonished, and moved, by the words which followed, and the low tone of regret with which he spoke them. 'I'm sorry for behaving the way I did. I should have known better. You don't deserve — that sort of treatment.'

He stopped, and turned to face her. 'I'd

121

had too much to drink, as usual. Not that that's any excuse, I know.' She saw the expression of profound remorse, and honest perplexity as he struggled to explain. 'Hell, Rose! I'm a rough diamond. You know that. I'm not cut out to be one of these smooth, polished sort of gents. To tell the truth, they scare me half to death sometimes — and you!' he blurted, with desperate truthfulness. 'Society ladies. They terrify me! I'm relying on you to get me through all this.'

He glanced around, waved his hand at the tossing trees, and the rolling fields they could see in the distance now, through the tall trunks. The land was still all part of the vast Strenshaugh estate, and she knew exactly what he meant by the gesture.

'I was never cut out for this. Not like you. Sometimes, I wake up in a sweat in the middle of the night, Rose, petrified! Many's the time I've almost made up my mind, to grab my bag and just take off. Head off and never come back again! I sometimes think it would have been far better if I'd never come here. Never been found the way I was!'

'That's nonsense!' Her voice shook with emotion. 'Grandfather — I've never known him so happy, all the years I've been living here. And myself.' Her voice sank to a breathy murmur, and she blushed fiercely, but bravely she went on. 'I was overjoyed when we heard you'd been found out in Africa. I've looked forward so much, to having someone — to having you here.' Shyness prevented her from looking at him now, but courage gave her strength to carry on. 'I haven't always been — as understanding as I should. I'm a simple girl, too, Johnny. With you — I have felt sometimes out of my depth — I'm ignorant about life. I've been tucked away here at Strenshaugh, an ignorant, unschooled country virgin. All the things you've endured, all the violence, the dangers you've faced . . . '

'We must help each other, Rose! By God, we must! We'll see it through, together. Oh, my love! Just give me another chance. We'll make a fresh start, you and I, from now on. I swear I'll be different. Promise you'll give me a chance, Rose, my love!'

She raised her eyes now, and met the full, dark blaze of his, felt the passion she saw there, and watched with a joyful helplessness as his mouth came down, and hers lifted eagerly to meet its consuming force.

11

Rose felt the strength of his hand, its warmth cupping the softness of her breast, separated from his flesh only by the thin cotton of her nightgown. His fingers stroked, and fanned, and she felt her hard, budding response to the tingling flame of the caress, and she moaned and shivered at her body's rebellion. Her lips were swollen, still wet with the imprint of his last passionate kiss. She twisted, fought herself free as he belatedly realized the extent of her struggle, and half-staggered a step away from him, clutching at her gaping dressing-gown, restoring her decency.

Her voice shook with her distress. 'Please! Johnny! You must not — don't treat me so, I beg you!'

It was the pleading in her voice, the lack of anger, which inflamed his own fury.

'For God's sake, Rose! What's wrong? We're bound to each other, aren't we? You'll be my wife in a few months — and I'll be your husband! Will you deny me then?'

'No, no! Of course not! But it will be different — '

'How? How will it be different? Because

we'll have a certificate, we'll have said a few words in front of a crowd?'

She stared at him, her eyes shining with tears.

'In front of each other, Johnny! And in front of God! Our vows, Johnny!'

'We're in front of God now, whether we like it or not! I love you, Rosie! You know I do!'

She did not even feel the normal quiver of annoyance at his familiar little cognomen for her.

'If you love me, you'll respect me, my feelings . . . ' she shook her head in sudden hopelessness, took a further step away, around him, and stared down at her bare feet, reminded yet again of the impropriety of what they were doing, what she had virtually condoned, by allowing him to visit here, in her own bedroom, before she was even dressed. And knowing all the time that it would lead inevitably to a situation such as this. *Hoping* that it would! she scourged herself penitently. Even now, she felt that shivering awareness of her flesh, her scantily covered flesh, its frightening depth of response to his embraces, which, only a few short days ago, she would never have believed it capable of. It was her fault, just as much as his, she castigated herself, that things had reached this pitch. She had been too complaisant of her own virtue, too confident in her power to conquer, to transform this new, wonderfully pliant Johnny, who had declared his love for her. Love clearly did not mean the same thing to both of them.

As though uncannily in tune with her thoughts, he cried vehemently:

'I'm talking about *real* love! Red-blooded love! Not your namby-pamby hearts and flowers and drawing-room poetry and love-songs! You're all shut in, Rosie, trapped in your polite society mannerisms, and your bows and your curtsies, the kind your Ned Lovatts revel in! Damned hypocrisy, all of it!' He gestured towards her, and she felt the deep rush of colour through her features. 'You're trapped as tight as the way your pretty flesh is trapped in those damned stays of yours! I think it's the first time I've ever truly touched you ... '

His remark about Ned had stung her hard enough, but it was the use of that hated phrase about 'red-blood' which truly hurt, for she remembered only too well how he had used it of Kate, in a comparison in which the mistress had fared far worse than the maid! The reminder of that humiliation gave strength to her argument now.

'You're talking of passion, not love. Passion

126

that even beasts feel! Love is what distin-
guishes us from those animal urgings. Love
comes from our sensibility. You say you love
me, Johnny.' She felt the heat invading her
cheeks once more, but she faced him, held his
gaze. 'What you feel is desire. To love me, you
must first know me. You know little about me,
other than the fact that you find me not
unpleasant to look at. As I know very little
about you. Love is learnt — '

'You said it last night. When we kissed. You
whispered it, when I was holding you.'

For an instant she faltered, but recovered
herself quickly.

'True. Because I *want* to love you! I want
to be a good wife, a proper partner to you
— in every way,' she added softly, despite her
embarrassment at such a forthright statement. 'I know, after the life you've led
— before you were restored to us — it is hard
for you, to adjust.' She hesitated, taken aback
all at once by her own reluctance to go on. 'It
is perhaps my fault for being somewhat lax in
— in — permitting . . . ' she waved her hand
about her, to indicate both the informality of
their surroundings, and her deshabille. 'It's
better if we do not meet like this, up here.
And we should try not to be alone together,
too much. It's difficult. There's so much
opportunity, here. We must try to invite more

guests. Parties!' She made an effort to brighten her voice, and her expression. 'With Christmas coming quite soon . . . '

He swung away from her, and moved over to the window bay, staring out at the ragged, wind-streaked clouds of the morning. She saw that he had picked up an ornament from the small, lacquered table in the recess. All at once, a hot wave of disturbing emotion ran through her, from toe to head, as she saw he was clutching a white figurine, made of alabaster. It was a translucent representation of a nude female, about eight or nine inches high. A slave girl, standing on a miniature plinth, her head lowered, her arms held in front of her, in an attempt to shield herself, the wrists shackled, linked by a short chain, in the case of the statuette a filigree as delicate as a cobweb. His thumb was pressing hard against the tiny protuberance of a breast. The effect on Rose was startling. She felt a riot of conflicting sensations, as though it were her own flesh he was touching, as indeed he had only minutes before.

To her mortification, he held up the figurine, thrust it towards her.

'See this, Rosie? What do you think of it? Pretty, isn't it?'

She struggled not to show her discomposure. 'Yes, it's a beautiful sculpture. Grandfather got it — a full fifty years ago now, when he was a young man. At the Exhibition. The original statue was there, a huge piece, in marble. It was the rage of the show, apparently. They sold thousands of those small models.'

'Yes. Funny, ain't it?' His features were stamped with that hard, cruel look that frightened her. 'You've got statues like this all over the place. And paintings, too. Like that Venus picture grandfather has hung in the library. What a beauty, eh?' He smacked his lips, and raised his eyebrows salaciously. 'She'd warm a feller's bed all right, eh?'

'They're works of art,' Rose began stiffly, but he ignored her.

'Naked women all over the place, and everything perfectly all right, as long as it isn't real flesh we're looking at. That's it, isn't it, Rosie, my love?'

Her eyes widened as he came closer, and held the statuette up once more, almost thrusting it in her face.

'Take a closer look at it, Rosie! That's what all you young society gals are like, it seems to me. Look! No nipples, see? Nice pointy little bosoms, but nothing like the real thing, are they? And look here!' He gestured again, at the flawless conflux of the smooth white thighs. 'Nothing! Nothing of what nature's put there, for our delight, my dear! Just a smooth white nothing! Cold marble! That's your high-class virgin, eh, Rosie?'

For a second, she thought he was going to dash the figurine to the floor, but instead he banged it down forcefully on top of her bureau. She found she was shaking, and drew a deep breath.

'You'd better go, Johnny. I'm going to ring for Helen. Then I've got some correspondence to see to. I'll see you for lunch.'

He shrugged. 'Maybe.' His glance flickered again towards the statuette of the slave girl. Suddenly, he thought of his mother, the misty shadow of her beauty, which was all he could remember. Thought of the murderer he had once loved as a father, who had condemned her to a shame such as that depicted by the little figure. He thought, too, of Lucy. She had taken part in one of the infamous *tableaux vivants* performed at Mrs Moss's, had played a similar role, and almost as comprehensively revealed. A choking sense of disgust overtook him, both with his own inordinate desire and the stifling conventions in which he and this beautiful girl before him were enmeshed.

He smiled cruelly. 'P'raps I'm too much in the way here. P'raps I ought to take off again. Go up to London for a spell.'

The wound his words made showed all too plainly, but she struck back.

'Why not? Things are more to your taste up there, I imagine. The *ladies* are not quite as cold or hard as marble up there, I believe! Nor as white as alabaster, either, I've heard!' The look of momentary wide-eyed amazement and dismay told her of the success of her retaliatory blow.

★　★　★

Lord Strenshaugh glared down the table at the two young people on either side of him. For once, he was dining alone with his grandchildren. The conversation had largely consisted of a monologue from him, punctuated by the necessary, minimal answers from Rose and Johnny. Impatiently, he waved the butler away, and waited until Mr Reece and the footman had left, and the door clicked shut behind them.

'What the devil is it between you two? Just when I thought you'd sorted yourselves out, the pair of you, here you are behaving like a pair of spitting cats again. I tell you, the whole of the staff will be wondering what's afoot! At least get on with each other in front of guests — and in front of the servants! I've a good mind to bring the wedding forward, and to hell with all the gossip-mongering. They can count off the months on their fingers and be damned! We'll have it before Christmas! The sooner the better!'

'I'm willing to play *my* part, Grandfather.' Johnny smirked mischievously, but the old man only grunted irritatedly. However, it was to Rose he turned, who was staring at him with undisguised horror.

'It's no good making those great cow-eyes at me, my girl! You'll learn to play Lady Strenshaugh to this young pup, even if you can't stand him!'

She kept her head down while she murmured her excuses and was given permission to leave.

'We'll join you in the library,' his lordship said. She recognized it as an order that she should go there and wait for them.

'I thought you'd started wooing her, Johnny!' The edge had gone from Lord Strenshaugh's ruddy features. They now bore a look of perplexity. 'She seemed quite ready to put up with you — and now!' He raised his hands helplessly. 'You want to go charging off to London, like a dog on heat, and she can't bear to look at you! You'll have to be a little more discreet about your peccadilloes! I hope you've given up that blackamoor you were parading around the town!'

Johnny shifted uncomfortably, and made to speak, but Lord Strenshaugh held up his hand.

'I've told you, there's a way for a gentleman to arrange these things. For God's sake, Rose is a pretty enough girl, isn't she? There's any amount of fellers would give their right arm to be in your shoes, believe me! Including that chappie Lovatt. You haven't quite won her yet, you know. Time you learnt how to handle your affairs in a proper manner. Get on with the business of wooing her. What do you think about bringing the wedding forward? Do you think she'll go for it? She's always been a good gel, done what's expected of her. But you'll have to play *your* part, my boy! One more trip up to town, and back here within a fortnight, you hear? And after that, down here you stay, unless it's to accompany your fiancée on her shopping-trips and sorting out her trousseau! There'll be plenty to keep you occupied, with a December wedding to arrange!'

★ ★ ★

Lucy came in from the bathroom next door. The close-cropped skull still had droplets of water gleaming like tiny jewels in it. She untied the sash of the flowered robe, and let it fall from her. Her fragrant body shone lustrously, and she stood proudly, letting the oblong of grey daylight from the window fall on her nakedness. She was conscious of Johnny's appreciative gaze, as he lounged on the bed.

'My proud little savage!' He smiled. 'You were not meant to be hidden beneath layers of clothing, my sweet.'

She advanced slowly towards him.

'Not in this climate, my darling pirate. You should take me back to Africa, if you want to keep me like this.' She coiled at his feet, let one long, thin hand fall upon his thigh. 'Do you think your little bride will be as accommodating? Perhaps you should take *her* there, on your honeymoon. She might shed her inhibitions along with her clothes!'

Johnny felt a spark of anger at her mockery. At one time he would have laughed loudly at any derogatory comment from Lucy about Rose. He was startled at the prick of conscience he felt now, and his shame on his fiancée's behalf at such remarks. Not for the first time, he experienced that wave of guilt when he thought of the beautiful, lonely girl waiting back in the gloom of the November countryside. He realized just how much he was looking forward to seeing her again, after more than two weeks' absence.

He was a fool to have kept away from her, he told himself. It should not have taken his grandfather's peremptory summons to bring him scurrying back. He could guess how furiously the old man would lay into him, and serve him right, too. He would take all his lordship's rage, and make up for the way he had treated Rosie. God, he was longing fiercely for Christmas, and the wedding which would be the chief element of that festive season! What had that shy little virgin done to him, he asked himself with a kind of rueful amusement? He was glad in a way that his wayward character had brought him here once more, for a last debauched fling, for he swore he would do his utmost to be faithful to her, once they were man and wife. She deserved nothing less, and he should thank his lucky stars he was to be given such a prize.

The spirit was so willing! But, oh, the flesh was so weak, he admitted, as he watched Lucy's dark hand steal imperiously up his paler thigh, and he squirmed lower in the bed, drawing her sinuous frame up, and over him, like a skin-tight velvet glove.

They were still lying coiled together, dozing in sated after-passion, when there was an urgent knocking, and Johnny heard his man calling out his name.

'Sorry to trouble you, sir! But there's an urgent message. A carriage is waiting. It's Lord Strenshaugh, sir. He's gravely ill! A seizure, they say!'

12

Johnny flung the cap and the heavy travelling-coat aside, scarcely acknowledging the greeting of the footman, who bent to gather them from the polished floor of the hall. Johnny was already bounding up the wide staircase, taking two of the rises at a time, but the brooding silence of the great house told him the worst, even before the grave-faced doctor stepped forward as he hurried towards his grandfather's room.

'I'm afraid he's gone, sir. About an hour ago. He never regained consciousness.'

Dr Ealey quickly passed on the details. 'His lordship went out for his usual afternoon ride, took the dogs with him. Apparently, after tea he complained of feeling unwell. A 'damned autumn chill' was how he described it to Mr Reece. He said he would take supper in his room, have an early night. His valet took him a hot toddy, helped to get him into bed. He told him he couldn't keep warm, but said he'd be fine in the morning. Told him to bank up the fire, and leave him. When his man went in this morning to wake him, he said his lordship couldn't be roused. He was highly coloured, making a peculiar, laboured sound, snorting. I came as soon as I could when I got the call. It was plain he'd had a seizure. There was little I could do, though I tried my best, of course. I stayed with him.'

The doctor paused. 'I'd warned him once or twice — you know what a choleric disposition his lordship had, sometimes. He was seventy, after all. The drinking — and he was still very active. Riding and so on. But then . . . if he *had* recovered, I'm sure it would only have been a partial recovery. His faculties would have been impaired.' The doctor smiled gravely, and lightly touched Johnny's arm. 'He wouldn't have liked that. This was quick. The kindest way.'

Johnny felt sick, and empty. His eyes had a lost look.

'I'll go in to him. Excuse me.'

The heavy drapes were drawn. A candle burned on the table by the bed, and another pair, in longer, spiralled holders, flickered either side of the narrow mantelshelf over the small hearth. The mirror over the fireplace had been draped with black cloth, as had the long chevalglass in its dark frame. The smell of the tallow mingled with a sharp odour of soap or disinfectant, overlaid with a heavy, sickly-sweet perfume from a bowl of crushed leaves and spices on a stand near the door.

Rose was sitting on one of the elegantly simple regency chairs, still favoured by her grandfather in his personal room, despite the various changes in style he had seen through his long life. Rose's slim back was upright, her form clothed in the formality of a black mourning gown. Probably one she had worn until only weeks before Johnny's dramatic entry into their lives, he guessed, as mourning for the old queen, who had ruled for almost the whole of the life of the figure who now lay so rigidly composed beneath the bed sheets.

Only when Johnny had quietly closed the door behind him did Rose's head turn. He came forward hastily, put his hand firmly on her shoulder, pressing her down as he felt her make to rise. He bent, his lips lightly brushed against the black lace of the shawl she had draped over her head. He smelt her fragrance briefly before he moved on to the side of the bed.

He was startled at first at the dark colour of the features against the snowy linen. There was a heavy, bruised look about the cheeks, deep shadows surrounded the closed eyes, the lids of which were empurpled. But it was the severity of the expression which struck him most; the etched lines about the turned-down mouth, showing through the whiskers, the set of that jaw, and prominent chin, the compression of the lips. It was his grandfather still, as stern as he remembered him. The arms, in the white nightshirt, were arranged on top of the sheet, folded, the fingers interlaced, and Johnny wondered who had carried out the task of laying him out. The hands were dark, too, the oldest thing about him, rope-veined, knuckles large, thrusting. Then Johnny remembered their last parting, those hands heavy and full of love as they hugged him, patted his shoulder. The look the old man had given him, eloquent in his love, and hope, for his future.

He reached out, touched their coldness now, and felt overwhelmed with loneliness and grief — and guilt.

'I should have been with him!' he said hoarsely. A great sigh welled up. The sob burst from him, the tears came, and suddenly he was clinging to Rose, she was there, holding him tightly, her arms about him, his face resting on the ruched lace and satin of the bodice, her lips kissing, lapping at the salt of his grief.

He struggled to get hold of himself, and succeeded. He lifted his head, smiled though his cheeks were wet with tears.

'He looks fierce, doesn't he? I hope to hell he's not still angry with me.' He gazed into her face, saw the strain, and the shock there, and again a deep sense of remorse shook him. 'Oh, Rose! I'm so sorry, my love. For everything. I'll make it up to you.' Very slowly and gently his fingers took the edge of the gauzelike shawl which framed her face and piled-up hair. Carefully he slipped the light cover back upon her shoulders, before, he moved to kiss her softly upon the lips. He felt their softness, their warmth. She did not stiffen, or pull away, and though the kiss was always gentle, he felt the return of the pressure, her willing response. 'I love you, Rose.' He whispered it solemnly, like a vow.

Outside, together, their new responsibilities were already waiting for them. Gooding advanced, holding the tray on which, already, lay a considerable pile of cards and telegrams.

'I thought I'd better refer these to you, milord.'

Rose, holding on to his arm, felt the shocked tremor pass through Johnny at the footman's style of address. She squeezed him tighter, sought his hand and clasped it to her side.

'That's right, Johnny. You're Lord Strenshaugh now.'

★ ★ ★

141

Gooding was staring at her, unable, despite his experience, quite to disguise his curiosity at Rose's reaction to the sight of the cheap envelope lying on the silver tray. She had almost gasped aloud when she saw it, and her hand had frozen in mid-air. Now she forced herself to carry on the movement, to take it up in her fingers.

'Would you like me to wait, miss? Will there be any reply?'

Spots of colour appeared in her pale cheeks.

'No, thank you, Gooding. That will be all.'

Johnny had disappeared somewhere. Gone out riding, in spite of his professed abhorrence for the pastime. Anything to escape the atmosphere of the house, she supposed. She could scarcely blame him, yet she could not help feeling secretly hurt at what she saw as his desertion of her. Shocking as it was, she looked back on those first few days after their grandfather's death almost with nostalgic regret now, despite their sadness. Again, she had felt that sudden, new closeness, the tenderness in her cousin which had so warmed her, all the more welcome because of its total unexpectedness.

It was a sadness somehow precious because they shared it. He really did care for her. She had glimpsed it briefly after the engagement party, only to have that dawning happiness snatched away by his shameful reluctance to accept the bounds of civilized society, the moral codes which must govern their lives, which were part and parcel of their privileged but responsible position in that society. It was, of course, tragic that it should have been the death of their grandfather which had brought them close once more, shown her yet again, the force of true feeling that he could display towards her, and — yes! She would admit it gladly — a feeling that she could genuinely return for him, that could indeed be the beginning of that love which she had prayed for, to seal their union for a lifetime.

He had been so tender with her. His kisses, their embraces, were so full of love, restrained as they were, that she was dizzy with relief and gratitude. He had shown at last the true sensitivity she had always hoped was there, behind that rough, at times shocking, ignorance and lack of concern for convention. This newly revealed love was wonderful; she felt guilty at the secret throb of joy in her heart when grandfather still lay in state, brought down into the small family chapel now.

But then the remorseless outside world began to press upon them again. As the arrangements for the elaborate funeral built up, so that the two young people felt a kind of helplessness, caught up in affairs which were inexorably slipping out of their grasp, the pressures built up, too. Sir Arthur Able, a cousin of the late lord and only a few years junior to him, had arrived, along with his loud and interfering wife, Lady Charlotte. Rose had seen little of them during her girlhood. There had been little familial affection on the part of his lordship or Sir Arthur, even though, her grandfather had bitterly reflected, Sir Arthur, and then one of his 'brood', would one day inherit title and estate. It was with a wicked glee that Lord Strenshaugh had hastily informed them by letter of the startling news of Johnny's discovery and imminent return. Sir Arthur and Lady Charlotte had stayed away from the celebrations to welcome the long-lost heir. Duty brought them now, sour, black as crows, for the funeral ceremony. Plain malice made them stay, according to Johnny, who took a savage pleasure in confounding them at every turn.

'Good heavens, young man! We can't leave Rose here unchaperoned. We'll have to stay on until alternative arrangements can be made. Perhaps Anne or Rowena could move down. It's so awkward. They have their own families to think of.' Lady Charlotte looked at

Johnny as though he were personally responsible for the whole sorry mess. 'Perhaps you could move out. Up to the town house.'

Johnny glared at Lady Charlotte, his angry dislike all too plain.

'This is our home. Rose's and mine. This is where we live. Good God! We'll be man and wife in a matter of weeks — '

'Don't be ridiculous, my boy! You're not serious? The wedding will have to be postponed. For at least six months! Surely, even you must realize — out of respect for your grandfather! The period of mourning . . . '

Rose had felt herself blushing deeply, both in sympathy and embarrassment for Johnny at his look of incredulity. His dark eyes actually turned towards her in incomprehension. 'No! We can't — '

'Of course we realize that the wedding will have to be delayed a little while, Lady Charlotte!' Rose cut in desperately. 'Until the spring. But Johnny has the running of the estate to learn. So many things. Now that he . . . ' she stopped, aware of the ruffled expression on the florid features of Lady Charlotte at this indelicate reference to Johnny's inheritance of the very position to which her husband and she had aspired until several months ago.

'Madam!' Johnny exploded. 'There are fifty rooms here, and a veritable army of servants! Do you think we could get up to anything untoward, even if we were so inclined? We've chaperons enough, thank 'ee, ma'am!'

'You are still perhaps unfamiliar with the ways of polite society over here,' Lady Charlotte answered sneeringly.

'I'm afraid not! I'm all too familiar — and heartily sick of them, I can tell you!'

He stormed out without another word, and Rose stared after him, her eyes blurred with tears. She knew how badly he had taken the news of the marriage postponement, even though he should have known it was inevitable. She sighed, bit her lip, and murmured an unconvincing apology on his behalf, all the while cursing Charlotte and her gloomy husband to hell and back.

For several hours after this exchange, Johnny had kept out of everyone's way, including her own. Things could hardly get worse, Rose had naively reflected. Now, in the afternoon post, had come this letter. She had recognized at once that ugly, square printing. She carried it up to her room, settled herself behind her closed door. For a long while, she stared at the envelope lying on the bureau. A fire had been newly laid in her grate, waiting only for the match to be applied. She should toss the envelope on it now, unopened. Consign it to the flames, where it belonged.

Her hand reached out to do so. She picked the missive up again, gave a small whimper of distress, then feverishly tore at the corner of the paper, pulled out the single, cheap sheet inside.

SO YOUR LORD HAS COME BACK TO YOU NOW, AND YOU'LL SOON BE HIS LADY! BUT HIS PRETTY BIRDS ARE ALL WAITING FOR HIM UP HERE. THEY KNOW HE'LL BE BACK SOON, AND SO DO YOU, DON'T YOU, MY DEAR? AFTER ALL, HE MIGHT LIKE YOU IN YOUR BLACK, BUT WHEN HE GETS BENEATH IT YOU'RE AS WHITE AS SNOW, AND LORD JOHNNY'S TOO HOT BLOODED FOR YOUR COLD CLIME, MY GIRL!

13

'I have a rather bad headache. I think I might be coming down with a chill. I'll have an early night, if you'll excuse me.' Rose nodded towards Sir Arthur and his grim-faced wife. She did not look at Johnny, who had come in late to the meal, and had slumped broodingly in his place, adding nothing to the desultory conversation, and drinking far too much wine. She heard the scrape of his chair as she hurried out, his muttered remark as he followed her. She could just imagine the outraged expression on Lady Charlotte's face.

In the draughty dimness of the wide hall, she turned, pulled her hand away as he reached for her wrist.

'Please, Johnny! You shouldn't! Stay with them. At least for a short while. For form's sake!' She knew that appeal was hardly likely to win over him, of all people, so she added, softly: 'For me!' She had slowed down, hoping he would turn back, but he stayed at her side, even succeeded in capturing her arm as she reached the foot of the grand staircase. 'I meant it. I do feel a little out of sorts. I'm going to ring for Helen. I'm going to bed.'

'We've hardly had a chance to talk for days! Not properly! Not alone!'

She was aware of the servants' eyes in the background. She did not try to release her arm. She gathered the skirt of her long gown with her free hand as she began to climb the stairs, Johnny at her side.

'That's hardly my fault!' she answered. 'You take yourself off somewhere every chance you get!'

'I can't stand it, being cooped up with them.'

'It's not as though you're taking the opportunity to start learning about Strenshaugh. Mr Kemp was looking for you today. You said you'd go round the estate.' Mr Kemp was the estate manager.

She felt Johnny's quick gesture of impatience.

'Kemp knows what he's doing, Rosie. That's why he's paid so much, to take care of things. Grandfather never bothered about the way things are run. He had more sense.'

'The world's changing so fast. We have to change, too, Johnny. Modernize. Grandfather chose not to, especially after he lost your parents — and you. Then there was my mother's death. But the old ways are changing. He was looking forward so much to you taking over the reins. I think — '

'I don't know if I'm cut out to be a farmer, Rosie!' Johnny interrupted.

His tone sounded harsh to her ears. She flushed, felt the upsurge of all the hurt and anger she had been repressing since she had read that filthy note.

'Hardly that! There are hundreds of people who depend on you for their livelihood!' She could not help the bitterness, which overflowed. 'But then, as you say, you can always leave it all to Mr Kemp and his staff! You can play the dissolute lord with your cronies up in London!'

They had reached her door, and he pulled her round by her arm, staring intently into her face.

'Rosie! What the devil's wrong with you? What have I done now — apart from trying to keep out of the way of that stout bitch and her bore of a bloody husband? Believe me — if it was up to me I'd have shown 'em the door the day after the funeral! If they don't clear off soon I might just do that anyway!'

His baffled frustration showed at the coldness of the look she returned. She echoed his question.

'What have you done? Examine your conscience, Johnny. Is it pure as snow?' He frowned at her strange words, and on a sudden impulse, she pushed open her door. 'Come on. Come on in to my room. Who cares what people think, eh? You clearly don't, milord! Perhaps I should take a leaf out of *your* book!'

He stared at her, even more at a loss as he stepped through the door and she banged it shut behind him.

'There! Let the servants gossip, eh? Let Lady Charlotte have apoplexy! Who cares?'

He was looking positively alarmed now at the untypical wildness of her expression and her behaviour. Her brown eyes sparkled with fire as she stared at him, with a strange smile stamped on her face.

'Maybe I've been playing the country mouse too long, buried down here. Why don't you take me up to London with you, Johnny? Show me how you and your cronies spend your time up in town! Perhaps it's *me* who needs educating, not you!' Her gown rustled as she moved quickly to her bureau and snatched up a sheet of paper, thrust it at him.

'It certainly sounds exciting enough! No wonder you were so reluctant to tear yourself away!' She saw the dark colour mount as he swiftly scanned the printed words, saw the look of naked dismay when he glanced back at her, his mouth opening, but hesitating to speak. 'And it's not the first such I've been

151

privileged to receive!' she said breathlessly. Again, she swept back to the bureau, lifted its curved lid and reached into the interior compartments. She pulled out the first note she had been sent, still in its envelope, and handed it to him. 'That came a few months ago, when you were making your first visit. Just before dear Kate left me! I was so shocked I showed it to her.'

There was a stillness about him now, like an animal alert to some new danger. He held the envelope, but did not take out the letter. He kept his gaze fixed on hers, heard the raw pain behind the anger in her tone.

'She didn't doubt its truth for one minute! In fact, she called you a whoring beast — forgive my indelicate language, won't you? I reprimanded her, of course. Quite severely. Things were never the same between us. She told me she was leaving just a day or two later. Go on! Read it, Johnny! It will make you smile, I'm sure.'

He hesitated, then took out the note, read it. His mouth thinned. Her voice was shrill, piercing.

'There! Don't you find it amusing? The bit about Kate blacking up my face for you?'

His dark eyes sparked with anger, too, now. 'Anonymous filth! Some cowardly sot — '

'That's what grandfather said!' She saw the

flicker of surprise on his features, and went on quickly, 'Oh, don't worry! I didn't show him the letter. I just asked him what you were up to in London. He assumed I'd heard gossip from the servants, passed on to me by Kate. Scurrilous nonsense, he called it. Is it?' She thrust the question like a dagger at him, waiting. He met her stare challengingly, but made no answer. 'Is it nonsense? This thing about the black girl, Lucy? And why was Kate so ready to believe such a wicked lie? What had you done to make her think such wickedness of you? Tell me it's all lies, Johnny! Tell me now!'

She met his gaze, saw the vulnerability there, behind all the rage. She waited breathlessly, half-hoping, half-dreading that he would deny it. She saw pain, and even shame, but he did not flinch.

'It's over now. It's all done with — '

She made a soft exclamation, compelled to go on. 'It's true, then? Lucy? It . . . '

'You want me to tell you? To describe it? You want the details?'

Her face was drained of its colour now, and her head shook slightly. The tears were starting to fall, but she took no notice of them.

'It's different, Rosie. For a man — for

153

someone like me. It's not the same. Our passions . . . '

She shook her head quickly, as though she did not want him to continue, wanted him to stop at once. Her voice sank almost to a whisper now, all the anger melted away, leaving only those great, silent tears rolling down her face.

'You said you'd find Kate. You never did, did you? Over two months she's been gone now. Why haven't you tried to find her?'

'For God's sake, Rosie! Enough! Things have been . . . ' he gestured around him, flinging his hand high. 'A lot's been happening.' She was staring at him, the channels of her tears glistening in the lamplight. 'I'll find her.' His voice sounded bitter, dead. He turned and left her standing there. Both letters lay on the rug, like dead leaves.

★ ★ ★

'Now then, Reece. I have to find this girl. Her people live in the village, don't they?'

The butler's face retained its impassive stamp, as did his voice as he answered evenly:

'His late lordship always accorded the style 'mister' before my name, milord. It's customary.'

154

'Very well, *Mister* Reece!' Johnny hissed through his teeth. 'Now! As I said, I need your help.'

He felt as though he were merely moving along a predestined path, towards his own failure, helpless to prevent it, when he set off through the parkland, following the path through the misty chill of the woodland, its trees stripped of foliage, the branches laced in black, jagged and bare. The very wood where, in leafy high summer, he had first made love with the girl he was about to try to find. He had picked her up in this very cart. His lower limbs were wrapped in a thick plaid rug. He put his gloved hand out to touch the buttoned leather beside him, and felt his manhood throb in recognition of the pleasure he had experienced from her eager young body. A pleasure whose memory was now tainted by his shame. And yet there was a foolish anger there, too, that he should be made to feel that shame, a frustration, both with his own inescapable conscience, and with Rosie's purity, the rigour of her morality, which threatened the hope of happiness that had dawned for both of them.

Damn the girl! Why couldn't she accept the fact that he loved her? He had only just realized it for himself, was coming to terms with the strange feeling of it. Was even preparing to sacrifice all his old, rebellious attitudes for her sake, to clothe himself in this strangling rectitude of the society he had been flung back in so unceremoniously.

He had tried to talk to her again this morning, striving to be calm, to be penitent, about those accursed letters. Even to do that, he had had to waylay her, practically manhandle her into the steamy heat of the conservatory to snatch a private moment, away from the ears of the hag Charlotte. He had spoken as a confessed sinner, with a disarming smile. He could not have been more honest.

'I've been a bad 'un, Rosie. What can I say? Guilty as charged, my love. But I swear, it's finished, from now on. On grandfather's grave I swear it. I want you to marry me, Rose. I won't look at another. That's my pledge.' He was shaken as he uttered the extravagant words to discover that he meant them.

He knew his leching had meant a lot to her, knew just how important on the scale of sinning it was. He thought of her beauty, the unspoilt innocence of it, and he loathed himself far more than she did for the heated arousal of his flesh at this thought. He must be gentle with her, even though every atom of him ached to possess her. And he would, too. He would show her, and himself, what love really meant. And felt like. He would teach her to release the rapture, the joy of physical love that lay hidden inside her. Though it made his blood race, his desire for her was cleansing. He would be worthy of her.

But first he had to win her back again. Who had written those letters? When he spoke against the cowardice of the anonymous writer, she had brought him back to the one painful fact.

'They were done to hurt you — and me!' he cried. 'To stop us being together!'

'But they are true!' That much was, unfortunately, undeniable. 'Perhaps they come from your African herself, from Lucy,' Rose had speculated. 'I don't know enough about — about that kind of life. That kind of woman. Perhaps they have feelings — sensible feelings, too. Perhaps she doesn't want to lose you, however low she is.'

Her suspicion startled him for a moment. But then he thought of Lucy, of how separate the passion she could share between the sheets was from the hard-headed reality of her tight-curled skull. Then, in his typical, impetuous fool's way, he had blurted out something which had added mightily to the already high barrier between Rose and himself.

'More likely to be your pillar of virtue, Mr Ned Lovatt!'

It was almost comic the way poor Rose's jaw dropped, her brown eyes popping out of her head. She had floundered like a fish on a riverbank before she could even speak.

'How despicable of you! How could you even think such a thing, such a lie?'

The injustice of it fanned his fury, until they were almost snarling at each other, and he was disgusted with himself for his pettiness in suggesting Lovatt's hypocrisy. He cut himself short, his weariness with the whole argument evident in his tone.

'He's no worse than most, I suppose. Makes damn sure he doesn't get caught, that's all. It's like I told you. Men are different. You'll just have to take my word for it, my dear.'

'*Some* men!' Then she had stopped, given him a long, level look, full of mystery, and all the more disturbing for the fact that he could not tell what was going on behind the look. He was not used to such subterfuge from one as transparent as she normally was. 'Find Kate for me,' she said quietly. 'Find out what has happened to her.'

He swore he would, but even as he said it, he had the feeling he was sealing his own fate, condemning himself to failure with the one he had only just found out he loved.

*   *   *

The village street began as a twisting, narrow road, then widened out to a huge space of bare earth, with spreading green common either side. It took him a while to ascertain where the Addys' cottage was, but eventually a barefoot boy led him there, walking in front of the horse. Several people gathered, in belated surprise, as they realized that the gentleman who had descended from the smart cabriolet was the new Lord of Strenshaugh. A few tugged at their forelocks, a couple of giggling women bobbed an awkward curtsy. As Johnny, distinctly nervous, smiled in acknowledgement, he heard a shout from behind him, then felt a blow on his shoulder, which made him stumble.

He turned to see a solid, ruddy figure in farm labourer's garb, his round face covered in stubble of several days' growth.

'Get away from this gate, you bastard! We don't want to see you, you hear? Keep away. She damn near died 'cos of you, and she might still, so be off with you, or I'll thrash you like the dog you are, lord or no lord!'

14

Johnny was not as appalled as he might have been at the rough simplicity and the cramped conditions of the cottage's interior. The memories of his own upbringing, the primitiveness of the surroundings he had grown up in, were too recent. But he *was* shocked, deeply, at the difference he saw in the wasted form and features of the young woman who had clearly just risen from the old settle in the tiny front room which served as parlour. She was wearing a drab, grey gown and darned woollen stockings, and had a knitted shawl about her shoulders against the wintry chill, despite the fire in the adjacent kitchen, the only other downstairs room of the dwelling. The smoke from this fire filled both rooms with a pungent haze.

'What have you come here for? What do you want?'

Kate's red hair was partly hidden under an ugly mob-cap, whose untied ribbons hung at her shoulders. The red, unkempt locks which straggled from beneath its cover looked dark and greasy. But it was the face that dismayed him most. Not only the loss of its beauty, the dark-edged hollowness of the eyes, the unhealthy parchment muddiness of the skin, but the pain-etched weariness of her expression, the dead shadow which had been stamped over the former, lively beauty. She was hunched forward, her shoulders bent, her hands formed into fists, pressed into her stomach. She moved stiffly, like an old woman.

'You shouldn't have come. You've no right to be here.' Her voice sounded hoarse, bereft of life, too.

'You should have told me, Kate!' he cried out, with raw anger. 'You shouldn't have kept it from me. I'd have helped — '

'Oh, yes! And I'd a been Lady Strenshaugh now, would I?' She gestured over his shoulder, towards the outer doorway, where the rectangle of light was still blocked by the figures pressing as close as they dared to gawp in. 'You've caused enough upsetment here Master Johnny! Get back to where you belong, and leave us alone. I want nothing from you!'

He felt the wound from her words, more than the swelling bruise on his cheekbone, where her brother's fist had smashed into him. They had fallen, threshing together, Johnny giving as good as he got in the brief brawl before the villagers dragged them apart.

Michael Addy had been hustled away somewhere, and Johnny had been restrained, too, until a modicum of order had been restored. In the small enclosure of a garden in front of the cottage, Kate's father, supported by his wife, had swiftly apprised him of Kate's sad recent history. Generations of rigid social caste had kept his tone respectful — he had even apologized for his son's physical assault on Johnny — but there was no disguising the underlying bitterness in his words.

Kate had simply told them she had quit her job as Miss Rose's maid, giving them few details, and flying tearfully 'off the handle' when her father had remonstrated with her. She had gone away to a neighbouring village to stay with her aunt for a while, where word came back that she was gravely ill, and 'like to die', which was when the whole sorry truth had come out. Carrying Johnny's child, Kate had sought traditional country help in bringing on a miscarriage. The 'remedy' she had taken had succeeded in terminating the pregnancy, but at a terrible cost. She had been close to death, and was indeed still at some risk.

'I fear she'll never be well again, sir,' her father told him. 'She's not even fit for work no more. She didn't want to come home, but

162

she's in no state to fend for herself, as you'll see.'

Now he *had* seen for himself, and he was smitten with conscience and anger made all the worse because he scarcely knew against whom he should direct it. Society, and its rigid protocol of upper and lower orders? Rose for letting Kate go, for suspecting nothing, and for making no effort to trace the girl's whereabouts? But the biggest betrayer of all was, he knew, himself, for he was very well aware that he was the root cause, that his unthinking lechery, or passion, had brought all this tragedy into being. It was just another example, the supreme one, of his irresponsibility, his failure to accept the code of the society he had been brought back into. Rose had been right all along. He had almost cost the life of this poor, ruined girl. *Had* cost the life of her unborn child. Not just her child, his, too! his sickened conscience reminded him.

'I would never have turned my back on you, Kate!'

His pain was evident, and his conviction, too, and Kate felt the old power of her attraction for him stirring painful memory.

'Aye! And we'd have all lived up at the hall, one big happy family, eh? You, me, and our love-child, and Miss Rose!' She gave a small groan, her strength seemed to ebb from her all at once, and she bent even further. Her voice dropped to a soft murmur. 'There's been enough damage done. Enough hurt. Go back where you belong, Johnny. Just look after her. She thinks a lot of you . . . '

'She wants to help, too. She's been asking about finding you. We'll take care of you.' He glanced about him, at the humble surroundings. 'Of your family. We'll make it up . . . '

'The best way you can make it up is to go back and make her a good husband.' As he started to protest, Kate held up her hand and her voice grew more urgent with her plea. 'Can't you see, Master Johnny? We can't let her know the truth. A girl like Miss Rose, in her position. She can't live with it. We've got to make sure she doesn't find out.'

'No! You're wrong. All that matters now is to get you well again. I'm going to bring the carriage, bring you back to the hall. Dr Ealey will take a look at you. You'll stay there, as his patient, and our guest. It'll be all right, you'll see.'

Kate shook her head. She gave another low moan, and her fists tightened at her stomach. Johnny moved forward quickly, and took her arm. Once again, he was shocked to feel its fragile thinness. She sagged weakly against him, as though resistance was draining from

164

her. He half-carried her back to the settle and lowered her on to it.

'I won't be long. I'll be back for you within the hour.'

She gave a cry, reached up and clutched at his hand to detain him.

'Johnny! Listen! Don't tell her the truth! Not all of it! Don't tell her about you and me! She doesn't have to know. Why hurt her? I'll just say it was — someone from the village — a lad!'

He quietened her, told her again he would return soon, with the carriage. Outside, the crowd was still gathered. Forelocks were tugged respectfully, but there was a buzz of murmurings, and Johnny knew what they were muttering. His fingers went to the throbbing, discoloured lump over his left cheekbone. The identity of Kate's 'secret' lover was too well known to be kept hidden. Not only her irate brother, most of the countryside around was aware of it. Rose would have to be told the truth. She would hear about it soon enough, in any case. He told himself he was glad that it was so. No more lies, no more subterfuge. No more anonymous notes about his misdemeanours. All that was over. She had whispered, once, as they kissed, that she loved him. He would soon know if that, too, was the truth.

★ ★ ★

Dr Ealey emerged at last from the room in which the sick girl had been installed. Rose and Johnny had been waiting anxiously during the long minutes of the examination. They had scarcely exchanged a word since Johnny had fetched Kate in the carriage, after sending word for the doctor to attend as soon as he could. Johnny swore to himself he would tell the full truth, at the first proper opportunity. He wanted a quieter, more reflective moment to make his confession to Rose. He knew how much it would hurt her to learn that he was the culprit. In spite of her illness, and her agitation at being reunited with her former mistress, Kate had flashed a beseeching look at him, begging him to keep silent. She herself had wept as she gave a brief, sorry history of her misdemeanour, clearly implying that the man involved was someone of her own station, unknown to Rose and not among the staff at Strenshaugh.

'Poor girl!' Rose said, when Kate had been put to bed to await Dr Ealey's arrival. She coloured a little as she went on, and Johnny had felt that tender mix of sympathy and irritation at the over-delicacy of Rose's sensibility. However, her words roused all his old fears and anxiety for the outcome of this unfortunate situation. 'She must have been — in her condition — when she left me. That's why she was so different from her normal self. Why she was so sharp — and surly. Who is the brute? She must be made to tell his name. He deserves to pay for his — his wickedness!'

Once more, Johnny urged upon himself the necessity of speaking to Rose as soon as possible, however much he feared her reaction. He could not allow Kate to go on protecting him — and Rose — by her silence.

Dr Ealey came forward to them, shaking his head.

'These country midwives! No better than medieval witches, most of them! They use these traditional herbs and plants, claim to know nature's ways, and concoct potions that can well be lethal. I'm afraid your maid's fallen victim to one of them. She's still seriously ill. But the fact that she's survived this long after the miscarriage is a good sign. There was some infection, but it seems to be on the mend. It will take a long while for her to regain her strength, but with care she should be able to make a good recovery.' He glanced at Rose quickly, as though acknowledging the candid nature of his disclosure. 'I doubt she'll be able to bear children. But then she's lucky to have got away with her life, the foolish girl. There's many in her position who are not so lucky.'

'It's the fellow who seduced her who should be punished!' Rose said hotly. 'She won't even tell us who he is! That sort always seem to get away scot free!'

The doctor's eyebrows flickered towards Johnny, with a hint of resigned humour almost, in complacent acknowledgement of male bonding.

'There's a good nursing-home, at the coast. Not too far. It's a charitable trust, excellent conditions. That's if you're prepared to accept responsibility for her, of course,' he added quickly.

'Certainly.' Rose blushed again, then glanced at Johnny for confirmation.

'Of course.' He nodded firmly.

'It will be a long haul, I think,' Dr Ealey continued. 'You wouldn't want her staying all that time here at the hall.'

'Well, she must stay here for now. Until she's stronger. We'll see how she is after a few weeks. We don't want to send her away too soon. I feel I've let her down badly enough as it is. If only she had felt she could have come to me! Told me what was wrong!'

'Well, you're doing your best for her now, eh?' The doctor smiled. 'Both of you.'

When Dr Ealey had left, after promising to

look in on his patient the next day, Rose said: 'I must go and talk to Kate. I hope Dr Ealey didn't mention that nursing-home to her. I don't want her to feel she's a burden to us here. She can stay as long as she likes. I feel guilty enough as it is!' She turned and came close, holding her hands out to him, her face lit up by her smile. 'And I want to thank you, Johnny, for finding her. I should have done it ages ago. So many things have happened. Not that I'm trying to excuse myself. You said you would, and — '

'Rosie!'

The intensity in his cry, the look on his face, stopped her in her tracks. She felt a sudden cold fear, like an icy touch, without understanding the reason for it.

'What is it, Johnny?'

'We have to talk! I have to tell you!'

'Tell me what?'

He took her arm. She felt the pressure of his fingers digging into her flesh. He pulled her along the corridor, towards her own room. Her heart was thudding, the fear grew, so that she was afraid to break the silence. She let him lead her to her bedroom, and into its neat quietude. He sat her down on the chesterfield, in front of the newly cleaned fireplace. He stood over her, and she almost held her breath at the tortured expression on his features, the brilliant plea of the dark eyes.

'Rosie! Love! Kate's lover! Seducer! That wicked brute! God forgive me, it was *me*, Rosie. I was the one who got her with child!'

15

'She cannot stay here! Not under this roof!' Rose's words, uttered with a low, trembling intensity, were spaced, came at Johnny like the projectiles from a gun. She felt an empty sickness inside, as though her vital organs had been sucked out from within her. She was still suffering from shock at the brutality of his confession, even though she had had several hours to absorb the horror of what he had done. When he had first told her, she had, quite literally, been struck both dumb and motionless. She felt the strength flow out of her, the trembling weakness of her limbs, which made her incapable of rising from the sofa, or of making a sound, beyond that first agonized, whispered, 'No!' She was giddy, thought she might faint, and in alarm he had sprung forward, seized her by the shoulders, tried to take her in his arms. She felt like a rag-doll, pulled back and forth, until she had managed to gasp out a few more tormented phrases. 'Don't — touch me! Leave me — get out!'

Still the tears would not come, only that swirling sickness, the gulping breaths. She bent forward, as though she had taken a blow, leant her swimming head down upon her hands, her elbows jabbed into her knees. Then came the nausea, so that she was afraid she would be sick on the rug, the rhythm of her blood roaring in her ears. When the giddy sickness eased, and she became aware once more of her surroundings, she realized, with a great sigh of relief, that she was alone. She thought she could not have borne to lay eyes on him again.

She made it over to the bed, and lay face down across it. Then the tears came. Savage, rending sobs, jerking her whole frame, while his words hammered around in her brain, until she became frightened at the violence and hysteria of her grief.

'Say it isn't true!' she wept, croaking the words aloud, and wondering who on earth she was addressing them to. After a long, long while, the sobs quietened, died. She thought longingly of dragging off her clothes, of crawling beneath the blankets, drawing them over her head, as she had when she was a little girl at her home in Derbyshire, to make a warm, safe refuge, hidden from the world. Except that she knew now that there was no such place, nowhere safe from the world and all its hurts. Her fond, girlish dreams, of being Lady Strenshaugh, of living with her lord and lover in their fairytale castle, were as foolishly unreal as all her childhood fantasies. There was nowhere at all to hide.

Her face was blotched, her eyes puffed and her nose red. Inexpertly, she strove to tidy the wild disorder of her tumbled hair, to pin the falling tendrils of rich blackness into place again. She would not ring for Helen. Could not face her, but her face burned anew at the thought of the gossip that must be humming below stairs like the telephone wires her grandfather had been so vehemently against when they were first installed at the hall. Instead, she went along the corridor of the broodingly silent house, back to Kate's room. She tapped and entered.

The wasted figure was lying back against the pillows, the long, red tresses dark against the whiteness spreading down on to the sheets. There was a fragile trace of her beauty still in the sharp angularity of the bone structure. Rose's heart welled with pity. Who could not feel sorry for the tragic figure, and the sorrow in that expression? Those great eyes turned on hers now, and the lines of sorrow deepened.

'You know.' It was a statement. 'Did *he* tell you himself?'

Rose's throat closed, she was unable to speak. She nodded. Kate nodded back, her pale hand rose and fell back against the coverlet, in a hopeless little gesture.

'I begged him not to,' she murmured. 'But I knew he would. He's too honest for his own good.'

Despite her best intentions, all Rose's feelings of pity were crushed by the overwhelming sense of betrayal and heart's pain, which filled her eyes with fresh tears.

'How could you, Kate? How could you do this to me, after all the time we've been together? I thought you cared for me.'

The teardrops formed, fell from the dark lashes, rolled down Rose's cheeks. Kate's grey eyes remained dry, but the sadness they carried was evident.

'I did. I do, miss. I would have died, rather than put you through this. I didn't want you to know. I tried to stop it . . . '

With yet another sense of shock, Rose was all at once aware, without anything being said, that Johnny and this girl had been lovers more than once. Had met, kissed, had assignations, over a whole period of time, here, under this very roof, and all the while . . . Her body seemed to burn now with mortification as, helplessly, she relived the feel, the passion of his kisses, his arms about her, holding her tight, the touch of his hand on her soft breast, proffered to him through the thin cover of her nightgown.

'How long? How long was it going on?'

'Not long, miss. Only in the summer. Before you became engaged. A couple of months. No more.' Kate's voice faded, as she realized how deeply Rose was wounded by her words. 'I didn't want you to know, miss!' Kate cried, her tone desperately alive all at once. 'He shouldn't have come looking for me. You would never have known. You'd have heard nought from me!'

How rough and uncultured her speech sounds! Rose thought inconsequentially. After only a few months away, back in the village. When her speech had become so refined, and ladylike with me. A few months away. Two? As long as they had been meeting, secretly, making love, in their dark corners, passion blazing, while stupid, innocent Miss Rose lay sleeping alone, and dreaming hotly, shamefully, of what it would be like when she and Johnny . . .

'I didn't want to come here, miss. I asked him to go away, to leave me alone.' And now Kate was crying, too, her voice hoarse with distress. 'I'll leave! Let me go back home, miss! I'm sorry!' She made an effort to thrust back the blankets and get out of bed.

Rose saw the white shins, the bare feet, and she moved forward, as though she would physically prevent the girl from rising.

'Don't be so stupid! You're sick! You've been very ill. You have to get well. His lordship must pay for — for his sins! We all pay. You more than most.'

Kate fell back weakly, while Rose firmly replaced the covers, and stood close by the bed. Kate took a deep, sniffling breath.

'It wasn't just him, miss,' she said bravely. 'I didn't — I wanted him to — to do what he did. What *we* did.'

Once more, Rose felt her whole body burning. Part of it, the greater part, was shame, for she recognized so much in the maid's stammered words. Or, rather, in what was *not* said. She remembered yet again, the feel of him holding her, the secret shameful strength of her own, ignorant longings for more; her anticipation of what it would be like to belong truly to him. But *I* waited! her mind screamed out in righteous protest. My thoughts may have been sinful, but that's all they were: thoughts. I did not offer myself, he did not take me. Because he had no need! an inner voice answered mockingly. He had this girl, stretched out in this bed before you now. Maybe, indeed, in this very bed! And elsewhere. Where? Her mind tortured her with its conjectures. Two whole months of their clandestine loving, within this very house. Did they laugh at her, share sniggering secrets about her: 'ice-water Rosie', as he had never tired of calling her?

'You betrayed me! The two of you! And now you've ruined — shamed me!' Rose's fingers curled, a redness blazed in her mind, shook her whole being so that she longed to strike and rake at this pathetic figure, score that pallid flesh the way her heart had been scored by their infidelity.

'He's not like the others, miss! I mean the gentlemen you know. He can't be like them. He doesn't know — I mean how to go on like them. How could he? You have to under-stand — '

Rose's voice choked, shook with her fury.

'You — you dare — to lecture me — to tell me how . . . ' with an explosive sound of disgust, she turned on her heel.

'You must forgive him, miss. It's because he couldn't have you — he loves you!' The cry rang shockingly loud in Rose's ears as she fled the room.

Steeling herself, Rose had rung for her maid, questioned her, even as Helen helped her to wash and to change her gown for the evening. It was harrowing, as well as excruciatingly embarrassing, but she sur-prised herself with the new determination she found. By the time they had finished, Helen was close to tears, but she told Rose all the buzzing gossip that was causing such a stir among the domestic staff. How the talk was all of his lordship's dalliance with Kate Addy, and its unfortunate results. Of the brawl outside the Addys' cottage in Garrowby, and the still-reverberating shock waves of his lordship's bringing Kate to the hall.

Rose had ordered Helen to bring a light supper up to her room, and to inform Mr Reece that she would not be dining tonight. When she had tried to nibble at the food, and drunk a cup of tea, she had waited until she could seek out Johnny in the privacy of the library. A fire burned brightly, the logs sending tiny sparks darting up the chimney. Johnny was sitting in what had been her grandfather's favourite spot, and in his chair, the bottle of brandy at his elbow. She could tell that Johnny had already drunk well through his solitary meal. He had a brandy-glass raised to his lips as she entered. He set it down so swiftly its contents slopped on to the polished surface of the table. He sprang to his feet.

'You should have eaten something. There's no point in making yourself ill.'

'You don't want *both* your paramours ill, I suppose!' She had not meant to speak so vituperatively. He winced visibly, and for an

178

instant she felt a stab of pity and compassion for the raw suffering she saw on his face. It disconcerted her so much that it caused her anger to flare once more. This time she spoke with deadly quiet. 'She cannot stay here! Not under this roof!'

Again that open look of hurt, of bewilderment almost.

'You wanted me to find her. You can't turn her away now!'

In some strange way, Rose felt as though she were observing herself from a distance, and it was like watching a stranger. Where had she found such cold, steely resolution, the capacity to hit back, the need to wound as she had been wounded?

'Oh, no! Of course not! I'm sorry, I forgot. I can't turn anyone out, can I, because I don't have a roof myself? It's you who own me, isn't it? You clothe me, feed me, provide me with a home. I'm kept by you, just as I was kept by grandfather since I was a young girl. It's I who should be leaving. I'll move out. Perhaps with Sir Arthur and Lady Charlotte. Or with one of their daughters. I could end my days as a governess to their grandchildren, perhaps.'

The Ables had been away for the last four days, seeing to matters at their home, and visiting their married offspring. They had insisted they would return to Strenshaugh Hall in a week or so. Rose had never given them a thought. Now she reflected just how violent their reaction would be to the scandal which had unfolded so dramatically during their absence.

'Don't talk like that!' Johnny answered her stinging word harshly. 'You know damned well this is your home as much as mine! More! I'm the interloper here, everyone knows that! Grandfather provided for you for life. Because you were closest to him.' He made a step towards her, raising his hands as though to plead. She was afraid for a second that he was going to embrace her and, even as she drew back from him, part of her ached for him to do just that.

'I'm perfectly serious, Johnny. Even without your confession — and without Kate's misplaced sense of loyalty in trying to keep quiet, the scandal could not have been buried. I know that the servants are ablaze with it, that all of Garrowby and the countryside around are aware of it. Aware of the wrong you've done, aware of your public brawl with Kate's brother. You can't keep her here now, Johnny! Even you must realize that!' He looked so youthful, standing there in hang-dog silence, that again that disturbing pity and tenderness flickered on the perimeter of her thoughts. She made a great effort to collect herself and clasped her hands together. She moved to stand beside him in front of the blazing fire, welcoming the warmth she could feel through her clothing.

'Good heavens, Johnny! Have you any idea what you're doing? How big a scandal this will be, when it gets out that you've brought home a girl you've wronged, made her a guest in your home — the home *we* share? The papers, every scandal-sheet, will be full of it. You're not some ordinary little citizen, Johnny! Don't you see what it means? You'll be expected to attend the coronation of your king next year! To take your seat in the Lords to vote on important issues! They'll hound you — *us* — to death!'

'To hell with them! We'll go away! After the wedding — as soon as we're married. We'll travel the world. I'll take you to Africa! You'll love it, Rosie. It's so wonderful. Nothing like all this!' He gestured around him, gazed at her in appeal, then stopped when he saw the strange, fixed expression on her face, her astonishment. He waited. 'What is it?'

'You surely — I mean you can't really believe . . . ' Her voice was breathy, underlying her amazement. 'There can't be anything now, Johnny. Not for you and me.

That's over. Our engagement is dissolved.'
She shook her head. 'You must know, we
can't contemplate a betrothal now?'

She was even more astounded at his look of
incredulity, that expression, as though a
thunderbolt had struck.

'You must know that everything is over
between us, Johnny?' she said softly.

'I love you, Rosie!' He came to her. She
could feel herself quivering, from head to toe.
She waited for him to seize her, to crush her
against him, to clamp his mouth over hers,
but all he did was grab her hands, to squeeze
them painfully. His face was inches away from
hers, she could feel the heat of his breath on
her. His eyes were black, piercing, brilliant
with his intensity. 'You said you loved me!'

Time seemed to have halted. All she could
see was his face, feel the blaze of all that
passion, that tremendous will, the merciless
crush of her delicate hands in his grip. She
fought to get her words out.

'I could not say it now! It wouldn't be true.
I've never said it to anyone but you.' And she
lifted her head challengingly, eloquently,
towards the ceiling, in unspoken but clear
accusation of his perfidy.

She felt him release her, his own hands
dropping to his sides. He seemed to crumble,
the tension draining from him. She cleared

her throat, fighting now against the great wave of desolation she could feel rising to engulf her.

'I'll leave tomorrow. I'll move — '

'No! Damned if you will! *I'll* go! First thing in the morning!'

Instinctively, she knew that the hardness now engraved on his features was masking the vast depth of emotion. He glanced round the comfortably appointed room.

'I wish to God I'd never set eyes on Strenshaugh Hall in the first place!'

16

A fierce gale blew up during the night. The wind shook the windows and shutters of the house, roared about the chimney pots, and continually blew downdraughts of pungent smoke into Rose's bedroom, so that she was glad to have Helen send one of the kitchen girls up to dampen the coals and put out her fire. Even with her warmest flannelette nightgown, nightcap tied under her chin, her bed-jacket about her shoulders, her feet encased in woollen bed socks, and with two hotwater bottles in her bed, she still felt cold huddled under the heavy blankets. The glow of the bedside lamp, which normally seemed so cosy when she settled down to read before sleeping, now served only to emphasize the hostile dimness of the shadows lurking beyond its limited circle of light. In any case, she was far too distracted to concentrate on the page in front of her, which remained unturned as the minutes ticked slowly by. Soon, she extinguished the lamp, and lay instead staring into the buffeting darkness. The storm was a perfect match for her violently agitated thoughts.

The chill that made her shiver as she lay with her knees drawn up, and shoulders hunched, came from within rather than from the external cold. Her wretchedness brought vividly to mind the anguish she had suffered after her mama's death. She was shaken to discover that her present sorrow and sense of lonely desolation was worse than at her grandfather's passing only a few weeks ago. Painfully, she acknowledged that then, in those hours of fresh grief, Johnny's presence at her side and, above all, the wonderful change in his character, his tenderness towards her, and the real love she thought he had revealed for her, were comforts that made her think there was no ill she would be unable to face, as long as he was there for her.

How cruelly he had shattered that dream. Even more cruel was the incredible fact that after such a devastating confession he had still imagined that they could share a future together, go on to be man and wife. How could he know so little of her to believe that she would still consent to the marriage? How could she have known so little of *him* that she could ever have dreamed of sharing the rest of her life with him?

Kate's words rang again in her brain. *He's not like the others.* True indeed! How could he be so shameless, so insensitive, as to think he could bring the person he had betrayed her with, and that person her very own maid, back to the house, to their home? She curled up tighter, hugging her knees into her chest, withering with shame as she thought of the notoriety, the scandal which would flare up, when the news of his action spread abroad, as it surely must. She was trapped. There was nowhere she could turn to escape the ignominy that must follow her, innocent as she was. She would never enter a drawing-room again without hearing that private snigger, the behind-the-hand whispers that she must inevitably construe as some mocking reference to her.

He wouldn't care. Wouldn't give a damn! She heard the profane phrase ringing inside her head, the sound of his declaration. What did he care for ignominy, for shame? How could he when he could not feel it? Kate was indeed right — he was far, far different from anyone she had ever known. Not that she had known many, she was forced miserably to admit to herself in the dark. Ned Lovatt. She blushed hotly as she recalled Johnny's scornful denigration of him, and of others in his circle. At least Ned would never have stooped so low as to disgrace her in this way, by dallying with her own servant! And she burned anew at the memory of Johnny's wicked assertion that Ned was a frequenter of those lewd places up in London which Johnny himself had visited. And had still displayed no real shame at admitting as much! She had done Ned a deep injustice even to consider what Johnny had told her.

The long night wore on, the wind beating against the old house, and her thoughts swept just as wildly through her mind. *We'll go away! I'll take you to Africa!* She, who had never so much as crossed the Channel. He would turn his back on all this — his title, his lands, all the responsibilities that went with the blood, his rank in society. And he had expected her to do the same! Again came that overwhelming desolation at the thought of the great gulf that separated them. It seemed so clear to her now that they could never have hoped to make a life together. 'The best of the blood', her grandfather had said. But he, too, had deceived himself. There was some fatal flaw in Johnny's character, some vital essence had been destroyed by all those important years of violence and lawlessness in a savage land, that had left their indelible mark on him.

Her thoughts came back to the immediate future and to the girl lying in one of the rooms above her. Not in the servants' quarters on the top floor, or over the stables and laundry, but in one of the lesser guest-rooms, only one storey above her own room, here on the first floor. The feeling of betrayal, like bitter bile in her throat, rose once more, and the same old question rattled around her head. How could Kate have done this to her? However wickedly persuasive he had been, how could Kate have been so cruelly selfish as to inflict such a hurt upon her?

Her maid was not one of those loose, immoral girls — there were such; even Rose, unworldly as she was, knew that, especially among those of the lower orders, brought up in such harsh surroundings, uneducated, insensitive — but Kate was not like that. The opposite, in fact. From the first, when they were both adolescent girls, Rose had felt an easy affinity with the red-haired girl, a friendliness, given the confines of their vastly separate stations, that led to a real closeness and affection. She had thought it mutual. The betrayal was a second, deep wound.

She tried to turn her mind from such painful reflections, and was powerless to do so. Helplessly, she found herself probing deeper and deeper into the mechanics of their deceit. Why had Kate given in to him? Had she even tried to resist? Rose heard the cruel, mocking whisper, the hateful chuckle at her own self-deception. You know fine well, miss. You know his kisses, the way they feel, the way they make *you* feel. His arms crushing you, the feel of his body — the caress of his hand on your breast, that beating need — she moaned softly, and rolled over, buried her face in the pillow, racked by a convulsive sob. Her body no longer shivered, but was scourged with a heat that made her tremble from head to foot.

★ ★ ★

The morning light of the December day came late and grey, with the last remnants of the gale blowing sleety raindrops like flung gravel against the leaded window-panes, and swaying the black branches of the trees back and forth in the parkland. Rose had lain awake through the early hours, so that she slept late herself, to reawaken drugged and dizzy with sleep, shocked to find it was already eight-thirty. She felt a great reluctance to stir. The bed was a warm and comforting cocoon now, a haven from an outside world which contained nothing but bitterness. The room was still in semi-darkness, for the thick winter curtains had not been drawn, and she lay on for some further minutes, glad

189

of her fogginess of mind, postponing the return of full consciousness, and pain. Then, with a sharp reprimand to herself for her cowardice, she reached behind her for the cord to summon Helen, with her morning tea.

The maid came swiftly, with her customary knock and murmured greeting as she entered. She set the tray on the bedside table, and moved over to pull back the curtains, to admit the subdued light, and reveal the rain-pocked window squares.

'Terrible morning, miss.' She came back to the bed, and began to pour Rose's tea. 'Mr Reece was telling us, miss. That foreign gentleman — can't say his name — he's done it, with that new machine thing of his. They've sent a signal, right across the ocean to him, over to Newfoundland. They call it wireless.'

'Yes. Mr Marconi. I read about him.'

The brightness of Helen's voice contrasted sharply with the listlessness of her mistress's answer. It was clear that Rose was in no mood for chatter, which was not surprising.

'Shall I run your bath, miss, or would you like to take breakfast up here? Before you have your bath?'

'Run the bath, please.'

Helen nodded. She gave a little bob,

preparatory to leaving, then nodded, pink-faced, at the tray.

'Mr Reece told me to bring that up, miss. Said it might be important.' She turned and left quickly.

The envelope was simply headed *Miss Rose*. She recognized Johnny's ungainly hand. The note was stark in its simplicity:

Gone to London. Won't be back. Be in touch when I've made all arrangements.

It was not signed.

She felt a shock, a catching of her breath, a jolting inside as though she had taken a soaring jump on horseback. Why should she feel the misery, like a blow, rising again? Surely she should be relieved that she did not have to face him again after all that had happened? She swung herself out of bed, shivering in the morning chill, and pulled her dressing-gown tightly about her. Helen looked surprised at her appearance in the bathroom doorway, even more so at Rose's words. Striving not to show the colour that she could feel mounting, she said:

'There's no need to wait on me, Helen. I'll bathe myself. Lay out my things, then you can go. I'll call you when I'm ready for you to lace me up.'

Helen was too startled to hide her surprise, but, after a distinct pause, she muttered: 'Yes, miss,' and departed, with a face as red as her mistress's.

The poor girl probably thought she had done something terribly wrong. But then again, Rose reflected, so many things had happened over the past two days that she might well simply decide that it was all part of the madness into which the world of Strenshaugh had slipped. But all at once Rose had been overcome by a sense of her own pampered uselessness, and an acute reluctance to display her nakedness to the maid, in spite of the countless occasions on which she had already done so. Shameful as it was, she could not help her fear that, just as she now viewed her body with a disturbing new awareness, Helen might, also. Tears of helpless anger pricked at her eyelids, and she railed inwardly against Johnny for the storm of emotion with which she gazed at her own reflection in the steam-misted mirror.

The unfamiliarity of bathing and drying herself, dusting herself with powder, then putting on her own underclothes and stockings made it a lengthier process than usual. She was still embarrassed when she rang for Helen to come and lace her into her stays, but Helen's own awkwardness at the departure from routine was clearly forgotten. Her round eyes, and the flush in her cheeks were the result of excitement now as eagerly she gave Rose fresh news.

'It's Kate Addy, miss! She's gone! Beatty took her breakfast up and she wasn't in her room. Then Mrs Fielding found out she'd cleared off. Got a lift with Kenny Foreman on the milk-cart, first thing.'

★ ★ ★

'It'll be the death of her, all this lot, miss!'

Mrs Addy's chin quivered. Despite the polite form of her admonition, Rose knew very well the depth of injury and indignation implied in the woman's tone, and in the glowering silence of her husband. He didn't look at Rose directly. His gnarled hands, with their huge red knuckles, were plucking at the rim of his cap, which he held in front of him, at his loins. Rose could only be thankful that there was no sign of the volatile son, Kate's brother, Michael. Even so, she could feel her legs trembling under her gown and the thick travelling coat, and she had to struggle hard to keep her voice from wavering with nervousness.

'Please let me talk to her, Mrs Addy. It's all been a dreadful misunderstanding. I'm sure you know how fond I was — am — of her. I still want to help.'

Rose was admitted at last, her boots ringing on the narrow, bare wooden staircase. A plain iron bed filled almost the whole of the tiny bedroom. Kate was looking ghastly, her complexion paler, her face stamped with pain.

'You silly girl!' Rose burst out, close to tears herself. 'You could have killed yourself, going off like that! Didn't Dr Ealey make it clear to you? You're ill, Kate! You need proper treatment, otherwise you'll never get well.'

'I'd be a darned sight better if you didn't keep pestering me! I just want to be left alone. I know the trouble I've caused. You should never have made him come after me, miss! I never wanted any of this!'

'You think I — we — could have just left you, to — to fend for yourself? Look at what you've done. You — '

'Maybe I deserve it! I bet that's what you think, isn't it? After my wickedness.'

Rose was a little taken aback by the aggression of Kate's reply, but she swiftly mastered any sense of shock.

'That's not so, and you know it. It's . . . Lord Strenshaugh knows how deeply he's wronged you. Please — you must let him at least begin to make amends, by taking care of you — your recovery.'

'Is it true?' Kate's tone was fierce almost in its accusation. 'You've sent him away? You're not going to marry him?'

Rose coloured, felt herself bested by Kate's intense stare.

'I couldn't,' she murmured softly. The look she returned was soft also, an appeal now, for understanding, so that Kate's bald answer was even more like a blow.

'Then you're a bloody fool, miss, and that's all there is to it. He's wild. I know it — and so do you, more than most. But he wants you, miss, whatever he might say, or do. And that's the truth. It's not easy for me to say so, but it's a fact. And you *are* a fool, if you can't see that — and forgive him for what he's done.'

17

Rose fought hard to conquer her feelings of injustice and outrage at her former maid's intransigence, and the girl's belligerent attitude towards the innocent victim of her wrongdoing. After all, she reminded herself, Kate was herself a sufferer, and a victim, too. She had paid dearly for her sin. Her health was seriously, perhaps permanently, impaired, her prospects in life ruined. She had as much cause as Rose to look back with longing on the uneventful peace of their former days together at Strenshaugh. Before *he* had come so catastrophically into both their lives. Their serpent in Eden.

But that uncomfortable inner voice of conscience stirred once more within Rose. Come now, miss! Strenshaugh was no garden of paradise before Johnny's entry. You were a mere shadow, an insipid country girl, ignorant of life and fearful of learning of it. Johnny's arrival came like the sudden gust of the gale, blowing through the stifling deadness, bringing *real* life to stir you up, to breathe true feeling into your unawakened spirit. The shocking intimation came to her that maybe Kate was right, that Rose was no more than a fool for refusing to accept Johnny's moral lapse.

Painfully, she explored for the first time the possibility of doubt in her own preconceived, firmly implanted and conventional standards of morality. *Ice-water Rosie, red-blooded Kate.* Johnny's words and, clearly, his sentiments, too. She glowed hotly for shame, not for the description, but for her own secret recognition of its inaccuracy. If only he had known how far from the truth it was; how, in private, her sensations were so far from his notions of her that her blood, rather than being still and frozen in her veins, sizzled and bubbled with the violence of the shocking new feelings he had aroused in her. Surely, he must have guessed, from the passion of their last kisses, the strength of that feeling? That she was waging a war within herself against those emotions, which ran counter to everything she had been brought up to believe in, those restraints of God-given morality which were our only protection against total license — and anarchy? Restraints which, sadly, Johnny had refused to recognize, or observe.

And which Kate had wantonly disregarded, too. True, she wept bitterly for her surrendered innocence now, but there were times — how the plurality of that word tormented

Rose: how many? she constantly wondered — when she had gladly yielded to their illicit passion. Even now, she had been at pains to share the culpability, refused to accept the partial salving of conscience offered by the convention of the innocent maiden seduced. And deep within, Rose, too shockingly and newly aware of the unruliness of her own blood, understood the truth of Kate's defiance, reluctantly admired her for her painful honesty.

But then came an even more bitter truth, equally hurtful and shaming to recognize. She was jealous of Kate! Tormented by the thought of their loving, their secret trysts, by her fearful, blazing visions of their fleshly sins, her torment made worse by the blur of her own ignorance. And with that jealous fury came powerful renewal of her outrage and moral rectitude. You wish *you* had made love with him! that inner voice taunted. Fiercely she repudiated its claim. No! She would have come pure to the marriage bed. Why then could she not expect the same from the one she accepted as her lover? He had taken Kate's virginity. The red-haired girl had told her so, and Rose believed her. He had been prepared to take hers, too, even though she had intended to make him wait until their wedding-night. And what would *he* have thought and felt if his bride had come to him already sullied with her impurity?

Meanwhile, through all the inner turmoil of Rose's thoughts, life ground on. Dismissed curtly from the sick girl's chamber, Rose's sense of rightness forced her to proceed with her plan to help her. Overcoming her embarrassment, which nevertheless imposed on her an attitude of stiff and formal correctness, she conducted a lengthy interview with Kate's parents. She convinced them, and urged them in turn to convince their daughter, that the help came from the conscience-stricken Lord Strenshaugh, and that it had nothing to do with her own design or even her wishes.

The eventual outcome was that the family accepted the offer of help to ensure Kate's treatment and convalescence at a sanatorium at the coast, together with a generous financial settlement to her parents, in compensation for the wrongs they had endured. It would also help, Lord Strenshaugh's solicitor assured Rose later, much to her chagrin, to ensure their public silence in the storm of scandal that must surely follow.

The first thunderclaps of that storm reverberated about the hall within the next two days. Since the death of the Queen at the beginning of the year, the more relaxed atmosphere of the new court, under the already jaded appetite of its king, did nothing to change the tub-thumping moral high ground of the press, to whom sensation was grist to its hypocritical mill. Rose herself, as long as she stayed within the boundaries of the house and grounds, could be protected from the baying pack of reporters, though the blood-sniffing journalists attempted to infiltrate. Thanks to Mr Kemp's vigilance around the perimeters of the estate, and Mr Reece's severe eagle eye on the house staff, intruders were kept at bay. The estate manager wielded his authority over the villagers of Garrowby, too, but breaches were clearly made, for several newspapers carried sensational headlines over the story of Johnny's precipitate transfer of Kate up to the hall, and the summoning of Dr Ealey. While not straying beyond the bounds of prurient speculation, they managed to proclaim clearly and luridly enough the sad recent history of the former lady's maid, and her association with the new Lord Strenshaugh. Sue us and be damned! they seemed to challenge boldly. Johnny of course did nothing of the kind. Instead, he seized one intrepid hack by the throat and threw him down the steps of the town apartment, and the sharklike feeding frenzy began in earnest, as they tore his far from spotless reputation to shreds.

It was no comfort to Rose to see herself paraded as the innocent dupe of his lechery, and her own maid's deceit. She stayed, pale and besieged, in the fastness of the old house, and bowed to the demands of Sir Arthur and Lady Charlotte that she should formally announce the breaking-off of the engagement in *The Times*.

'You'll have to winter abroad,' Lady Charlotte declared. 'There's a place in Switzerland, belongs to friends of ours. It will be ideal. You must stay out of the country for four months at least.'

The look of consternation on her fleshy features when Rose obdurately refused to countenance such a move was almost comic. Rose surprised herself with the new assertiveness she found to stand up to Lady Charlotte's overbearing manner.

'You can't bury yourself out here. What are you going to do when that young reprobate decides to come home again? The disgrace he's brought down on us is already too much to bear. Surely you don't intend to add to it? Surely you can see how completely impossible it is for you to remain here now?'

'I don't think he *will* return.' Rose's voice was a throaty murmur. 'Not for some time. Besides, this is my home. My grandfather would wish me to remain here.' Pop-eyed and puce with indignation, Lady Charlotte found her domineering ways entirely useless against Rose's quiet determination. 'I'm sure you and your husband have devoted far too much time to my affairs since grandfather's death. I shall manage very well on my own, and I thank you for all the kindness you have shown these past weeks,' she told the outraged couple. 'I'm sure you can appreciate that I would prefer a period of solitude. So much has happened lately. I need some time alone.'

'Very well, young lady!' the older woman fumed. 'But please don't come running to us when that young degenerate returns and you find you dare not stay under the same roof without forfeiting your honour!'

'Indeed, I can assure you I won't!' Rose answered, with a coolness belied by the inner churning of emotion at her own effrontery.

The Ables departed the following morning, grim-faced and tight-lipped with disapproval, in spite of Rose's polite leave-taking as she saw them into their carriage from the steps of the hall. The day after that came news of the proposed visit by the senior partner of the family's firm of solicitors, and an assistant. It was a mere ten days before Christmas. The tall tree in the hall, and the decorations, restrained as they were, were a mockery against the brooding atmosphere of the house. The meeting took place in the library, where, again, the cheerfulness of the cosy room, with its crackling log-fire, and the wintry sun falling in oblong patches of brightness on the faded rugs from the long windows, were in painful contrast to the tense sombreness of the quartet of figures who took their place at the table.

Mr Parr, the senior partner, nodded to his young assistant, who proceeded to fill the polished wooden surface with the plethora of official papers he drew from his bulky case. The round and naturally cheerful face of Mr Kemp, the estate manager, took on an unaccustomed look of solemnity. The lawyers had particularly requested that he should be present. Rose could feel her heart thumping, was sure its movement could be seen against the satin bosom of her black mourning-dress. She felt the encasing constriction of her stays squeezing her ribs at the deep breaths she was taking, and she wiped surreptitiously at her sweating palms with the lace-edged handkerchief she clutched in her right hand.

Mr Parr nodded at the papers spread before him.

'We have received instructions from his

lordship.' His dignified face was set in deep lines, which, along with the gravity of his tone, seemed to Rose to convey his profound distaste for the task facing him. 'He wishes to assign power of attorney to you, Miss Martingale, in all matters pertaining to the running of the house, and the estate. Everything, in fact. He has abdicated all responsibility for the affairs of Strenshaugh, everything except the title itself, which he cannot bequeath to you.'

He paused, as though waiting for her to say something. She stayed silent, her face drained of colour, her dark eyes brilliant, fixed on him like a bird caught in a trap. He cleared his throat.

'It is a most unusual step, and, I must say, as I told him, an ill-advised one. You are not even come of age. Indeed, you are in law his ward. But, also in law, it is a step he may take, provided you consent. If you do so, you will have our support and help, to the utmost of our ability. Mr Kemp, I am sure, will continue to serve the estate faithfully, and will be there to guide you all the way.'

He looked at the manager, whose ruddy features darkened even more as he nodded and gave a strangled grunt, which was meant to be an affirmation of his pledge.

Mr Parr gathered a sheaf of the spread documents.

'These will all require your signature. But before you do that, his lordship asked me to give you this letter. You should read it before you proceed.' He made to move. 'Perhaps you would like us to retire, give you an interval of privacy?'

She took the sealed envelope from him and hastily got to her feet, stretching out a detaining hand.

'No, no. If you will excuse me, I will just move over by the window. Mr Kemp, will you see to drinks?' She gestured towards the trolley. 'Or there is coffee and tea there, should you prefer. Excuse me a moment, gentlemen.'

She knew well enough now the hand which had scrawled her single name, *Rose*, on the envelope. The sheet of notepaper shook visibly in her hand when she withdrew it from the envelope. The three men began to talk quietly in the background, as though to emphasize the privacy of this interval. She turned towards the brightness of the window, and faced out to the short grass and winter-black trees of the park. Her eyes moved quickly over the single page, to read its contents before they blurred with her tears.

Dear Rosie,

I won't trouble you again. I make one last appeal to you to throw aside all your anger and hurt at the wrong I've done you and tell me you'll still marry me. I did wrong by you, and by poor Kate, whom I hope you'll forgive. You mustn't blame her for what happened. The fault was all mine. She's not as strong as you, not many of us are. I meant what I said when I told you I love you. I just wish I could be the way you always wanted me to be. I'd try my best to make it up to you and would try never to hurt you again.

If I don't hear from you, and if the papers come back all signed, then I'll be leaving as soon as I can, and you won't hear from me again. I want to leave Strenshaugh in your charge, Rosie, for I know you'll look after it. You deserve it, far more than I ever did. Whatever happens don't let that old buffer Sir Arthur and his frogfaced wife get their hands on it. Not till I'm good and dead anyway. I'd give title and all to you if I could. Sorry, my love, for everything. In time you might not think so badly of me. Forgive me one day if you can.

Yours ever,

Johnny.

She groped for her handkerchief, and dabbed at her eyes. She stood for a while staring out at the scene lit by the thin sunlight. She felt empty, as cold as the wintry paleness spread before her. She was scarcely aware of any thought passing through her brain, until suddenly there came the clear, ringing condemnation of Kate Addy's voice. *You're a bloody fool, miss, and that's all there is to it.*

She shivered, then drew herself up, and shook her head, dismissing the phantom voice from her mind. She turned back towards the three men, and to the table covered with the sheets of paper. Her chin was lifted high.

'The documents, Mr Parr. I'm ready to sign them now.'

18

'Were you at the meeting with Mr Lloyd George yesterday, Lord Strenshaugh? Is it true you support the cause of the Boers? That you're against the war?' The speaker was a short, stocky individual, with an abundant brown moustache, neatly trimmed, his chin clean-shaven but showing the faint bluish tinge of his efforts with the razor. He was smartly dressed, though the glinting tiepin, the bright colour of his waistcoat, and the flash of the ring on his little finger betrayed the flamboyance associated with one of his profession. The reporter had given up any pretence at disguise, and fired his questions rapidly at Johnny, taking advantage of the younger man's apparently relaxed good humour, which might dissipate itself at any second.

Johnny smiled back easily. He tightened his grip on Lucy's arm, which he had felt tense. He knew she did not welcome the glare of notoriety which came with being so closely associated with him in these turbulent days.

'My trade depends on discretion, Johnny,' she had said. 'A whore's fame has to be selective, as you know. They all know me at Mrs Moss's. But I don't expect my gentlemen to bid me good day in the Strand, or in the park, with their wives and sweethearts on their arm.'

She knew he was even more careless now of his reputation, that his parading of their relationship in the more fashionable watering-places of the capital was a gesture of defiance against the hypocrisy of high society. She was also aware of the harm such a high profile might do to her. But, underneath all his bravado, she sensed his lonely, even desperate, need, and she felt far too deeply for him to deny him. Her sympathy and compassion went against every grain of self-interest she had learnt in the hard school of her upbringing, but even a woman of her mercenary profession had a heart, and, in this case, it was the heart rather than the head which dictated her behaviour. Not that she stood to lose financially from her sentimentality, she reminded herself wryly.

She had definitely not been present at last night's affair, this pro-Boer political meeting, which had degenerated into a flailing riot, from which Johnny and a few cronies had returned to Mrs Moss's, dishevelled and bloody-browed, and full of high-spirited excitement. Johnny's excess of energy had been spent later, in a more private and more passionate manner, in the tumbled sheets of his bed, which Lucy was once more sharing on a regular basis.

She listened warily as Johnny answered the reporter's questions.

'You can see from last night that there are plenty of folk who don't agree with what's happening out in Africa. I'm sure you occasionally read the stuff your own papers are writing, don't you? Chasing women and children, burning them out of their farms, locking them up in camps, and starving them to death or disease! Is that something to be proud of?' For an instant his words rang with conviction, then his face split with the familiar, devilish grin. He raised Lucy's gloveless hand in his, lifted its thin darkness to his lips. 'Of course, I support the noble efforts of our lads to free our black brethren — and sisters — from the yoke of oppression, eh, Lucy?'

She snatched her hand from his, and struck him with hard playfulness on his shoulder. She spoke in a convincing impersonation of a rough cockney accent.

'I dunno nuffin' about that, milord. All them heathens out in them foreign parts! I only know I tries to be a good gal for you, Mr

Johnny, so's you don't take your whip to me black hide, sir!'

The reporter's eyes lit up for an instant at the inflammatory possibilities of the girl's speech. Then the explosive laughter of the handsome couple burst over him, and he smiled with rueful good nature. He patted the notebook, which had remained all the while in his pocket. He had material enough for a good storyline, and thanked his good fortune and dogged perseverance in tracking down the young rake and his doxy, and finding him in such an expansive mood. He rose to take his leave, and nodded in genuine and grateful respect.

'Don't forget to put in the bit about my cut-throat days as a buccaneer! All the poor folk we sent down to Davy Jones!' Johnny laughed and turned dismissively back to the black girl, their faces nuzzling in flagrantly public affection.

In the swaying privacy of the hooded hansom later that night, with the outside lights of the city flickering across the drawn blinds, Johnny ran his hand up over the inviting shape of Lucy's leg, under the rustling gown. As his fingers encountered the frilled garter and the gathered roll of the stocking top, he pictured with throbbing anticipation the exotic spectacle of the dusky body, innocent of cover except for the pale silk of the stockings. She made no coy pretence of preventing his frank examination, but lay back in his embrace, and returned with unassumed eagerness his kisses.

'If you're going to do me here, you'd best hurry,' she said. 'We'll be home soon.'

Johnny laughed, withdrew his hand from under her skirt.

'Everything comes to him who waits!' He kept his tone light. 'Are you sure you won't change your mind and come with me?'

She stared back levelly at him, with her dark, smoky eyes.

'Now why should I want to go out and live among a load of savages? You sure you won't change *your* mind and stay here? There's nothing you'll find out there that I, and a lot of good girls like me, can't give you. Who knows? She might change her mind in a month or two and decide she wants you after all.'

He laughed, and shook his head.

'Not our Rosie! You don't know what these good girls are like! Rocks will melt and hell will freeze over before she'll forgive me for what I've done! Just as well, eh? I was never cut out for respectability, Lucy!'

The dark hand fell across his lap, and with careless skill caressed his hardening flesh beneath the thick cloth.

'Then I'll just have to make the most of you while I've still got you, my lusty lord!' She laughed deeply in her slim throat, and her plump lips parted to cover his willing mouth, as their tongues probed and tangled in their firing passion.

★　★　★

Two days after Christmas Johnny embarked at Tilbury on a steamer bound for the East African territories. Mr Parr himself informed Rose of the departure, by letter. She had received no communication from Johnny, apart from that one note brought by the solicitor himself. It was the gloomiest and loneliest Christmas Rose had ever known, including the first after her mother's passing. Stirred by pangs of conscience, or a sense of duty, or perhaps by less noble, more mercenary considerations now that Rose held such formidable reins of authority in her inexperienced hands, the Ables had invited her to spend the festive season with their family at their home. She declined politely.

'Give as many of the staff as you can the holiday free,' Rose instructed the impassive butler.

'You can't spend Christmas on your own,

213

miss!' Helen declared, horrified.

'It's scarcely more than a month since my grandfather's death,' Rose reminded her. 'I can hardly celebrate when I'm in deep mourning.'

'Yes, but even so, miss. You oughtn't to be alone like this. Not over Christmas!'

'I prefer it this way.' Rose's cheeks coloured, but she met Helen's concerned gaze steadily. 'After all that has happened this past two weeks.'

'Yes, miss.' Chastened, Helen desisted in her protests, and Rose kept her solitary vigil. She spent the day in the library, with a blazing fire, and only a silent Gooding to bring her meals in to her. The silence of the closed-down house seemed to echo with its loneliness. Try as she would, she could not keep her thoughts from speculating on how Johnny was faring. Of course he won't get in touch, not even today, of all days, she reprimanded herself, and hated her weakness for the forlorn hope that she would be proved wrong.

The day was endless, and Rose hated the countless stares she received from the pallid, waiflike figure, unbecomingly garbed in black, each time she looked into the mirror. You drab, pathetic little mouse! she castigated herself. Why should you want to hear from him? From someone so base, who has proved so unworthy of your love? She wondered how he would be spending this special day. Not pining and weeping alone, that was for sure. She thought of the black girl, Lucy, tortured herself trying to picture the exotic figure, to picture the pair of them together, touching, kissing, loving . . . she flung herself along the length of the sofa, torn by the convulsions of her weeping, and buried her face smotheringly into the cushion, biting savagely at its silken material to prevent her howls from being audible. Her fists pounded furiously at the upholstery, her heels waved in the air and her body threshed about, possessed by her helpless fury.

The hysterical fit left her exhausted, but at least the wildness of her torment had been expunged from her. She was glad that she had given Helen the whole day off, and that she was attended by Lottie, one of the younger maids still in training for upstairs duties. The diminutive figure was too nervous to do other than concentrate wholly on performing her tasks correctly, and when she had attended Rose in her bedroom to see her into her night things, both servant and mistress were greatly relieved at their parting.

Many of the staff were not even present in the house on Christmas night. Traditionally,

Boxing Day was the occasion of the servants' ball, a lively celebration which went on from early afternoon, soon after lunch, until the early hours of the following day. Rose and her grandfather and their few guests had always attended for the concert, the meal, and the opening of the dance. His lordship dispensed presents and prizes, and made a speech in praise of their loyal service. Rose always looked forward to Kate's vivid account of the later proceedings, the scandals and the intrigues which took place as the night's festivities wore on. In spite of the period of mourning, Rose had anticipated the pleasure she would take from being at Johnny's side for this event, muted as it must be. Now, she made no reference to the event, and no information was passed to her that it would take place. If it did, it would be without her presence. And two days later, came the news of Johnny's abrupt departure from England.

★   ★   ★

The new year came in with seasonal iron-hard frosts, and Strenshaugh Hall was lonelier and gloomier than ever. Large sections of the house were virtually shut off, the furniture covered in the spectral white shrouds of dust sheets, though Mr Reece ordered fires lit periodically in the various silent rooms to combat the effects of the cold and damp. Rose felt more ghostlike than ever. Solitude and silence became the norm. Even Helen's efforts at respectful friendliness withered and died against her mistress's remoteness. Rose had learned to bathe and dress herself, except for the lacing of her stays and the arranging of her hair, and soon even these tasks were performed largely without conversation.

Helen was hurt at the transformation in the shy but always friendly girl, but she quickly became inured to it. She could even understand it, for her red-haired predecessor had been the chief instrument of change in the pale shadowy figure. Opinion was quite sharply divided below stairs as to the degree of Kate Addy's accountability for the gloom which had descended on Strenshaugh. Some said it was wicked that she should be luxuriating in some private nursing-home, and that her family should have so benefited from her wantonness. There was a general reluctance to blame young Master Johnny for his undoubted role in her predicament, and most found it hard to understand Miss Rose's uncompromising attitude towards his little peccadillo with the former maid. 'Too stiff and starchy for her own good!' was the opinion in the main. 'Forgive and forget is best,' they agreed, advocating a generosity of spirit not always evident in their own doings.

There was no doubt however that Rose was altered mightily by her unfortunate experience. Hours went by when she would not speak, except to convey minimally the necessary orders to get through her day. Social calls were so actively discouraged that the few faded rapidly to none. Dr Ealey tried, using as an excuse his reports on Kate's progress at the sanatorium. He struggled manfully to maintain conversation over the tea or coffee he was offered, while Rose gave him her polite attention.

'They're becoming concerned about the outbreak of smallpox up in town,' he informed her, one icy January day. 'Over two thousand cases now, they reckon. And in this terrible weather, too.'

One of Rose's self-imposed tasks was to read through the morning paper every day. She drew the line at imbibing it with her breakfast, as her grandfather had done, but its newly ironed pages were laid out in the library, where she sat and conscientiously ploughed through it, so that she was at least *au fait* with the outside world even if she was not part of it. However, as the first bitter month of 1902 came to an end, part of that world was waiting to thrust itself dramatically into her consciousness.

She was in the library as usual, and flurries of ominously small snowflakes were swirling in the greyness beyond the windows and clinging to the square panes, when Mr Reece entered. The very set of his impassivity was a warning of something untoward.

'You have a visitor, Miss Rose,' he announced, in his most formal tone. Rose looked for the tray, and the card to show who this unannounced arrival should be. There was no tray, no card.

'It's your father, miss. And his lady wife. Mr and Mrs Martingale.'

19

The seven intervening years since she had spoken to her father seemed to have dissolved. Inside, Rose felt again all the quivering revulsion and fear of the fourteen-year-old she had been when they had last met. When Mr Reece had brought news of his arrival, a wild idea had sprung up in her mind that she could not possibly face him, and she had thought of telling the butler to convey her refusal to meet him. She had recognized her own craven cowardice and had overcome it quickly enough. She was less certain that she could successfully disguise her trembling unease, especially at her first glance of that fleshy, overbearing countenance, with its stamp of haughtiness, framed by the bushy, greying side-whiskers, the distinctive rising tuft of hair at the front. She fancied from her first contact with the cold blue eyes that she could read all the old contempt in which he had always held her. She actually felt faint, could not move, as he strode purposefully over to her, and placed his heavy hands on both her shoulders, as though pinning her to the spot, while his scented visage dipped frighteningly close to hers, and she felt with private disgust the brush of those whiskers as his dry lips touched briefly on her cheek.

'My dear Rose! After all that's been happening to you these past days, I felt I had to come. We've been estranged too long, dear girl. We must let bygones be bygones. I'm sure you will welcome our support in these difficult times. It's been so painful to see your name spread over the newspapers this way, to see that young scoundrel degrading you so wickedly. I feel so bad about it, leaving you to fall prey to such an evident bounder. I suppose one can't really blame your grandfather. He'd lost touch with the world, shutting himself up in this mausoleum of a place, and you with him, it seems! He must have been in his dotage to let the young blackguard make such a fool of him — and of you, too, my poor girl!'

Rose could feel herself growing more and more agitated. She wanted to cry out for him to be quiet, to tell him he had no right to appear so suddenly in her life once more and to voice such obnoxious sentiments. But she could scarcely trust herself to speak at all and so she remained silent.

'I said to Amy, I must go to the poor girl. We can't leave her all alone in the world at a time like this.' He turned to the figure at his side, drew her forward. 'Come and kiss your stepmother, Rose. You should have met long before this. I blame myself, though I know his lordship was at pains to keep you from me. This is Amy. My dearest companion!'

She was fashionably dressed, her carefully coiffured hair was fair, a coppery gold. It was piled high, and perched on its crest, tilted towards her brow, was a small hat, trimmed with sable, and sprouting two small feathered wings. The short dark veil was caught up, revealing a face which was almost beautiful, that of a woman in full bloom, and certainly much younger-looking than her husband. She was full-bosomed, voluptuous, but then Rose noticed, with something of an unpleasant shock, the thickening waist beneath the open mantle, and the gown whose loose flowing style clearly allowed for the fact that she was pregnant.

She stepped forward, her gloved hands held high. Rose steeled herself not to pull back. She stood, turned her cheek to receive the kiss from the rouged lips.

'I'm so sorry, my dear. I was so sad when I saw your announcement. I positively wept for you. But at last we meet, Rose, after so long. You look so pale! And thin! Really! You must let us cheer you, take care of you from now on!'

'And we have news of our own that will cheer you up, I hope!' Rose felt her stomach churn at the unctuous pleasure oozing in her father's tone. 'We are to increase our family, Rose. You are to have a little brother or sister in a few months. I'm sure you'll wish to offer your congratulations, won't you?'

A wave of faintness came again, and Rose swallowed hard, gave an indeterminate murmur, all the while hearing again her mother's weeping, her father's thick, angry voice coming through the muffled darkness. She was suffused with a choking rage, spreading like molten lead through her veins. This child will be no brother or sister of mine! Sired by your lust, with this woman — this stranger, who is nothing, less than nothing, to me.

'Rose! Are you unwell? You're as white as a sheet, girl. Perhaps you'd better sit down. Here. Let me assist you.' He moved to take her arm, and there was a second of deep embarrassment, and shameful truth, as she shrank away from contact. She did not wish to feel his touch on her again.

'No, no! I'm fine! It's just — it's been something of a shock, seeing you again. I haven't — I'm not used to visitors any more. You should have warned me you were coming.' She sat hastily on the sofa, her pallor tinged with colour now, at the awkwardness of the revealing moment.

'Not an unpleasant one, I hope? A man may call on his daughter without leaving his card, I trust!' Rose heard in his strident tone all the old assumption and arrogance, the dominant masculinity he had exerted over her mother and herself. I am not that child any longer! she urged herself mentally, while she sat with fists clenched in her lap, every muscle locked rigid. It was as though he could see into her mind, was asserting that dominance all over again, as he continued. 'You *are* pleased to see me again, aren't you, Rose?' There was a hint of threat behind his probing question.

His wife sensed the uncordial atmosphere, and in an attempt to overcome it sat herself down beside Rose. She put her arm around the stiff shoulders, and said, in a voice that gushed with a false girlishness: 'I've been so looking forward to meeting you, my dear! Especially now!' She patted her stomach briefly with her free hand, with an expression of coy and complicit intimacy, as though to establish their exclusive bond of femininity against the imposing figure standing over them. 'After all, we're all family, aren't we? We should be there for one another, whatever happens. That's why we came — when we heard about your trouble, Rose.'

'Can I ring for some drinks? Tea for you, my love.' It was a statement, not a question, and his wife nodded complacently. Rose sat there helplessly, with a sense of the years unravelling as she experienced all the old impotence of her childhood. Her father made some joking reference to the antiquated fitments of Strenshaugh as he yanked at the bell-cord to summon the butler.

'Tea for the ladies, and I'll have a whisky and soda, I think. But don't drown it!' He laughed. The butler's face retained its usual impassive neutrality, as he moved to the drinks cabinet, which had, all the while, been no more than six feet from Walter Martingale, and poured him his drink. 'Reece, isn't it?' Rose's father said, preening himself on his ability to remember the name. 'You were here before, I remember.'

'I was under-butler then, sir, to Mr Knight. I took over his duties seven years ago. Just about the time that Miss Rose came to us.'

'Hm. Can you have a guest room prepared for us? And make sure it's warm, and the bed's thoroughly aired. This damned weather, eh? My wife's in a delicate condition.'

Mr Reece paused, and turned towards Rose, his eyebrows lifting in eloquent, silent enquiry, and her father's colour heightened.

'It's all right, isn't it, Rose? We came with our bags. You can put us up for a night or two. Not as though you haven't got enough room, eh?' He gave a short laugh, which did not disguise his irritation with the butler's firm acknowledgement of Rose as mistress of the house.

'Shall I prepare the Green Room, Miss Rose?'

'Yes, that will be fine, thank you, Mr Reece. Tell cook we'll have guests. And tell Lottie she's to wait on Mrs Martingale.' The last name seemed almost to stick in her throat. She watched the butler nod, and retire. All the while, this sick helplessness and sense of invasion spread through her, pinning her like binding restraints to her seat on the sofa.

'You have to watch these fellers.' Her father frowned, gazing after the departing Reece. 'Think they own the place after they've been here a few years. Make sure he remembers who he is, Rose!'

'He's excellent. I couldn't manage without him.'

'Nonsense! He's not indispensable, and you mustn't let him think he is!' He stood, in front of the fire, blocking its heat, legs apart, the tails of his coat parted. As though he owned the place! Rose thought, bitterly echoing his words. 'But don't tell me you're living all alone in this miserable pile! I thought old what's-his-name, Sir Arthur and his wife, were staying?'

'They've gone. They were very kind — but — I manage very well. I prefer my own company these days.'

'Oh, my poor lamb! Well, you're not alone any more, my sweet. You've got us now, and we won't desert you!' The arm came up again, encircling, to draw her in close embrace, and Rose strove not to show her reluctance, as that golden head, and fashionable little winged hat, dipped towards her in spurious sistership.

★   ★   ★

In spite of her own unease, Rose sensed as the day wore on a certain tension in her father, a restlessness like the coiled energy of a spring. It even drove him out for a while into the murk of the falling snow, which was now lying to the depth of several inches. Rose was relieved to see him go, after refusing his offer that she should wrap herself up against the weather and take a turn with him. Amy had retired to bed soon after lunch, which had been taken in the formal chill of the dining-room. They did not linger over it.

'I generally take my meals in the library,'

Rose confessed. 'It's the cosiest room in the house. Grandfather always preferred it.'

'Yes, I suppose you've had little chance to play hostess,' Walter said. 'At least until that young blackguard turned up on the doorstep. And God knows what riff-raff he brought home with him.'

Rose was stung into defending him, which she did instinctively.

'No. He never — he was always proper in his conduct here. I don't know about London — '

'Not always proper!' Walter countered, with vindictive pleasure. 'Not from what we read in the papers! With your own lady's maid! That must have been a doubly cruel blow for you!'

Was he mocking her? It certainly sounded so from that sneer in his tone. She choked up, unable to reply.

She noticed his steady drinking as the day progressed. By the time he and Amy entered the library again after they had changed for dinner, his complexion was florid, his speech even thicker through the effect of the whisky he had taken. And far more careless. When the butler attended them before the meal, Walter called out:

'Reece! Is there any decent wine left in the cellar, or did young Mr-Johnny-come-lately and his drunken friends clean it out? What about it, Rose? A decent vintage to celebrate our reunion, eh? And the happy event to come, of course!' He raised his glass of whisky in his wife's direction.

'Please see to it, Mr Reece,' Rose murmured quietly. 'Something suitable.'

Although a smoky fire had been lit in the dining-room, there was a chill about its imposing size which seemed to indicate the infrequency of social gatherings that had taken place there recently.

'About as convivial as dining in a vault!' Walter observed bluntly, staring at the panelled and portrait-hung walls. 'What a crew, eh? No wonder the title's ended up with a pirate! Blood will out, I suppose.'

Rose's heart hammered, but she could not refrain from saying: '*My* blood, father!'

'Only on the distaff side, my dear. Be thankful for that!'

Rose felt her throat close again. She was impotent to answer him, and her eyes misted with tears. The meal was an ordeal, punctuated with his virtual monologue, to which the women were expected to listen and twitter their agreement.

'Smallpox is running rife in London now. I suppose that's one advantage of being buried away down here. Still, not surprising, eh? Did you read the census figures? Six and a half million now! Like rabbits!'

How could he be so insensitive, she wondered, with his pregnant wife sitting opposite him? The diatribe flowed on.

'At least we seem to be getting on top of those damned Cape Dutchmen at last! I believe our bold and bad new lord is all in favour of the rebels! That's why he's headed out there, perhaps! To throw in his lot with the Boers, eh? So maybe he'll get his come-uppance after all!'

When the meal was finally over, Mr Reece came forward and placed the twin decanters close to Walter's elbow, along with the cigars.

'Damned if I'll sit here all on me own!' He snipped at a cigar, struck a match and drew heavily on it. The blue, pungent smoke billowed, then rose in a cloud above the heads of the three diners. Walter squinted at the port, then reached instead for the brandy, and slopped a more than generous measure into the balloon glass. 'I'll accompany you ladies to the library.' He nodded dismissively in the butler's direction, and the attendant Gooding, standing in his formal, old-fashioned uniform in the background.

Amy excused herself after only a few minutes before the warmth of the library fire.

'I shall take my leave. I need early nights in

my condition,' she added archly. 'The young girl will do fine,' she said, in answer to Rose's enquiry. 'I don't like to make a fuss. Do come in and say goodnight, won't you, my dear? I know we're going to become the best of friends. More sisters than mother and daughter.' Rose felt the tug of her facial muscles as she forced a polite smile.

'Don't be too quick to steal her away from me,' Walter said. 'Remember, we have a lot of lost time to make up for. I'd like a time to talk with my daughter.'

His words hung in the air after his wife's departure, and Rose's heart sank, as she was trapped in this new intimacy. Her feeling of tension and anxiety increased. She waited for him to speak, felt that inner tremble once more when he came and sat close beside her on the sofa, and, worse, reached out for her hand, which he took and held in his own. She had to fight not to withdraw it from his grasp.

'One reason why I came to find you — a quite pressing one — was my speaking with an acquaintance of yours. Someone you knew rather well, I believe. A young gentleman who thinks very highly of you, even now, in spite of the unfortunate events you have been involved in. Someone I understand you held in high regard, until that rogue of a cousin came along to upset the apple-cart. He's still concerned, deeply, about you, Rose. Still has those feelings. You know who I'm speaking of, I think. Young Ned Lovatt. As fine a young chap as you could wish for. Solid family. And as true a man as you'd find anywhere, even if he doesn't have a title!'

20

It appeared to Rose that with the introduction of Ned Lovatt's name and his apparent abiding tenderness towards her, her father had revealed the true reason for his sudden re-emergence into her life. She found herself wondering, with her new-found worldly cynicism, what debt Walter owed Ned, or the Lovatt family, to cause him to press the young man's suit in this fashion. The family was certainly wealthy, and influential in many business circles, which was where her father made his own income. A modest income enough, as she recalled. There had always been unpleasant rumours that he had married into the Able family, with its connection to the Strenshaugh title, because of the prestige it would bring, the access to influence and wealth it would afford. Could it be that a similar desire had motivated him to act as broker for Ned? She had no idea of her father's financial status. Her grandfather had assumed all such responsibility for her, had taken her as his ward, and had provided for her for life, and deeply grateful she was for it.

On paper, the Strenshaugh fortune was a

large one, though it was tied up in property and land. Her grandfather certainly had been far from profligate, living a withdrawn life at the hall after the loss of his two children. And now, contrary to everyone's expectation and assumption, Johnny had released a very modest sum for his own use, and handed over the whole structure of the Strenshaugh finances to Rose, under the guidance of those experts such as Mr Parr, and Mr Kemp, who had served the family faithfully and ably over the years.

It occurred to her that her father might be looking to better his own interests with her, now that, in theory at least, she had such powers under her signature. On the other hand, the Lovatts were much more diversified in their dealings, much more commercially orientated, in circles where her father made his living. Whatever the reason, it became quickly and embarrassingly apparent that he was an advocate of Ned Lovatt as a suitor, and it made her even angrier towards him for his belief that he could manipulate her like his bundles of share certificates, under the guise of his concern for her well being.

He was far from subtle. No doubt he thought he could browbeat her into acceptance the way he had dominated her during her childhood. She tried to scotch his plan at the very outset, hating herself for the quaver she could detect in her voice that betokened her nervousness.

'There was never any *understanding* between Mr Lovatt and myself, father, whatever impression he may give. He was an amiable enough gentleman, and I met him in company on several occasions during my season, and last year, too. He has visited here, with his mother, and with his sister, Estelle.' She could feel the colour mounting warmly to her face but she struggled on. 'We — liked each other well enough. But there was never — nothing formal was ever said, or hinted at . . . '

'Young Lovatt thinks you were keen enough on him! And his lordship was ready enough to accept him as your intended, until that young devil from Africa turned up, like the bad penny he is!'

'That's not true!' She could not hide her agitation. 'Nothing, *nothing*, was said at all, by me — or by grandfather, I'm sure, to make him think that!'

'Whoa there! Methinks the lady doth protest too much!' His rubicund face stared at her with all his old belligerence. He waved his hand in dismissal of her gasp of protest. 'In any case, there's nothing to stop you now, is there? He's a good, honest fellow, and he'll make you a good husband. You won't find a better — and you damn near found a sight worse, young lady! You can thank your lucky stars you found out in time. Young Ned's worth ten of your lordly rake, and you'll be a fool to turn him down!'

Rose's face flamed.

'Perhaps you don't know him as well as you think you do! He's no paragon of virtue, as you seem to think.'

His eyes narrowed. She saw the light of something there which made her feel uncomfortable, as though something unpleasant had touched her. His features took on a worldly smirk, which so clearly expressed his scorn for her girlish ingenuousness that it made her toes curl inside her shoes with her fury and embarrassment. The deep chuckle which followed made her long to attack him.

'So the young rascal tried it on with you, did he? Well, this may not be what you want to hear, my girl, but it's the truth, and something you ought to be aware of, now that you're grown up. That sort of ardour is what every man feels, Rose. It's not the stuff of polite drawing-room conversation, but it's real. What was it? An embrace that was more than a polite peck on the lips? More than that? Well, at the risk of shocking you, let me tell you that such passion is a compliment to you — to your attractiveness. You're a beautiful girl — or at least you could be, out of that damned mourning, and with something to cover that pallor of your face!'

He swung on his heel, flung his arms in the air in exasperation. 'It shouldn't have been my place to talk like this! It's a mother's task! But your mother's gone!' He turned to face her again, and she saw the downward turn of his mouth, that gesture of contempt. 'Not that your mother would have explained such things to you. She was never — '

'Please be quiet! Don't go on! I don't . . . ' her voice broke on a sob, her chest heaved with her emotion. 'You're right. It isn't your place! I don't want to hear any more, about any of it. Believe me, I am not as naïve as you think me — as I once was. I understand something of the way of the world, even of men. Young or otherwise!'

The tears came in earnest, but she met his gaze, flung her challenge at him, and saw his reaction of surprise, and intuitive grasp of her words. She was shaking like a leaf. She felt her strength and courage draining from her.

'I — don't want to quarrel. But now — now is not the time for me — to be thinking of anyone — of committing myself to any relationship. I would have thought you would realize that. Tell Mr Lovatt not to entertain any hopes — any false hopes — in that direction. Excuse me, please, Father. I can't talk any longer.' She turned, no longer trying to hide the force of her weeping, and fled from the room, feeling his eyes boring into her as she ran.

Rose was ashamed of her lack of courage, and her subterfuge, when she sent a message via Helen the following morning that she had developed a cold, and would stay in bed for the day. The maid acted as doorkeeper, and succeeded in keeping Walter out of the bedroom, while Rose curled up with the blankets pulled up to the crown of her head, and feigned sleep. Later, though, after Helen had brought her some hot soup and fresh rolls, and had temporarily deserted her post, Amy came tapping softly and slipped in before Rose could stop her.

'I'm glad I caught you.' The blond figure, looking glowingly healthy, spoke in a whisper, and glanced back over her shoulder as though she was keeping her visit a secret from her watchful husband. She came over to the bed and perched on its edge.

'I'm sorry you're not feeling well, Rose.' She was still wearing her dressing gown and glanced proudly down at the curve of her pregnancy. 'The things we women endure, my dear! If men only knew a tenth of what we go through!'

She chatted inconsequentially for several minutes. Rose answered minimally, without being downright rude, in the hope that the older woman would take the hint and leave her in peace. But soon, to Rose's discomfort, her stepmother broached the real reason for the visit.

'I hope Walter didn't upset you yesterday. I can understand how awkward it must feel between you, after all this time apart. But lately . . . ' again she glanced down significantly, cradled the slight bulge beneath her gown . . . 'especially since we found out about the happy event, he has been thinking a lot about you, my dear.' Her hands moved, and reached across the bedclothes to take hold of Rose's as they lay on the coverlet. Rose did not withdraw, but her own hands lay unresponsively in Amy's grip. 'He *does* love you, whatever you might think of him. It's not always easy being a parent.' She smiled winningly, again with that hint of youthful shyness she was so ready to parade. 'As I'm sure I shall find out before long.'

Her voice seemed to shoot up an octave, making transparent the insincerity of her effort to sound casual as she continued; 'Has Walter mentioned, we met an old friend of yours? I say old! I mean a very handsome young fellow. Ned Lovatt.' Her lightness of manner died away magically, and her face assumed an expression of great concern and compassion. 'He's so worried about you, Rose. He thinks a great deal about you. He told us how anxious he was, about how you were feeling, managing after this terrible thing with your cousin. Ned's far too sensitive to get in touch with you himself, but he urged us to see if we could help in any way. As I said, Walter had made up his mind to get in touch in any case. He was worried in his own right. But Mr Lovatt's concern tipped the scales.'

Rose felt the grip on her hands tighten, and the golden crown of hair bent forward, until their brows were almost touching. Again came that embarrassingly girlish look, like schoolfriends sharing secrets, as Amy smiled.

'That young man is sweet on you, Rose, you mark my words. He's far too modest to speak on his own behalf, but I could tell at once. But I don't have to tell you that, do I, my dear? You must know what a passion he harbours for you. A girl knows these things. And why not? A girl as lovely as you! What young gentleman wouldn't fall for you, eh?'

She giggled, and Rose writhed with shame under the bedclothes.

'Please!' She gazed at the smiling woman in genuine distress. 'I really couldn't entertain such ideas, not now! With everything that has happened so recently. I'm sure Mr Lovatt must realize how inappropriate it would be. I just need to be left alone, in seclusion, for some time. I don't know how long it will be, before — if ever — I could think of such attachments. Will you make sure he is aware of my feelings? Please?' Now she *did* return the pressure of Amy's grip, and gazed with earnest, troubled eyes at the figure leaning towards her. And saw disappointment, tinged with veiled annoyance, as Amy shrugged and released her hold.

'Very well. But such young men don't grow on trees, my dear. And such a handsome, well set-up young man! I'm sure there must be girls up and down the country who would leap at the chance!'

★ ★ ★

Ned came across the thick carpet, and slumped down in a vacant chair, acknowledging the greetings from the select group gathered in the ground floor lounge of Mrs Moss's. He was dressed in evening attire, with white tie, and a silk scarf hung carelessly at his neck. His lean good looks were stamped

241

with relaxed weariness, the crinkled eyes at odds with the smooth youthfulness of his features. The blond moustache was immaculately groomed, the locks of golden hair that fell like curling wings at each brow added to his handsomeness.

'Well, have you managed to see her yet?' Sir Charles Forsythe put out his hand possessively and took Lucy's bare arm. Her chair was close to his, and his contact was a clear statement that she was his, occasioned, Ned thought with bitter amusement, because of his own arrival. The black bitch was far too haughty. One of these days he would have her, he vowed yet again, though Charlie had asserted his claim once more in the wake of Strenshaugh's abrupt departure. Damned pirate's cast-off! But he'd teach the bitch what a real man was like — and he wouldn't have to play the moonstruck lover to do so!

She was smiling in that enigmatic, superior way of hers. It probably merely meant that she could hardly understand a word of what the conversation was about, the heathen! Even though she put on such airs and graces. Ned grunted, and shook his head in answer to Sir Charles's question.

'No. Just got to show a little more patience, I suppose. The poor girl's still in mourning for her grandpa — and for her young pirate fleeing the coop like that!'

'I'm sure she's not the only young lady who's doing that!' Lucy put in. She felt Charlie's grip tighten painfully on her skin. He dug his thumb cruelly into her thin flesh, pressing in to the bone, but she did not show any sign of pain. He would make her pay in private, she guessed, but it would be worth it, for she knew her lightly barbed taunt had hurt just as much as any probing thumb.

'And you're one of them, are you, Lucy?' Ned smiled tauntingly.

She gave him that slow, contained smile in return again, and shook her head. A thin band of shining white silk fitted round her brow, standing out against the darkness of her skin, and the tightly kinked black curls that hugged her skull. A single pearl was embedded in the silken band, right at the centre of her forehead, while at the back a short white plume rose, about six inches in height. Her dress was a pale cream and fitted very tightly over her slim figure. The gown was sleeveless, and its bodice was very low, so that her small, high breasts showed prominently. It clung to her form so closely that it seemed impossible for her to be wearing anything beneath it, except stockings, for her delicate ankles showed below the hem, clothed in pristine white.

'Not me, Mr Ned, sir. To tell the truth, I was quite glad to see the young rascal go. He was a randy young bucko! Far too peppy for my old black bones! In fact, I was almost as relieved as *you* were, I bet, to see the last of him!'

She chuckled, and he fought to keep the smile on his face.

'So! Old Charlie here isn't quite so demanding, eh?'

'Far more satisfying, I must confess. You young blades are all huff and puff and blow the house down! No finesse! It takes experience to know what a girl really wants.' She took Sir Charles's hand and placed it squarely and provocatively over her right breast, where the dark skin met the white of the gown.

Charles let his hand lie there.

'Did her old man put in a word, as he promised?'

Ned frowned. 'So he says. Lucy's right, though. I mustn't be in too much of a hurry. Sofly softly catchee monkey, eh, Lucy?'

'Perhaps Mr Johnny queered your pitch with her,' Lucy observed, her eyes holding him steadily. 'Maybe he told tales out of school about what you get up to.'

He grimaced. 'Wouldn't put it past the bounder at that! He certainly had no idea how a gentleman should behave.'

'Perhaps he thought he was getting his own back. For someone doing the same to him. Letting his little cousin know what a naughty boy he was up here.'

Ned shrugged dismissively, but, in the slight flicker of his eye, and the perceptible darkening of his fair features, the black girl thought with inner triumph that she detected the truth.

21

Johnny pulled off his wide-brimmed hat and wiped at the sweat which clung to his brow. He let the filthy red bandanna fall back around his neck, and stared with distaste at the monotonous lines of bleached canvas tents, and the rows of small white bungalows, with their glaringly new tin roofs. They looked like hen-coops. He slapped at a large fly buzzing persistently in front of his face. So this was Nairobi!

'What a dump!' he groaned, and urged his mule forward wearily. At least he could look forward to a bath of some sort and a decent meal, now that the long journey was ended.

'Don't you worry!' Willy de Voss laughed. His unshaven jowls shook with pleasure, his bulky frame galvanized into action as he motioned his plodding beast forward. 'In a year's time you won't know this place! It will be booming, mark my words! Come! We find Charlie's hotel. Tonight we drink plenty, yah? You enjoy a nice Masai girl, or maybe hot little Kamba!' He roared encouragingly. 'And I let you meet Rosa, yah? She sure be tickled to meet a real live English milord!'

'Stow it, Willy, you great Boer baboon! Nobody gives a monkey's toss about titles out here, so don't go blabbing off your mouth, all right?'

'Sure thing, bwana!' de Voss chuckled.

They approached the township along the well-worn trail from the east. Already a whole development of sprawling sheds and stacks of timber and other materials spread out along both sides of the simple iron track of the railway, which only a matter of months ago had reached this swampy plain. The short rains had started, and the vast sky was darkly bruised with threatening rain-clouds towards the west, providing a scene of sweeping beauty as the sun lowered, with colours ranging from the deepest indigo to rich salmon and fiery yellow, fading to the palest of blue-white washes over their shoulders.

The long, wide main thoroughfare, rejoicing in the patriotic name of Victoria Street, ran parallel to the tracks. Because of the earlier shower, its surface was a darkly churned mass of mud, into which the feet of the animals, and those of the small party of native bearers in their wake, sank with a soft sucking noise. Knots of men gathered on the *stoeps* of the wooden buildings on either side of the road stared with brief curiosity at the newcomers, then turned away when they saw the unimpressive size of the caravan.

Narrower roadways, full of puddles the colour of milky tea, led off at right angles to the main street, and it was down one of these that Willy de Voss turned. He made for a wooden building considerably larger than its neighbours, of two storeys rather than the usual one. There was a railinged veranda running around it on all sides, and wide steps leading to the double doors of the entrance. The timbers were still raw and new looking. A large wooden sign was inscribed STORR'S HOTEL.

Mules and wagons were hitched to every available post, and the veranda was crowded with men sitting drinking at the benches and trestle-tables. A cheerful babel rose from inside, also, where the large, square front room of the bar was packed with customers.

'Bloody hell! We're being invaded! It's that bloody Boer back again! Careful, Willy! We might intern you, you Dutch bastard!'

There were several such greetings as many recognized the portly figure who swung down gratefully from the saddle and grinned in return.

'God damn it! You Britishers are thieving all our land down south, so I thought I'd come up here and steal some back off you fellows!' The headman nodded at Willy's rapid stream of orders in Swahili, and led the animals away to the stabling area in the rear. 'This is, er, Johnny Able. Another poxy Englisher, but not too bad. Grew up down on the coast, with the Zanzibaris. So watch him! He'll cut your throat for ten rupees!'

There was a laughing welcome, and an eagerness to talk to a new face, a feeling which Johnny himself well remembered. Soon, he was sitting in the shade, swigging beer and parrying the questions about his background, which soon eased off when they perceived his reluctance to talk about it in any detail. He was happy enough to feed them more general news about 'home', which a good number sentimentally craved for. 'So, she's finally gone, eh, Queen Vic? Can't imagine the place without her, can you? Poor old Teddy's not so hot himself, is he?'

Charlie Storr, the hotel's owner, a tall, thin, stooped figure, with a bobbing Adam's apple and a long, straggling moustache which added to his generally lugubrious air, came and chatted for a long time. He too seemed to know de Voss quite well. As Johnny listened to the banter, and the good-natured, profane insults which flew on all sides, he marvelled once again at the lack of animosity between the representatives of two nations locked in war. It was so different from the jingoistic attitude in England. He recalled the bitterness with which David Lloyd George had been attacked when he spoke out at the meeting in London against the death toll among the population in the camps where the Boer civilians had been detained, and the ensuing mayhem, in which Johnny and his cronies had joined with savage enthusiasm.

Johnny had met Willy de Voss not long after he had disembarked at Mombasa, and was idling away his time at the club and other less salubrious spots, before he stirred himself to make the arduous trek down the coast to the wild region where he had misspent his youth. He hardly knew why he was undertaking the pilgrimage. He had tried during his months in England to institute enquiries about the fate of his parents, particularly his mother, and that of the *Venturer's* crew, without success. Since arriving back on the East African coast, he had managed to unearth some stories about mariners' graves not so far north of the region where Capitano had established his stronghold. Willy de Voss had helped him kit out a small expedition, and accompanied him, on what proved a fruitless quest.

When they reached the village where the graves were said to lie, no one could show them the exact location, and no evidence of their whereabouts was forthcoming. They pressed on, found the creek where the bandits' ship had been sequestered. There was a flourishing trading-post there now, all very respectable. The encampment in the bush, close to the sea, was still there, but deserted. The blackened stumps of the burnt-out buildings were already half-smothered in the undergrowth, even after such a short time. As Johnny stood there, reliving again the startling dawn arousal during the attack, it seemed more like a century than a mere year or so since those events had taken place.

In the neighbouring native village, once the inhabitants had recovered from their suspicion of the red-neck strangers, the *wazungu*, there were a number who recognized Johnny, and even one or two who greeted him with some enthusiasm. Gukimi had gone, they told him in answer to his question. To Zanzibar, or maybe Pemba. They grinned, and Johnny smiled fondly. No doubt she was doing what she did best, and no doubt making a success of it.

Meeting with his disreputable youth made Johnny even more restlessly aware of the pointlessness of his pilgrimage, and the general purposelessness of his life. Sitting round the camp-fire, sharing a bottle of whisky with his new companion, Johnny found his thoughts drifting back to the country from which he had so recently fled, and Rose's beautiful, sad face. He kept seeing her, in her mourning black, like a pale ghost in the tomblike emptiness of Strenshaugh Hall. The more he drank, the angrier he became at his inability to drive the mental image away.

De Voss glanced over towards the ruined huts, catching something of the flavour of Johnny's sombre mood.

'You can't bring back the dead!'

Johnny gave a twisted smile and nodded, reaching for the bottle again. The trouble was, he thought, his ghost wasn't dead; she was very much alive, and very far away.

When de Voss put forward his plan, Johnny welcomed the chance to seek solace in strenuous action.

'Your goddam government is going to annex the territory up north any time now. The railway's nearly through to the Lake itself. Another year at the most, and it will be there. There's a fortune to be made, I tell you! The whole place will be opening up. Taking supplies in from the railroad. Mule trains, getting produce back from the farms. People will come flocking out now. We could even get some land ourselves. Get in first. There'll be townships springing up all along the line — they'll all need to eat. To ship goods in and out.'

Although Johnny smiled sardonically at the 'we', he knew the Dutchman's words made sense. The idea of a mule-packing transport business appealed more than the farming. Though he might purchase some land, put a trustworthy fellow in charge while he wandered about the interior. After all, it wasn't that he didn't have the means. But he wanted the title of Lord Strenshaugh kept quiet. He wanted to succeed as Johnny Able, even if his wealth *had* come from the family he had never known until a year ago. He would create a new fortune, entirely through his own efforts. Then, perhaps, in a few years, he could return to Strenshaugh Hall. See again that gentle, lovely face which would not leave his memory, and which filled him with such bitter self-disgust when he thought of the unforgivable insult he had offered to her innocence and her breeding.

Meanwhile, there were diversions. As he discovered a couple of hours later, when he was lounging blissfully in the galvanized iron tub, in his upper room at Storr's Hotel. There was a tap at the door, the sound of a scuffle and a series of shrill giggles. Willy appeared, his red face glowing, and innocent of the thick stubble he was used to seeing on it. 'I couldn't find you a Kamba girl. Not tonight. But these two will do, I hope! See you later!' He thrust the two girls through the door and slammed it shut behind them.

★ ★ ★

'You cannot shut yourself away like a nun for the rest of your life!' Lady Charlotte's face was flushed with her indignation. 'It's ridiculous! You made a big enough fool of yourself over that wastrel, letting yourself be inveigled into an engagement, when anybody but poor William could have seen how totally unsuitable such a match would be. The boy would never be fit to take his place in decent society. Thank God you found out the truth in time, and didn't make a bigger fool of yourself by marrying him!'

Rose drew a deep breath, tried to still the trembling fury she could feel within. The hated tones were going on, drilling like some infernal instrument into her brain.

'If you ask me, William was far too ready to accept the story the young boor put about. I should have been much inclined to look closer into his claims than your grandfather did!'

'How can you — the family resemblance alone — why, he is so like the pictures of

Uncle George . . . '

'A happy — or, rather, unhappy — coincidence, if you ask me! That's probably what gave him the idea in the first place!'

Rose opened her mouth to make reply, then closed it again, with that feeling of hopelessness which overcame her whenever she tried to argue with the older woman. It was a matter for regret to Rose that the long, severe winter, which had made Strenshaugh a snowbound refuge, had broken with the spring thaw, for it had brought with it this odious interruption to her months of virtual solitude. The hateful voice bored on.

'I don't know why you should seek to defend him! It would have been better for you — for all of us — if he had perished in the jungle, along with his unfortunate parents. If indeed, he was poor George's son!'

'Please, Lady Charlotte!' Rose cried out in anguish. She put her hand to her mouth to stifle the sob she could feel building up within her. 'I know you mean well, but honestly! All I want is to be left — '

'Nonsense! You'll send yourself into a decline buried away down here! You've never been up to town once! No wonder people are gossiping! It's enough to start another scandal, the way you're hiding yourself away! What on earth will they be thinking?'

All at once, Rose caught the drift of the woman's meaning. She blushed crimson, but her new outrage gave her a new strength.

'I don't know! What will they be thinking? What are you implying, Lady Charlotte? Tell me plain!'

'You know fine well what I mean, girl! Even *you* can't be that naïve! They'll be thinking you're afraid to show yourself because you've a guilty secret to hide. A shame as great as that little slut of a maid he played you false with!'

Somehow, Rose managed to contain the searing anger choking her inside. Instead, she stood and turned, posed very deliberately in silhouette, and ran her hands down from her waist to the hips of her black day-gown.

'You see how I am, madam? Do you notice any new fullness of figure? I am indeed naive, as you say. But my clothes hang on me, and I swear I am thinner now than ever. More like the schoolgirl I was than the grown woman I am! Ignorant as I am, I know where babies come from, ma'am — and how they are got! I assure you, your concern, and that of others, is quite needless.'

'You are not in a fit state of mind to see reason. I shall not try. Sir Arthur insists you should accompany us to the celebrations. And to the coronation itself, of course, in June. I hope you recover sufficiently to remember where your duty lies to the family.'

She swept out without a farewell. For a few seconds, Rose stood, hot-cheeked with the shock of her own daring. Then the reaction came, and that disgust with herself at the despair which had turned her to this poor creature, who shut herself away like a princess in a tower, and shrank from any contact with the real world outside her self-imposed prison.

22

'If that's what you have heard about me, Rose, I fear I have been grossly misrepresented.'

Ned Lovatt's handsome face was flushed. He turned away, gazing out over the buzzing auditorium of the theatre, his profile sharply silhouetted against the dim lighting of the box. Sir Arthur and Lady Charlotte had moved to the foyer for their interval drinks. The heavy crimson drapes were drawn over the door, sealing Rose and Ned in momentary but complete privacy.

Rose was well aware this was all part of the great conspiracy. Her father was out there somewhere, too, enjoying the whirl of summer celebration the capital had been plunged into, despite the fact that his wife, Amy, still 'delicate', was at home nursing their three-month-old son. Rose had so far managed to avoid seeing the infant, Walter. What other name could have been chosen for her peacock-proud father's one and only male heir? She was filled with nothing but bitterness when she thought of her mother's unhappy life, cut short through his insatiable desire to father a child — a boy, to make up for the abiding disappointment of Rose's birth.

Rose had striven hard to keep the world outside the grounds of Strenshaugh Hall at bay. She had felt relief when the king's ill-health had meant postponing the coronation from June until August. Yet, she had to admit, if only to herself, the solitude of her life, when only Mrs Fielding's menu told her which day of the week it was, apart from the tolling of the bell from the estate village, and the short, Sabbath carriage-ride to the loneliness of the front pew in the small church.

In spite of herself, every day, she still felt that sudden quickening of heartbeat when Mr Reece brought in the post, her eyes swiftly scanning the envelopes, searching for that ungainly hand which she would instantly recognize. It was never there. Why should it be? He had sworn she would hear no more of him, and, for once, it seemed he was determined to keep his word. As for herself, not a day passed without his being in her thoughts, on her first awakening, and during her prayers at night. During the seasons' progress through spring into a gloriously fresh early summer, the pain of her existence grew beyond her resistance.

So, if she were being completely honest, she must acknowledge that it was not entirely the browbeating tactics of Sir Arthur and Lady Charlotte, assisted by her father and his wife that had eventually brought her out of seclusion, but her own pathetic need for some human contact. Her youthful need for companionship, seared as it had been by her misfortune, was not, it would seem, completely dead. However, this latest piece of social engineering was clearly the work of those within her limited family circle, and none of her own doing. It was not the first time she had been reunited with Ned. He had been in the party she and the Ables mingled with at the Claridges' Ball, though, to her great relief, he had exchanged only a stiff greeting and a couple of minutes' stilted conversation with her, and had seemed as embarrassed as she at their being thrown together.

However, on this occasion, her embarrassment was much greater than his. It was clear he was party to this conspiracy to trap her alone with him, also clear that he was desperately determined to proceed beyond the bounds of inconsequential chitchat to the former closeness, proper as it had been, that they had enjoyed. It was that, and her feeling of being the dupe in the games of others, that had made her speak more bluntly than she had ever intended, and to declare her knowledge of his acquaintance with the less reputable aspects of London nightlife.

As she heard his vigorous denial, she wondered if the heightened colour spreading over his features was due to guilt, or to his justified indignation at her accusation. He did indeed look shocked and angered, she admitted to herself. She felt a strange sense of disloyalty almost, as she acknowledged once more his fine looks. Then he turned back to her with a candid gaze, and she felt the tension of his annoyance fade. He gave a small, rueful smile, which affected her deeply with a sense of her own hasty ill-judgement.

'I have enemies, it seems.' Now his look was one of wounded appeal. 'I met your cousin several times, I confess.' He hesitated slightly, his embarrassment as plain as his reluctance to go on. 'The truth is, he was beginning to cause a stir, appearing all over town with — well, some pretty disreputable companions. I was afraid it would cause some kind of scandal, that it might get back to you. I knew — I didn't want it to cause you any grief. I tried once or twice to reason with him. It seemed to me, after your engagement . . . ' he stopped, gave a little shrug. 'Anyway, things got rather heated, I'm afraid.

There was nothing more I could do. Except hope that he would learn at least to be more discreet, and that you wouldn't hear of his . . . conduct here. But then came the breaking off of your engagement, all that business.'

Now she felt the warm colour mounting; she stared down at her gloved hands, clasped in her lap.

'I wanted to get in touch. Believe me! I couldn't stop thinking — but then, I knew there was nothing I could do to ease the situation.' His voice sank lower. 'I knew you wouldn't want to hear from *me*, at such an awful time.'

His voice was so humble and so full of pain that Rose felt her heart moved with pity for him. And an even greater pain in her own heart that Johnny, God forgive him, could have tried to blacken Ned's character in the way he had done. She cleared her throat.

'Yes,' she murmured. 'It has all been very distressing for me. I couldn't really bear to face anyone. You know of course he has returned to Africa. Left everything, the running of Strenshaugh, everything, in my hands. Oh, I have help, of course. Plenty of good men to see that I don't ruin things. They take care of it all — and me.' She glanced up, gave a smile that equalled his in its sadness. 'It *is* good to see you again, Ned. I mean it, truly.'

They heard the returning voices of people taking their places. Their eyes met, held one another for an instant. She raised her hand in a gesture of farewell. He seized her fingers and lifted them, kissed them lightly with his lips.

'I have never stopped thinking of you, Rose.'

The blue eyes blazed with his intensity, then he turned and was at the door as the first of the party came to take their seats.

★　★　★

The coronation trappings still festooned the streets of the capital. London seemed to have been celebrating for weeks on end, from Lily Langtry's wedding to a politician, the change of prime minister to the Conservative, Mr Balfour, the triumph of Lord Kitchener's return as the victor of South Africa, to the splendours of King Edward's crowning itself. Ned Lovatt felt as limp and listless as the faded flags and bunting which hung motionless in the balmy September night, as he acknowledged the greetings of the denizens of Mrs Moss's discreet establishment.

'Good evening, Mr Lovatt, sir. Long time

no see in these parts.' Despite their polite form, Lucy's drawled words, in her deep, rich tones, carried all the undercurrent of veiled mockery that made Ned's skin tingle with irritation. Brusquely, he brushed aside the eager embrace of his regular partner at Mrs Moss's, the blonde girl, May, who had raised her painted lips like an affectionate puppy for his kiss. He glanced around, and took a seat beside the black woman. May decided it would be better not to try to sprawl all over his knee. Instead, she perched on the chair's uncomfortable arm. The thin négligé slipped off her limbs to reveal the dark stocking and broad frill of the garter which held it to her pale thigh. The delicate satin slipper swung from her toes. As always, May strove to hide the unease she felt in her presence, for she knew Mr Ned's desire for Lucy's body, which was even stronger than his dislike of her cool, taunting character. In a way, May wished he *would* find opportunity to satisfy his lust for the African, get it out of his system — except she was afraid that, once he had tasted Lucy's delights, he would not be satisfied to return to May's more conventional charm. That woman had a knack of holding on to her men, of keeping them in thrall. She remembered the young Lord Strenshaugh's fascination with her — and old Charlie

Forsythe, who had run after her like a lapdog before young Mr Johnny had come along, and who was now back in favour, and paying accordingly for the privilege!

'What's wrong, Mr Ned?' the deep voice pursued, with daring mischief. 'Has the sweet and lovely Miss Martingale fled back to her country retreat, and left you all alone? After all your gallant efforts at squiring?'

'For the moment, yes.' He tried to look relaxed, and amused. May sat there, fuming inwardly, damning the black bitch to hell, and wishing there was some way she could stand up to her. But there was many a girl who had tried to do just that, and had the scars to prove it. May hated the way the smooth figure sat there, turned out like a lady, and acting like one, too, putting on her airs and graces as though she wasn't one of the biggest 'Daughters of Joy' in the whole of Mrs Moss's.

Ned affected to glance around.

'And where is *your* lord and master tonight? Don't tell me you've slipped the leash at last?'

Lucy laughed. 'You know me, Mr Ned. You won't find a better-trained bitch in all of London. I sit when I'm told to sit — and I come when I'm told to come! Charlie will be late tonight. It will probably be nearer dawn

— he's at some dreary do or other.'

'One of those wives and sweethearts things, is it?' he probed maliciously. 'One where respectability rears its ugly head!'

She chuckled again, and nodded her head in agreement.

'That's right, sir. And in those places, my old black hide would stand out like Satan in St Paul's!'

'I can't persuade you to a bit of private sport while you await your master's pleasure, can I?'

May sat there, mortified, burning with inner shame and hate at his slight. Lucy grinned. The dark eyes fixed on the discomfited May, and surveyed her with a slow assessment that brought little consolation to the blonde girl.

'I'm flattered, Mr Ned, but no, thank you. I may be a bitch, but I'm a faithful one. To whoever owns me. Besides, I'd say you've got your hands full enough, with this pretty young dolly.'

May's body prickled, her fingers curled in murderous hunger to inflict damage, but she said nothing. Ned's hand fell heavily on her gartered thigh.

'True enough. Come on, May! To work!'

But there was more in store for her than his usual hectic and supremely selfish pleasure.

When that was done, and they lay sweatily entangled in the bed, he slapped at her flank again.

'Up you get, my girl. Tell me, can you write, May?'

''Course I can!' she answered indignantly, then added, less certainly, 'Not that good, I'll admit. And my spelling's not that hot! But I can copy neat as anything! Why?'

'I want you to write a letter, my love. I'll tell you what to write. I'll even help you with your spelling. Not that it should be *too* good. We don't want to give the game away, do we?'

'Game? What game?' She stared at him suspiciously.

He rose from the bed, picked up her flimsy robe and flung it at her.

'Put that on. For once, I want you to work with your clothes on. You do this task well, and,' he added significantly, 'keep your mouth shut about it afterwards, and I'll pay you damned well for it. Wait. I'll get pen and ink and paper. We'll see how a good a hand you are! Not that it matters — as long as it can be read.'

'Who am I writing to, Ned?' she asked, intrigued now.

He grinned at her, tapped the side of his nose.

'To a young lady, May! A young lady who I hope will one day be my wife!'

23

Mr Parr himself was waiting to meet Rose in the front office, and led her past the busy clerks, through a door and up the narrow stairs to a corridor, off which stood the solidly comfortable offices of the senior partners. Safely behind the closed door of his own chamber, he gestured towards one of the two upholstered wing-chairs, arranged either side of the tiled fireplace, where a fire burnt with cheerful brightness against the unseasonable chill of the windy day.

'So good to see you up in town again, Miss Martingale.'

She accepted the glass of Madeira he offered her. Ignoring the huge old desk, which was covered with buff-coloured files, and sheets of loose papers, he took the chair opposite hers near the fire.

'Are you staying in town long? You should have let me know. I could have arranged to come to the apartment. Saved you the bother of coming in here.'

'No, no, it's fine, Mr Parr. I was close by. I wanted to see you. To ask you to arrange some regular funding. There's an extremely worthy cause I'd like to support.'

He nodded, waiting to hear more. She was looking so much better these days, he reflected. Almost radiant. Of course, being out of mourning helped. Black definitely did not suit her complexion. It had been a long and miserable year for her, losing her grandfather so suddenly, and then the awful scandal of the broken engagement, and Mr John's trouble. The lawyer had thought it a fortunate escape for Rose, but it soon became apparent that the young lady herself did not see it in the same light. In fact, he had been surprised and dismayed at the effect the young lord's flight had had upon the girl he had always thought so serious and level-headed, free from the flightiness one might have associated more readily with her youth, her good looks, and her elevated social position. In a couple of weeks it would be her coming of age. His mind went back to the celebration of her birthday a year ago, the grand ball, such as Strenshaugh Hall had not seen for many a year, and the announcement of the cousins' engagement. How beautiful Rose had looked that night, and how happy his lordship had been to see them betrothed! Yet, within weeks, the old man had gone, and the new incumbent had brought disaster down upon himself, and tragedy for his poor fiancée, and all because the young dog couldn't keep his breeks buttoned up with the servants in his own ancestral home!

Full of surprises, our Master Able. Just when he would have wagered a fortune on the young wastrel laying into the family wealth and squandering it on a life of debauched excess, the new lord had virtually handed everything over to Miss Rose on a plate. Taken what was really quite a modest sum for his own use, and decamped to the African territories, with apparently no intention of returning. Just as well for the girl who sat smiling at him now. Freed of her obligation to abide by her grandfather's dearest wish, she might find some happiness for herself at last with Mr Lovatt, who had a wise and level head on his shoulders, and family wealth enough of his own to be no threat to the Strenshaugh estate.

Rose passed over a letter for Mr Parr's perusal.

'I'd like you to read this. I haven't really discussed the matter with Mr Lovatt yet. He was quite distressed when he discovered that Miss Thompson had communicated with me.'

The solicitor saw the slight touch of colour to her cheeks, the shy downward glance, as she continued:

'He didn't feel it was something I should be concerned with, or involve myself in.' She hesitated slightly, then raised her eyes to meet his serious gaze. 'However, I think it's a most worthy thing that he's doing, and wish very much to be associated with it. I see no reason why young women such as myself should be so sheltered, so protected from the realities of the modern world, however unpleasant.'

'Indeed, I quite agree, Miss Rose. Allow me a moment, if you please.' He read quickly. The letter was perfectly legible, the handwriting neat, its roundness slightly laboured and childish. It must have taken the writer both considerable time and effort, he surmised.

Dear Miss Martingale,

I hope you will forgive me writing to you a stranger like this but I feel I must do something after I have heard from some of my friends how dear Mr Lovatt fell out of favour with you and some of your friends because of him befriending some of us unfortunate girls who canot be seen as part of polite world you know. You consider us shameful Im sure and you are right to do so, but Mr Lovatt bless him has tried only to help us and lift us from the life of shame we have lived.

We heard people of his class such as your good self have thought the worse of him for mixing with us fallen women and its not fair when all he has done is try to help us to mend our ways. He helps with money to free us from our wickedness and in other ways, to find employment and such like and make a new start for ourselfs. He is a good man miss and I cant bear to think of you thinking such bad things about him when he has been so good to me and some of my friends.

He will be very cross if he finds out I have wrote this letter to you but I know how deep his feelings for you are so I have told you the truth. Please miss don't let on to him as it will upset him so much. I will give you address where you can get in touch if you wish but I don't want him to know. I hope now you will think the best of him and remain

    Your humble servant,
        May Thompson, age 18.

'Have you replied to this letter, Miss Rose?' He handed it back to her. 'You are quite satisfied as to its genuineness?'

'Oh, yes. I haven't been in touch with the girl, but I *did* tell Ned — Mr Lovatt — that I had received it.' She smiled. 'He was, as Miss

Thompson says, most upset. But he has indeed founded a charitable trust, in his family's name. It's supported by the clergy, and has already done much good among the women of Miss Thompson's — situation.' Her colour deepened as she sought a suitable word. 'I have the details here, and I want to make immediate and regular contributions. A considerable sum, for such a worthy cause. I wanted to meet Miss Thompson — I hope I will, some day soon.'

She gave another shy smile, and a small gesture of deprecation. 'I'm afraid Mr Lovatt was shocked. He is most reluctant that I should involve myself with — with that sort of thing. I'm afraid he takes the traditional point of view: that we young ladies are too delicate to be exposed to the harshness of the real world. We're hothouse plants, to be protected at all times!'

From the indeterminate nature of his throat-clearing, Rose deduced that Mr Parr was of a mind with Ned and those like him.

'I must work patiently to convince him otherwise. In this new twentieth century I feel that women will have a greater role to play than has hitherto been assigned to them. I often feel how disadvantaged I am not to have attended school, but to have remained at home, at the mercy of governesses.'

'Well, you have responsibilities enough now,' the solicitor said encouragingly. 'We can set up the contributions to this fund without any problems. You've got all the details there, I believe? Good.' He rose and went over to his desk, where he pressed an electric bell set into the wall. 'We'll take care of it right away, and you can sign the documents before you go.'

When instructions had been issued to the clerk, who withdrew to complete the paperwork, Rose cleared her throat, in an effort to make her tone sound casual.

'Have you heard anything — is there any news of Lord Strenshaugh?'

'The last we heard he was in Nairobi, in the Kenya colony. Things are opening up there, now that the South African business is over. He was setting up some kind of trekking business. Mule trains, that kind of thing. The railway will open up the interior no end.'

She longed desperately to ask for more. Had he written personally? Did he ask after me? she wanted to say, but her embarrassment gagged her. Mr Parr seemed glad to switch the conversation back towards home.

'It's your coming of age in two weeks.' The awkwardness was still there, as the unspoken remembrance of the engagement party hovered between them, and the solicitor went on rapidly: 'Will you be coming up to London to celebrate?'

'I expect so.' She paused. 'But I'm thinking of holding a party at Strenshaugh, for the actual birthday. I've entertained so little — buried myself away, rather.' Her embarrassment was palpable.

Mr Parr smiled enthusiastically. That's my brave girl! he thought admiringly. She was blushing visibly now.

'We'd be very happy to see you and Mrs Parr down there, if that's possible.' There was another pause. 'Mr Lovatt was saying — we should make it a memorable occasion. He — his family — that is, his sister, Mrs Berkeley-Kerr — have agreed to help me.'

The solicitor nodded vigorously.

'Very sound young feller, Mr Lovatt, in my opinion, Miss Rose!'

★　★　★

'I never seem to have much luck with roses!' Johnny said tightly. 'I always seem to find the thorns instead of the petals!' He let his arms fall from the slim figure stiffening against his embrace, which had begun half-playfully, though his blood was racing with desire.

'What do you mean?' Rosa da Silva stared at him keenly, her own confused emotions suspended at his strange remark.

'I knew a girl called Rose in England. She wouldn't have anything to do with me, either! What is this fatal lack of charm I have with women?'

The richly tangled, lustrous black waves of her loose hair tossed.

'That is not what I hear from Charlie Storr's place!'

'Hah! The bar girls! Anyone can have their love for ten rupees!'

'Yes. Please, don't forget, eh? I am not a bar girl!'

The words transported him at once, over 4,000 miles, back to England, which would be wrapped now in that flame and golden autumnal beauty, as it had been that night at Strenshaugh, exactly a year ago, when the old house had blazed with light, and was full of music and laughter, the carriages rolling up to the steps in quick succession. He contrasted the slim, girlish figure in his mind with the full-blooded vitality of the mature woman who stood before him now. The Arab and Portuguese blood had worked to meld the most outstanding features of both races in a beauty which took men's breath. At thirty, Rosa was ripely blooming. Her flashing, dark-eyed allure, her coffee-cream breasts, generously on display over the scooped neckline of the white, gypsy-style blouses she favoured so much, the roll of her hips, and the supple waist unrestricted by any confining stays or corset, under a wide flowing skirt which ended daringly at mid-calf, to reveal the tight boots of shining leather, together composed a portrait of a woman to turn every man's head when she entered a room.

That she could, and did, survive so independently and successfully in such a male-orientated, frontier society was a tribute to the force of her character. She had helped to organize various railhead canteens, and now that the railway was almost in sight of its western terminus at the great Lake Victoria, she had settled in Nairobi, managing the feeding and accommodation of the ever-swelling ranks of railway workers, and others associated with this magnificent venture. She ruled over her large staff of Indian and native labour practically single-handed, and there were few who could best her in an argument, or match her iron will.

He had already found out as much, to his cost, in the months he had known her. Tormented by the spectre of the pale English girl who haunted his memory, and his conscience, Johnny had sought escape in the way most familiar to him, indulging himself with the girls of easy virtue and of virtually every shade of colour who were to be had in plenty around the frontier town. Rosa was different. Her beauty was a challenge, even though part of him, the most decent part, recognized and respected her seeming immunity to his charm, and her incredible loyalty to the unlikely object of her devotion, his partner and friend, Willy de Voss. That had to be the reason for his failure to woo her, Johnny told himself. That and his own nicety of conscience against his undoubted lusting after Rosa.

All modesty aside, Willy was not the most prepossessing of men. His rotund figure, and flabby jowls, usually with several days' growth of dark stubble, was hardly the stuff of which girls' dreams were made. Certainly not those of exquisite beauties of Rosa's calibre. Nor were the couple tied by marriage, or any formal agreement.

'He helped me a lot when I was down in Mozambique,' she told Johnny. 'I could not have survived without him.' She would not elucidate, but clearly she felt herself under an obligation to the Boer. She was generally acknowledged as his 'woman', though never in her hearing. Willy treated her with an almost embarrassing respect at times, and was extremely wary in his relationship with her. And why not, Johnny thought, if it kept him exclusively in her bed at night?

Johnny was frustrated. He felt he owed it to his masculinity and his freedom to make a sexual play for Rosa's affection, yet there was a restraint there, too, a mutual restraint, which disturbed him deeply. Whenever he had the chance, he would make a grab for her, sometimes playfully, sometimes with clear and serious intent. Always, firmly, he was rejected. And yet they stayed the best of friends.

'This girl — this English Rose — she must have been a very unusual girl, no? To turn down such a handsome catch!'

She was teasing him, but he didn't mind. He had talked little of his recent past. Willy had blabbed to her of his title of milord, unable to keep from boasting, and she teased him a great deal about that when they were alone. But she respected his secret. All at once, he found that he wanted to talk of Rose.

'She was.'

'It is as I thought! You are in love with her! That is why you come here, to try to forget her! Yes?'

'No!' The mood of tenderness broke,

leaving a taste like ashes. He gave a harsh, brittle laugh. 'She was your typical English virgin! Ice-water for blood, and afraid of any real feeling in her pretty little bosom! And she'll probably die a virgin, too! Afraid of real life to the end!'

24

'Rose! You know perfectly well my feelings for you. I have refrained from speaking of them. I even stopped myself from getting in touch for all these months. But — it's been a year almost since you became free again. Those feelings have never changed.'

He had caught hold of her hands, in the long white gloves. She felt the pressure of his grip, tightening, in keeping with the emotion in his voice. Once again, that sneaking feeling of dismay came upon her, which had ambushed her thoughts so often during these past hours. You little fool, to pick this birthday night of all nights to try to lay the ghosts that fill your mind! The laughter, the buzz of voices, and the band's rhythmic playing, highlighted the irony of her reflections. She felt trapped in the lamplit seclusion of the little room, its closed door sealing them from the gaiety of the party. The sound of celebration, of thronging guests, seemed so alien in the old house. And yet, a year ago, the hall had carried just such a noise; identical sounds of happiness, of rejoicing.

No! Furiously, she denied it. Not identical!

Johnny was gone, her grandfather was gone! As Ned had reminded her, a whole year had passed. Times had changed. So must she! She had made such an effort, to revive herself, to wake herself from her deadness, to take up with life once more. She must not let herself be trapped, defeated, by these private, painful memories. She made herself relax, thrust the stab of dismay from her.

'I know that, Ned. I'm only sorry that I cut myself off from everyone. From you. And I must beg forgiveness, for ever . . . doubting you. Your decency . . . ' her voice trembled, emotion caught her. He was crushing her hands now, holding them to his chest. She saw the love and the hunger in his face, saw its beauty as it bent reverentially towards hers, hesitating even now. She closed her eyes, lifted her mouth, her lips parting. They were kissing, their lips met softly, then pressed ardently, their mouths twisting, worrying, opening to the passion which shook them, welded them in its beating force.

He had released his hold on her hands. Hers were round his neck, hugging him to her, his were at her waist, pulling him into her, crushing the tulle and the lace of her pale ball-gown, and the stiff petticoat beneath it, until she could feel the hardness of his body through the clothing. They were panting audibly when at last their kiss ended, and she clung giddily to him, while those lips nuzzled and whispered at her ear.

'Please, Rose. Tell me there's hope for me. I love you so much. I want you for my wife. There can never be any other for me.'

Daringly, improperly, his mouth sought her neck, the fragrant delicateness, felt the coils of hair behind the dainty earlobe, and she quivered, shivering with sensation throughout her frame, her gloved fingers digging convulsively in the stuff of his jacket.

She gasped, and squirmed. Passionate! Like Johnny's kisses! The traitorous thought flashed through her bemused head, and she whimpered softly. She reached up, for the fine, sleek, fair head, swivelled, her mouth wildly seeking his once more, offering herself to all the flaring passion transfusing them.

They broke again at last, and now he could feel her trembling. He relaxed the tightness of his hold on her, and she was crying softly. She kept her wet cheek against his, leaning on his shoulder, hiding her shyness, leaving the trace of her fragrance on him, as she whispered:

'Ned — I feel I have treated you so unkindly. I didn't — I'm honoured by your feelings for me. There's no one closer — no one at all.' She leaned weakly against him, rested her head against his solid strength, weeping still, tormented by the inner voice hissing accusingly at her. *Traitor! Liar!*

★   ★   ★

The contract was made, she committed herself to it, that night. But he understood perfectly the inappropriateness of any announcement. She was grateful for that understanding, for the sympathy, which was so reassuring; part of his quiet strength, the dependability she welcomed so much. Their engagement was not formalized until just before Christmas, while Rose was staying at the Lovatts' imposing country estate in the north Yorkshire dales. Rose could not help feeling that the pleasure with which the betrothal was greeted by both families was strongly coloured with relief.

Her father expressed it with his customary insensitivity, when he danced with her during the ball, which was held on the night itself.

'Well, all's well that ends well, eh? I must say, I thought old Grandpa William had lost his marbles when he paired you off with that young pirate! Thank God the young hound blotted his own copybook and took off with his tail between his legs! Merciful release for you, my girl, make no mistake about it! You won't find a solider young feller than Ned.

Fine family, too. At least you know he won't be after your fortune. Could buy and sell Strenshaugh twice over, I should think!' And he glowed with pleasure at the thought of the benefits which would flow from such a splendidly fitting match.

★   ★   ★

'You're bloody joking, aren't you?'

May turned from the dark-framed mirror of the dressing-table, where she had been arranging her hair into order after the wild exertions on the bed, which had sent it tumbling in disarray. Ned was propped up on the pillows, half-covered by the tangled sheets, and enjoying his cigarette, after the strenuous activity, which had left him tired but replete.

'What the hell would I want to go into service for? I've had my fill of that, I can tell you! Started when I was ten! Worked for a fat butcher and his wife, and their foul brood of kids! Slept with the birds and mice up in the attic on a straw mattress. Skivvied from dawn till late at night. Did the lot — washing, scrubbing, fire-lighting, kids! And all for three bob a week and blooming scraps to live on! Half a day off a fortnight, and never even saw my wages! My pa came round and collected them every Friday, straight from the missus, then into the pub and boozed 'em! All gone by Saturday morning!'

Ned listened impatiently to her tirade. 'Shut up and listen! I'm not asking you to go into service, you little idiot!' He chuckled, patted the rumpled bed. 'You give good enough service here. Born to it, you might say! Why let such a God-given talent go to waste? No, what I'm saying, if you'll just shut up and listen, is that you'll have to go along with it — the idea. We'll have to concoct a note, saying that you've been for the interview. That you've been fixed up with a job — somewhere far enough away, and obscure enough so that nobody's going to be able to check it. It'll keep Miss Martingale happy — and all the other do-gooders in our scheme. She's taken quite a fancy to you, my little fallen sparrow! In fact, I've been hard put to keep her from meeting you.'

'God forbid! I couldn't look her in the face . . . '

'You might have to! As I say, she's become very interested in our worthy cause. And especially in saving *your* shabby little soul! I may have to dress you up like a respectable girl and let her take a look at you. You'll need some coaching . . . '

She stared, eyes wide in alarm.

'No, Ned! I mean it! I couldn't do that, not to her face! Writing's different. But chatting to her! I couldn't! Poor soul! I'm no actress. Wouldn't be right!' She stood, came back to the bed, gazing earnestly at him, and sat down on its edge, facing him. 'You got to promise me I won't have to meet her. I mean it!'

He reached out and grabbed her arms, pulled her across his lap, and she lay back, staring up solemnly at him. She was still in her scanty underclothing, her white bodice unhooked.

'You'll do as I tell you, my girl!' he said lightly, smiling. But his handsome face was hard, his grip on her thin upper arms painful.

'Anyway,' May pouted, 'she'll soon have other things to occupy her, won't she? When's the wedding? March, ennit?'

'Why? You hoping she'll ask you to be a bridesmaid?' His grin was mocking.

'You're a right bastard, Ned, you know that? I feel sorry for your young lady, I really do! She don't know what she's letting herself in for, does she?'

His hands were still clamped around her arms. He lifted her thin form up closer to him, and she saw the sadistic hardness in his visage.

'It's different with young ladies, May.

287

They're delicate creatures. Weak. Easily broken. That's why we need girls like you, my sweet. Girls who can take the rough with the smooth. Who know what we really want, eh?' His fingers peeled back the edges of her bodice, exposing the small breasts. Those fingers dug into the warm, soft roundness, squeezing painfully, then his hands moved down to displace the thin silk from her lower body.

He lowered her roughly on to the rumpled sheet, knelt purposefully over her, pinning her arms above her head.

'God! You're never satisfied, are you?' she gasped, wriggling to accommodate his urgent manoeuvrings.

'The word is insatiable, my little hussy! And aren't you mightily glad of it?'

★ ★ ★

When Rose alighted from the carriage, she felt that rush of anger at the prurience of the small knot of onlookers who stared so dumbly but boldly at her. She glanced at the cottage, reflecting on the last time she had been here and the painful embarrassment of her interview with Mr and Mrs Addy. They stood at their gate now, waiting to welcome her, he clutching his cap, his balding head bared, his wife, a little plumper, head shawled, bobbing in obeisance. Rose nodded to the gawping spectators, moved forward through the open gate. The ground was speckled with the patchy crust of the snowfall, which was melting almost as soon as it had fallen. There was a spattering of rain in the air now, and the sky was a uniform grey. She had just been reading in that morning's paper of the rain of 'blood' which had fallen in southern England the previous day, the precipitation discoloured, so the experts said, by the sands of the distant Sahara Desert. An omen! her mind had intoned, before she dismissed her fanciful imagination.

Kate's stiff little note had arrived yesterday, offering her belated good wishes for the wedding in three weeks' time, and asking if she might call and see Rose some time? She was home on a brief holiday, from work near Reading. She had found a position as maid to a gentleman farmer's wife, and to assist in the managing of her three young children. Rose had supplied references for the position, which Kate had held for the past three months and more.

Rose's first reaction to Kate's request to come to the hall had been one of dismay, and even indignation. After all that had happened between them, she had expected her former maid to recognize the awkwardness of meeting again. But then she was ashamed of her own narrow squeamishness. She thought of all she had learnt in the past year; of people like the young women dear Ned tried so hard to help, the tough and unpleasant realities of the world, from which, she was so fond of declaring, the modern young miss did not need to be protected.

Still, it would be too embarrassing, not only for Rose but for Kate, too, to have her reappearing at the scene of her downfall, and start the whispering gossip below stairs off again. So she had sent word she would call at the cottage. She wanted to see how the family was progressing, to make sure the improvements to the cottage had been carried out satisfactorily, as she had ordered.

The place had been cleaned with painstaking thoroughness. Rose could see that as soon as she stepped over the threshold. She was directed into the tiny parlour, off the main living-area. Kate was waiting, in spotless white bonnet, brightly knitted shawl and checked gown. She sank in a deep and practised curtsey. The red ringlets framed a face that was thinner, more angular than before, though it had regained much of its beauty. It was a quieter beauty, more reflective, and stamped with the world's difficulties. Her form was sparer, her manner, unsurprisingly, more subdued and formal.

'It's good to see you again, Miss Rose.' She waved to the highbacked chair, clearly the place of honour, set close to the brightly burning fire in the small hearth. She waited until Rose had seated herself before she perched on the edge of the old settle, which almost filled the room.

Rose nodded. 'How are you, Kate? Well, I hope?'

'Oh, yes, miss, thank you. Fine now. I just wanted to see you — to wish you well, for your wedding. Three weeks, isn't it? I wish I could be here to see you — go to the church, I mean. You'll make a lovely bride.'

Rose blushed a little.

'Thank you.' All at once, a wave of emotion rose within her, so that she swallowed painfully, and she felt the prick of tears behind her lids. In her young imaginings she had always pictured the red-haired girl beside her helping her to prepare for the great day, the two of them united in their excitement and anticipation. She studied the slender form, and unbidden came those tormented visions of the lithe body, the red hair falling, in Johnny's arms . . .

'I'm sorry for all that's happened — come between us,' she whispered huskily. Her breast heaved. She had meant to be so calm, so serene, and now the tender sadness welled, and she choked on a sob.

Kate moved quickly, fell forward on to her knees, seeking Rose's gloved hands, pressing herself against the girl's knees. The white-bonneted head bowed, the red hair swung at her cheeks.

'Oh, so am I, miss, I truly am. I can't ever forgive myself!' She sighed deeply. 'Bless you, Miss Rose. I hope you'll be very happy.' But the voice was full of sadness, and a tear splashed to mark its dark roundness on the pale material of Rose's glove.

25

The sun shone for the wedding, bright and dazzling. But the high, cotton-wool clouds were shredded by the forceful, chilly wind, which buffeted the old churchyard in Garrowby, and sent Rose's veil billowing in a gossamer streamer, threatening her flowered head-dress, flattening her wedding gown against her body. She clung to her father's arm, glad of his support, as they bent and hurried through the applauding crowd to the shelter of the porch.

She had not wanted him at her side. However much she urged herself to follow her Christian precepts of forgiveness, she could not in her heart forgive him for what he had done to her mother, and for the years of his willing abandonment of her, however relieved the young girl undoubtedly was at his having done so. She had cried, alone in her bed, when she had woken on her wedding-day, her head aching and muzzy from lack of sleep, in the blustery dawn. Cried for her dead mother, and dead grandfather, wishing fervently that he could have been the one to lead her on his arm up the aisle to her wedding. And that was all she was crying for, she swore to herself, and groaned with shame at the thought of Johnny. She prayed for him, every morn and night, and now she was tormented by her need to expunge him from her consciousness.

In spite of her weariness, and the dawn chill, she flung back the bedclothes and rolled out of bed, to drop to her knees, shivering, and moaning softly, her lips moving. *God bless him. Keep him safe*, wherever he is. And now, please, God, on this day of all days, take him from my mind, all thought of him, all memory of him, please, God!

She was hollow, sick with fright, she realized, as she crawled shivering back into the warmth of her bed, curled up, and pulled the blankets up over the very top of her carefully bound and night-capped head. Appalled, she discovered she wanted only to stay there, never to emerge from this safe, solitary cocoon. She could be ill! A sudden, serious illness, making it utterly impossible for her to move, to get up, to bathe and dress, to set foot outside, on the path of her new life. Was she still praying, she wondered?

Miserable little fool! she castigated herself. You have a good man, a man you're not worthy of, waiting to give himself to you, to be your partner. You don't deserve him!

Don't deserve his love, his kindness, his compassion.

She was shocked at the wild transformation of her thoughts, the violent switchback of her emotions, as she found herself wishing that the day was over, that she could be alone with him — she felt the heat mount through her shivering frame — here, in bed! That this ordeal, of vows and giving could be over, that she could belong to him, in body and therefore in spirit. She was gripped once more by that feeling of helplessness which she had been experiencing for days now, through all the long preparations and rituals leading to the marriage. Like a victim, a sacrificial virgin, she had been led along the tortuous path — the trousseau, the wedding-dress, the guest-lists, the gifts, the whole ritual. Wedded and bedded — how significant the rhyming of those words! That was what she wanted, she told herself feverishly. That was all.

The moment of the first part came. She was not aware of the church, packed with faces, familiar and strange. Her vision was curtailed, hemmed in, appropriately, by the insubstantial white tulle mist surrounding her, blurring her world. Appropriate, too, the echoing quality of the music, the voices, to the dreamlike atmosphere in which she was engulfed. Her own voice was the most ethereal of all. Did she actually speak the words aloud? 'I take thee, Edward Arthur Simon, to my wedded husband . . . to have and to hold . . . to love, cherish, and to obey, till death us do part . . . I give thee my troth . . . with my body I thee worship . . . '

The words, the sacred music, seemed to swirl about her as mistily as the pale insubstantiality of her vision, mingling and fading like the spectral new messages carried on the ether by Mr Marconi's invention. The vicar's voice boomed with sudden clarity, imposing itself on her awareness.

'Saint Paul, in his Epistle to the Ephesians, teacheth you thus; Wives, submit yourselves unto your own husbands, as unto the Lord. For the husband is the head of the wife, even as Christ is the head of the Church: and he is the saviour of the body. Therefore as the Church is subject unto Christ, so let the wives be to their own husbands in everything.'

Then they were outside again, in the bright, blowing world, standing in the shelter of the porch, and the bridesmaids were fussing, and a fussy little, morning-suited man was arranging her train, and her veil, and her bouquet, then scuttling back to his boxes and plates, and disappearing beneath the black shroud of his camera.

'What's wrong with you, Rose? Pull yourself together, girl! You look as white as a sheet!' Her father's voice hissed in her ear, and she gazed at him dazedly. She winced as she felt his fingers pinch her cruelly on her satin-clad arm. His false laughter boomed out as he said with loud joviality, 'Come on, my girl! At least *look* as though you're enjoying it!'

The ride back to the hall, a slow, triumphal progress in the open carriage through the village, before they entered the rolling parkland, put some colour in her cheeks. She smiled, and waved, and people described her as 'radiant'. But she felt as though it were happening to someone else. She was curiously detached, observing it all, and her hand in Ned's felt icy, and lifeless.

The rooms had been transformed. Garlanded, packed with guests, and with the scores of extra, liveried staff, Strenshaugh teemed with light and laughter, excited voices, music. Rose smiled through it all at Ned's side, her arm in his. There were more photographs, in the grand hall, at the foot of the staircase. Groups interchanged, facial muscles ached with the effort of maintaining the visible evidence of happiness for endless minutes, while the photographer darted back and forth, fussed and fretted, before diving under his hood, and his victims stood like frozen waxworks, trying not to breathe, for posterity. At last Ned released her and Rose stood alone on the wide stairs, her train falling like a white river of ice down over the shallow steps below her. She stared at the tripod, the shrouded hump. She did not smile, and there was a momentary pause, a stillness, which transferred to the watchers, as they looked at her solemn, vulnerable beauty. The virgin bride. Icewater Rosie. The phrase leapt into her mind, pierced the numbness like a needle.

The wedding-night was to be spent at Strenshaugh. Rose had wanted to sleep in the room she had known for all of the eight years she had lived there, but, as with most things, the decision had been taken out of her hands, or, rather, she had stood by and agreed with her stepmother and Lady Charlotte and Ned's family. One of the grand and seldom-used chambers on the first floor, complete with decorated four-poster, had been transformed into a bridal suite.

She wore her wedding-dress through the long day: for the midday meal, with its succession of toasts and speeches, and for the grand reception afterwards. It was dark long before she had the opportunity to change. From inside, the long windows reflected the colour and splendour of the festive scene. Before she left, to go up to her old room and prepare for the ball, Ned joked about the flickering gaslight and the candled chandeliers.

'Good heavens, Rose! We really must catch up with the twentieth century! It's time we had electric lighting installed here, my love! It will be one of your first tasks — to bring Strenshaugh into the modern world!'

Helen and Lottie were both waiting up in her bedroom.

'Your bath's ready, miss. I hope it's just right for you.'

Rose was glad that she had established the practice of bathing herself, though she could smile wryly at the notion of her being shy to show herself naked in front of the servants. Why, with Kate she had never given it a thought. She had enjoyed being attended to, pampered. But that was before . . . before Johnny . . . before Kate and Johnny . . . she struggled to push her thoughts away, lay back in the fragrant caress of the water, and breathed deeply. She savoured the solitude. Her last moments of true privacy, and independence. All at once she felt a quickening, a physical stirring, that made her catch her breath. She was vividly aware of her body, the pale and rosy gleam of flesh, the sensation of her touch. She stood, caught an indistinct glimpse of her head and shoulders, the dark hair piled up under the cap, the pale blur of her face, the dark eyes, in the steamy mirror. This was the last of Rose Martingale.

She stepped out of the tub, wrapped herself in the warm towel. You're not Rose Martingale, she told herself. You're Mrs Edward Lovatt. Before God and man. But that shivering little frame she hid under the towel was still that Rose. Until tonight. She felt the heat mount, rise through her. This was the last time she would be herself, be this private, shy and timid girl. She let the towel fall, moved closer to the mirror, and stared at herself, with curious, shameful candour. She could feel her body rousing, responding to her frank examination.

'What have I done?' she whispered helplessly to her own pale image.

★ ★ ★

Rose kept her eyes closed, her head turned away on the pillow, while Ned clambered out of the bed.

'There's some water — and towels and things. Behind the screen.' His voice was clipped with embarrassment. She maintained the ridiculous fiction that she was asleep, had suddenly dropped off at this defining moment in their relationship. 'I won't be long.' She heard the rustle of his pulling on his dressing-gown, and then the clicking of the door as he left her alone.

He meant that she should rise now, clean herself, restore order, before he returned. She was biting fiercely at her lower lip, holding her breath as long as she could against the fiercely burning pain. Now she was no longer Rose Martingale, no longer the innocent, ignorant little maid of all her former years. She must move, she knew, and quickly, but she was afraid to do so. He had hurt her, badly, brutally, so that she had been rigid with shock and fear. He had cried out her name in a gasping, tormented sort of way, his hand had pressed on her brow and her hair, had crushed the coronet of dark green leaves and the white blooms they had found laid out on her pillow and which she had placed on her brow. Then the fingers were all over her, pressing her face, the hollows of her eyes, her cheekbones, digging into her fragile shoulders, both his hands, pinning her down; then he began that brutal, plunging ride, battering her body, crying out, grunting all the while, and she had felt his sweating flesh slamming into her, battering at her. She cried out, and his mouth, wet, searching, had bitten and sucked at her neck, and she couldn't hold back the tears.

It did not last long. There was the final lancing of pain, her cry at its flash of agony, and he was collapsing, inert, crushing her, their mingled breath thundering in her ears. He was up and gone and now she was alone, fearful of the stinging pain, the pungent wetness, afraid of what she would find. No one had told her. How could she have known that it would be like this, that he would transform himself into this strange brute? This was what God had ordained? This was the sacred act, this was the oneness of flesh she had dreamed of? Her cheeks were wet with tears, but there was a savage laughter booming around in her head as she forced herself to move and to discover that, after all, she was not seriously wounded, or bleeding to death; the modest stain of her virtue was quite unremarkable as she crouched stiffly behind the screen, where cloths and towels, and the tepid, scented soap and water, had been laid out in readiness for the closing act of this sanctified joining of flesh.

26

In the first weeks, and then months, of her marriage, Rose never lost her feeling of guilt. She felt secretly that she was unfaithful to her husband, that she was somehow failing him; that, after all, she did not love him as she had promised, and as she had tried to make herself believe. She would honour, and obey. But she could not love. It was a desolation to her, and she shut it away, in a secret compartment of her heart, like a walled-up prisoner. She kept this shocking truth isolated from the rest of her consciousness, her life. Alone, she prayed tearfully that she would change, that this shut-away, shameful captive of hers would die, that one day she would love Ned as she had vowed.

She became sure, as they gradually became more used to each other, that he sensed it, too, for there was something about his attitude towards her, a kind of reserve, almost a wariness, that was so different from the tender and easier relation of the months of their engagement. Of course, she strove even harder to deny this — tried to be the warm and loving helpmeet he had the right to expect, and deserved — but somehow she failed. She knew it, without being able to define it exactly. He held himself back. There was a division between them. Things were not as they should be. They were not one, body and soul.

Nowhere was this more apparent than in the 'bodily' relationship. For the rest of it, away from the bedroom, she could compartmentalize it, keep that secret feeling of failure locked securely away. They were considerate, almost too polite to each other, too eager to please, as though they hardly knew one another, and wanted to create the right impression. She deferred eagerly to him, encouraged him to fall into his role of lord and master, while she took on the mantles of 'dewy-eyed bride', and 'little woman'. Disturbing self-accusations of duplicity were thrust firmly away from her.

When they got back from their three-week honeymoon in Italy, she flung herself enthusiastically into the renovation of Strenshaugh Hall, under his encouragement and benign guidance. It was good to be so occupied, to have her life so busily filled. It gave her 'something to do' — a belittling phrase tossed at her by his sister — during Ned's frequent spells of absence up in town.

'Do you *have* to go?' she asked, hanging on

to his hand, twisting it, and with that youthfully pouting ingenuousness that the detached part of her could observe with wry and mocking amusement. Like some stupid little courtesan! She condemned herself for her play-acting. It occurred to her that she could have framed the question perfectly seriously, without the posturing. It required a serious answer. Each of them had brought wealth to their union. She had been taken aback at the brevity of their honeymoon. She had never travelled, and had looked forward to the new experience of exploring the Continent. They could well have spent three months abroad, instead of three weeks.

It was disappointing that Ned did not share her enthusiasm. Of course, travel was not new to him, as it was to her. Yet it dismayed her that the treasures of Rome, the beauties of Florence and Venice, seemed to be worthy of such little regard to him. And when they *did* come home, to begin their married life after their brief 'idyll', it struck her as incongruous that he should have to take himself off to the capital, dashing off to 'work', like some lowly clerk, and frequently absenting himself for two or three days at a time.

'Men must work,' he philosophized good-humouredly.

And women must weep? She completed

the adage in a silent question to herself.

She saw that it was important to him. He was involved in a world which was totally alien to her, of commerce and industry. Just as the running of the estate, and its farming fraternity, were foreign to him. She had hoped that he would assume the position of lord of the manor (and she his lady) under the expert guidance of Mr Kemp and his staff, but Ned had made it plain that country life held no interest for him.

'You keep yourself busy, my love. There's plenty to be done here, with the house. That's your task, and a formidable one it is, too!'

He was right. Keep busy. That was the trick, the answer to all those unasked questions of herself, all those shut-away secrets, which must not be released, or explored.

Except that, despite her busyness, she could not keep from asking in her mind, over and over. One of the most persistent, and disturbing questions was the enigma of their sexual union, or lack of it. Time and again, she endeavoured to steel herself to talk about it. The bedroom was the best, the only place, to raise the issue, but always her courage fled at the crucial moment, for how could she mention the 'unmentionable'? It had shocked her to realize how unprepared she had been for the sexual initiation of the wedding-night. It was painfully evident — how apt the adverb — that Ned had known what to do, through instruction or practice, she supposed, and bluntly he had got on with it. Yet more than the fragile barrier of her hymen had been shattered that night. She knew not how or why, but somehow her instinct had told her it ought not to be like that — a terrifying and brutal experience, the furtive groping and stabbing in the dark, her nightgown hauled up, for that furious assault, and the shameful, severing silence afterwards. Even her body told her so, after that first shocking baptism of fire. Her flesh pulsed with new sensations, with desire, with its own needs for a fusion far removed from that hasty invasion. She tried to imagine what it could be, what it was she was yearning for.

It was the greatest abiding disappointment to her. After all the holy words about it, the blessing of the church for it, to be reduced to this shame, the muffled tumble under the hot blankets, the grinding shame of it! That was how *he* felt, how he made it, fumbling at the hem of her nightdress, the fury of the brief passion, the brief assault, for that was what it felt like to her. He wanted only for it to be over, and when it was done, they were worlds apart. So why, then, did he repeat it during those first nights, as soon as they had doused the light, with an urgency that was not to be resisted? Not that she ever thought of resisting. After all, it was her duty, she had promised before God to be his, to worship him with her body. But why did she have to be his nightly sacrifice?

In Italy, in an effort to alleviate her very real dismay, her fanciful mind viewed it as some kind of Gothic novel, or an enactment of Stevenson's Dr Jekyll and Mr Hyde. The transformation of her loving husband into the beast of the bedroom, disturbing but soon over. But all her attempts at gallows humour did little to lessen the distress it caused her. She kept thinking of her mother. She understood now far more clearly what her mother had suffered. Was it to be her fate, too? And all the time, that nagging inner voice, like water dripping on stone, telling her it should not, need not, be so.

Just as hurtful, too, was the slow realization, once they were established back home, that the other intimate, physical signs of their love, which had been so wonderful to her, were no longer forthcoming. The embraces, the passionate kisses, which had so fired and aroused her during their courtship, had vanished altogether. Indeed, Ned had looked positively shocked when she plucked up courage one night to remonstrate with him. In bed, as he turned to turn down the lamp, she murmured:

'Kiss me, Ned. You never kiss me — the way you did . . . ' she reached out for him, put her arms round his neck, to draw him close, and thrust her body, her limbs, against him.

'Rose! Please! Don't! In a wife — it's not seemly!'

She felt his hands pull at her wrists, dragging them from his shoulders. Dazedly, she saw the shocked look, of undisguised horror, as though she had committed some terrible, wanton lewdness. She shrank away, the tears coming, and, instead of the sexual rite she had anticipated, he moved away, leaving a gulf between them, withdrawing to his side of the bed.

'Good night, Rose. We'll sleep now.'

And she lay, wetting her pillow with tears, her back to him, withered inside with shame — and hating him for that prim, outraged tone and expression, when every other night he exercised his right in that brutish assault on her yielded body.

What can't be cured, love, must be endured, love. That was the line of a song Kate had been fond of singing when they were young girls together. Rose followed its homespun precept, and threw herself into the work of modernizing the house. Apart from the installation of the electric lighting, she improved the plumbing, replacing the old fixtures with the more modern ceramic sinks and basins and toilet bowls. The bathrooms and the lavatories were retiled, with exotic new designs, to complement the Arts and Crafts wallpapers she introduced in the living-rooms, the bold floral patterns of Mr Morris and his school. Only the library she left in its shabby, panelled splendour. She had not the heart to change it, redolent as it was of the memory of her grandfather. She even left the great old draughty fireplace intact, though in the morning- and drawing-rooms she had the old vast stonework bricked up, and the smaller, tiled hearths, with their hoods of dimpled copper, fitted.

She bought new bamboo furniture for the conservatory, with bright sunflower- and butterfly-printed cushions, and filled it with the black-and-gold lacquered artefacts and spindly furniture, which imitated the Japanese style. Most popular of all, was the grand kitchen range she had installed, to the nervous delight of Mrs Fielding.

'It's going to take me a while to get used to this beauty, Miss Rose!' the cook told her. 'There might be a few burnt offerings before we get the hang of it all!'

'It's all costing a fortune!' Rose informed Ned, when he came home from a three-day sojourn up in the city. She tugged him by the hand, dragging him through the hall, along the corridor towards the double glass doors. 'Come and see the conservatory!'

One of the maids came hurrying by, with a quick little bob, and murmured greeting, and Rose felt Ned pull his hands away from her grip.

'My dear! Don't get so carried away!'

'Oh, pooh! It's all I've got to get excited about! Don't be such a stuffed shirt! We *are* married, you know!' She had seen his eyes on the disappearing maid, and though she kept her tone light, she felt that prick of hurt and anger at his starchiness.

'Exactly! We're not some country bumpkin and his lass sparking in a village lane!'

★   ★   ★

It was May before Johnny learnt of the wedding, and he might not have done so then, had it not been for one of Willy's cronies, who had joined the Boer, Rosa, and Johnny, as they sat on the veranda of Rosa's bungalow sipping the first of their sundowner beers. British papers took weeks to arrive out in the colony, and up from the coast, so the copy the Britisher was perusing as he sat with his dusty boots on the wooden railing was two months old.

'Hey! They're still going on about that bloody war we fought against you lot, Willy! Reckon we're on our uppers now, because it cost us so bloody much! They want a commission of inquiry set up to look into it.'

He grinned, and winked at Johnny. 'Still, at least we won the bastard, eh?'

Willy grunted. 'Hey, you watch your mouth, yah? There's a lady here, don't forget! And stop pretending you can read that bleddy paper! You know you're only looking at the corset advertisements!'

Their guest was turning the inner pages. Suddenly, he drew his boots from the rail and sat up, peering more closely at the small, columned print. Newspapers were precious, and most people read them painstakingly, from front to back page.

'Here! Isn't this from your part of the bush?' He directed his remark at Johnny, who raised his eyebrows in enquiry. 'This is you, mate! Look! You're in the paper. Bloody famous!' His voice was raised in excitement. Slowly he read out the brief announcement of 'the wedding of Miss Rose Martingale to Mr Edward Lovatt.'- He went on, ''Miss

312

Martingale was formerly engaged to her cousin, the present Lord Strenshaugh.'' He stumbled over the unfamiliar word in print. 'That's you, isn't it, Johnny?' The word had got out about his title, in spite of his reticence. It had not bothered him unduly, for people out in the colony set little enough store by it.

The visitor continued to read aloud the summarized version of Johnny's early history, and of his decamping to Africa after inheriting the title. With practised skill, the journal hinted at the scandal involving his exit from England and the broken engagement.

Johnny stood up. The sinking sun was behind him, so they could not see his face clearly, only the lean shape of him, and the long shadow. Rosa watched him closely.

'Well well! Good old Rosie! I never thought she had it in her! And with Ned Lovatt!' He threw back his head and gave a sudden, loud bark of laughter. 'I'm going to have a quick wash, and off to Charlie's! This calls for a celebration! And I never even sent them a card! They'll never forgive me!'

27

Johnny forced his gaze away from the enchanting valley between Rosa's breasts, displayed over the deep plunging neckline of her evening gown. The dark eyes glistened in the flickering lamplight. She smiled sympathetically.

'And how are you feeling now, milord? Fully recovered? I heard it was one hell of a celebration, even for Charlie Storr's. Every *malaya* in town is still talking about it.'

As always, Willy managed to look like a prim maiden aunt when Rosa referred to the good-time girls who tended to the basic needs of the male population. He grunted eloquently as he reached for another helping from the large joint of game meat on the table before him.

Johnny grinned in return, responding to her gently teasing tone

'It was a trifle expensive, I admit, but worth every penny. Eh, Willy?'

Willy frowned at him severely, every bit the portrait of one of his righteous forebears.

'It was a bleddy foolish thing to do, yah? We can't afford to be throwing money around like that if we're going to make this business pay.'

Johnny saw the look which Rosa flashed at him, and rightly interpreted it as a silent apology for Willy's *faux pas*. It showed how close she and Johnny were in so many ways, for he knew she was thinking that it was Johnny's money which so far was paying for everything to do with the new venture. Just as, he reflected with some discomfort, she could see through his deception, the brave, light-hearted front he had thrown up to disguise the hurt the news of the marriage had inflicted.

'I'm moving into that shack at the west end of town next week,' he told them. 'I've had enough of Charlie's place. I thought we could set up the front room as an office. I'll live out back.' He gave a wolfish grin. 'Might even buy a little Somali girl on our next trip, to be my housekeeper.'

Rosa returned his challenging look.

'So! Romance is really in the air, since you heard the news of your English Rose's wedding!'

'She was never *my* Rose, Rosa.'

'No?' Her soft response sounded more like a contradiction than a question.

'No!' he answered firmly. 'She's got far too much good common sense to be taken in by a wastrel like me. I reckon she could teach you a thing or two about men. I still can't fathom how you come to be mixed up with an old reprobate like Willy!'

De Voss coughed loudly.

'Have another beer, and shut your mouth — milord!' He seemed anxious to change the subject. 'Now then. What about we hitch a lift on the train? They've got out as far as the Mau escarpment already. We can head on west from there. We can scout out the Kavirondo country. Plenty of Kaffir farmers down there.'

Both men had quickly seen that the greater part of their trade as mule packers would come in future from the native tribes of subsistence farmers, who were slowly learning of the opportunities that the opening up of the interior provided to sell some of their corn and maize and other produce in exchange for goods or money. Johnny shrugged. He recognized the foolishness of his own inner resentment at the changes which were overtaking the vast continent, with the coming of the 'iron snake', as the natives called the trains running on the track that penetrated ever further westward. He eyed the slim young houseboy, who brought him his fresh drink. The lad was dressed in an immaculate, long white *kanzu*, with the broad red cummerbund tied about his middle.

'It's like dining at the Ritz!'

'We're no longer living in the middle of the bush, Johnny. Nairobi's going to be a proper town one day. Maybe bigger than Mombasa. New people are flocking in every day!' She frowned with mock severity at Willy. 'This one wouldn't even shave or put on a clean shirt if I didn't nag at him.'

Willy grinned guiltily. 'You don't know how lucky you are, my young friend. You stay footloose and fancy-free!'

Rosa stood, and the men rose, too. She led them to the cane-and-raffia furniture, with its lumpy cushions, set out at one end of the small room. She pushed Willy down on to the settee, and then, with an untypical show of affection, arranged herself on his plump lap, with an arm draped around his shoulders. She gave a little kick of her feet to dislodge the flimsy slippers of brocaded felt. She was not wearing stockings, and Johnny stared at her narrow feet, and the golden tones of the slender ankles she revealed. Was this unusual expression of her closeness to the portly Dutchman for his benefit, Johnny wondered? To demonstrate yet again that, in spite of his own nefarious attention towards her, she would never be unfaithful to de Voss?

She was tempted, though, Johnny was

certain. There were times when her rebuttal of his snatched embraces was a touch tardy. He had detected in her supple frame and fragrant lips a conflict, a fight against a bodily urge to give in. Perhaps his careless talk of taking a slender Somali girl to his bed had made her jealous. Then, unbidden, came that sudden wash of disenchantment with his own pathetic carnality, the jaded quality of his lust. Again he recognized that part of him would be bitterly disappointed if this beautiful woman should break her self-imposed vow of loyalty to his partner.

She bent her head and nuzzled the beaming red face close to her bosom, giving him a swift kiss on his cheek.

'Aren't you jealous, my love? Don't you wish *you* could bring a lovely young native girl home, to warm *your* bed for you, too?'

The broad hand came up and gave her a bear-like hug, while the adoring look he directed at her was an answer eloquent enough. She glanced across at Johnny, who was convinced he could plainly read the challenge in her eyes.

* * *

'Well, Johnny, my boy! Here's to nineteen-oh-three, yah? It's been a good year for us. I think we get bleddy drunk tonight!' Willy's dirty stubble-covered face shone with sweat. He was beaming from ear to ear. He let his hand fall companionably across Johnny's shoulder as they turned away from the small ceremony they had just witnessed and walked back down the dusty track, through the throngs of Indian and African workers milling and cheering wildly, some of whom looked as though they had begun the celebration much earlier.

The formidable, corseted figure of Florence Preston, the Chief Engineer's wife, complete with parasol and elaborate feathered bonnet, had just clumsily driven in the last key in the last rail of the iron track, which virtually halted at the glimmering surface of the huge lake spread before them. Port Florence, or Kisumu, as it was known to the natives, was the terminus of the great railway. Through the ravages of disease, man-eating lions, and, latterly, the hostilities of the warlike Nandi tribe, the great engineering feat had progressed over the past six years, through almost 600 miles of some of the most inhospitable country in the world.

Johnny and Willy had travelled often up and down the line during the past months, using its various stopping-places as heading-off points for their own expeditions into the interior. There were no roads anywhere, after more than a few yards from the primitive halts that acted as stations, and the two led their pack-mules through largely uncharted territory, to establish the trading networks by which they hoped to prosper. It was a perilous business in more ways than one, not least because of the volatile situation created by tribes such as the Nandi, who resented this unlooked-for intrusion by the red foreigners into their lands, and were quite prepared to kill to prove their point.

At first, it was mostly a matter of luck and daring that the two white men survived, but they quickly built up a small but loyal and well-trained band of followers, so that they could be a formidable force if called upon to defend themselves. And more and more of the native population was beginning to accept the dramatic changes taking place, and to discover the usefulness of the metal coins the white men were willing to pay for their corn. Already, Johnny had ordered a portable mill from England, and awaited its arrival at Mombasa early in the new year.

'We grind their corn for them, and buy their flour, too!' Willy exulted. 'We'll be millionaires in no time!'

They had set up camp in the shade of a clump of trees, on a low bluff overlooking the lake, some distance from the bustle of the railhead. The official celebrations were taking place in the long, shedlike buildings at the station, behind which a makeshift jetty was already being constructed as a dock for the steamers which would extend the transport service across to Uganda. Willy, sitting comfortably in the sagging canvas of the safari bath, his face considerably cleaner and shinier, watched Johnny's lean figure as he bent at the small mirror fixed to the tent pole and scraped at his chin.

'You getting rid of the bum-fluff?' he joked happily. 'You looking for black *bibi* tonight, eh, stallion? How many you get through, you reckon?'

'Not as many as you, you fat old goat!' Johnny returned, removing another wedge of the thick white lather on the keen blade.

De Voss exploded in indignant denial.

'You know that is not true! And don't you go spreading your poxy lies about me when we get back to Nairobi! Not that Rosa believes anything you say!' He levered himself up and out of the high-sided bath with difficulty, the water pouring from him. The ragged figure in voluminous khaki shorts stepped forward, holding out the towel, in which de Voss draped his bulk. The flesh of his body was white, in great contrast with the mahogany hue of his forearms and the V at his throat.

Johnny straightened up and stepped agilely into the scummy grey water Willy had just vacated, wrinkling his nose in fastidious disgust.

'Look at all the muck you've shed!' He shook his head. 'What the hell a girl like Rosa sees in a fat old lecher like you is beyond me!'

'It's love!' Willy declared simply, a moon-struck expression on his open features.

'They say love's blind. By God, they're right!' Johnny paused, lounging back in the cooling water, and waved at the boy standing patiently by. 'Juma! Any more hot water? *Maji moto!*' The boy grinned and nodded. He hurried out.

The bulky figure turned indignantly. 'At least my brains are not attached to my private parts! Not like some I could name! You think of nothing else!'

'You don't even enjoy it, do you? All you Bible-thumping Boers are the same. Full of doom and gloom, the wrath of God. If heaven's full of you lot, I hope I don't end up there!'

'You don't need to worry on that score, my friend!' de Voss answered, before his head disappeared beneath the flapping shirt. Juma came back with a *debi* full of steaming water, and Johnny drew up his legs while the boy added its contents to the bath. Johnny's thoughts continued to centre around the enigma of Rosa's stubborn faithfulness towards Willy de Voss, and, in particular, of the beautiful woman's refusal to allow his young partner to taste her physical charms. And that in itself led to another puzzle — his perverse feeling of relief that, in spite of his undeniable physical hunger for her, she had the strength to remain loyal to the Cape Dutchman. He had become almost glad of these long spells on safari, away from the temptations Nairobi offered, and the cloudiness of his thoughts.

Never mind! As Willy had intimated, there were consolations to be had along the way. And especially tonight, he guessed, in the mood of wild celebration the encampment was undergoing. Besides, it would be Christmas in four days. Peace and goodwill. Unwillingly, his thoughts drifted back to his one and only Christmastide (that he could remember) in England, two years ago. Though he felt his manhood quicken at the vivid recall of Lucy's exquisitely eager dark body, his conscience ached tenderly at the memory of Rose's lovely face, the hurt in her eyes the last time he had seen them, before he had left without even bidding her a final farewell. It pained him, as it always did, when he thought about her. And he thought about her too much! he told himself severely.

He drank a great deal, and went off into the shadowy compound of native huts afterwards, blundering back into the tent in the grey dawn, protected by that special deity who looks after drunks in such circumstances. And still Rose's sad, dark eyes swam into his mental vision, and he groaned at her haunting of him. God! It was two years and more since he had last seen her. 'We never had our Christmas together, did we, love?' he muttered to the dimness, empty despite the heavy snoring of the unconscious de Voss. She'd been Mrs Ned Lovatt for almost a year now. The name filled him with bitterness, as harsh as the drink that burned inside. 'I hope you're happy!' he breathed, and didn't know if he were wishing her well, or cursing her, before he sank into welcome sleep.

28

'And you're still quite happy, down here in the country?' Amy Martingale asked, the disapproval evident in her tone. Her face was still young-looking, but her figure had remained over-plump and matronly since the birth of her son, who would be two in the spring. Rose derived a certain amount of wry amusement at Amy's portrayal of the devoted but harassed mother, when in reality she saw the infant in the morning, only after he had been dressed and breakfasted; in the afternoon, for a whole hour before his nanny whisked him away for his bath and supper, after which he was brought in to his doting parents for a tender goodnight scene, to disappear up to the nursery in nanny's capable arms until the following day.

'The joys and the trials of motherhood, my dear!' Amy would sigh, when she visited Strenshaugh. The faithful nanny was always in attendance on such visits. 'And when will Walter have a little playfellow to be his chum?'

Rose smiled, with the right mixture of bashful uncertainty and hope. Inside, she squirmed with both embarrassment and anger. She had a feeling sometimes that it was a question in everyone's mind, if not on their lips. It was one with the wordless, grunting urgency of the sexual congress Ned insisted on — when he was home to share the marital bed, which he was able to less frequently these days. Rose was ashamed that this infrequency was becoming more a matter of relief for her than disappointment.

Even though she had quickly become caught up in the task of modernizing the house — and she soon discovered that it was no sinecure, that Ned really intended that she should shoulder full responsibility for overseeing the work — she had suggested, when his absences up in London became more frequent and prolonged, that she should spend at least part of the week up at the Lovatts' town house with him, but always he argued against it.

'You know you don't like being up in town. You'd hardly see more of me — I work late. Most nights I'm dining with business associates. You'd find it very dull stuff, I'm afraid. Ladies generally do, and quite rightly so! We're like a crowd of crusty old bachelors. We keep our own company, there's never a petticoat in sight!' His resigned little laugh was a full stop to the conversation.

The grim exercise of marital rights, which took place with such regularity, could only be for the purpose of procreation. There was no jot of pleasure, it seemed to her, for either of them. Shocked though she was at her own speculation and at the strangely stirring, powerful sensations of her own flesh, she still felt that this was not how sexual 'love' should be. Yet there was no one in the world she could turn to for help. It was not a matter she could mention to anyone, least of all the man to whom she had given herself. It hurt to realize that she was as lonely now as she had ever been.

Driven by her own instinctive needs, she had occasionally tried to show physical tenderness, to solicit him for an equally tender response. And each time there was that sense of shock on his part, a scarcely hidden revulsion almost, and fastidious distaste for something inexpressibly vulgar that she had done. It withered her each time, striking at the most sensitive part of her nature, so that she sobbed bitterly when she was alone again. Eventually, she suppressed those faint sparks of desire, and lay dead and receptive to his brief, furious use of her body.

'How are you feeling? Are you feeling well?' As the weeks passed, Ned's unfailing question on his return to Strenshaugh Hall carried more and more clearly the hidden meaning behind the enquiry. In the early days, Rose was weighed down by a deep sense of failure when she answered in the affirmative. She even managed to sound apologetic for reporting her good health. She was both apprehensive of becoming pregnant, and ashamed of her inability to become so. Clearly, it was something lacking within her. Ned was playing his part. She had ample, and painful, proof of that. She was afraid — she could not wipe out the memory of her mother, and her constant weakness, her failures to come to term. Perhaps it was something she herself had inherited from her. She was made aware once more of how isolated she was. There was no one she could turn to for help — no young woman, or even older female, to whom she could disclose such intimacies. Even though Amy had so recently given birth herself, the very notion of Rose's confiding in her was abhorrent to the lonely girl.

Even more painful was the reflection that one of the only people she could think of sharing such confidences with would have been Kate Addy, if only fate had not worked so cruelly for both of them. It was a double irony that the act of conceiving had driven Kate frantic, so much so that she had almost killed herself in order to reverse her situation, whereas it was Rose's incapacity to get with child that was causing so much grief, and proving daily more of a stumbling block to the happiness of her marriage.

Her relationship with Ned was uneasy enough as it was, without this added strain being put upon her — upon them, she conceded reluctantly, for her husband was as anxious as she was for her to produce a child. Why else did he insist on this cold and joyless physical contact whenever they slept together? She began to dread those nights, and to admit to a feeling of relief at the fleeting kisses they exchanged on his departure.

Then, in October, seven months into their marriage, came the first sign that she was pregnant. During that long week when her menses failed to appear, she experienced a tumult of contrasting emotions — relief and excitement, followed by apprehension and real fear. She said nothing to Ned, let him leave for London after the weekend, still unsure whether she had in fact conceived. Filled with anxiety, she looked for other indications. There was none. Physically she felt no different, no discomforts, no sickness. Ned was away for three days. Still she waited a further day. But her agitation was noticeable. 'Are you all right?' he asked her, after dinner. 'You seem rather quiet. Any problem — everything going ahead with the workmen?' The casualness of his enquiry told her that he was quite unaware of the reason for her change of manner. Perhaps he, too, had given up hope of late that she should perform her natural function as a procreator.

To her annoyance, she found herself blushing vividly, and stammering, hardly able to look at him as she gave him the good news. Then, unexpected, tears came, at the look of sheer delight transforming his handsome features. And relief, she had to tell herself later. But, in those first minutes after he had learnt of her condition, she was moved by the deep emotion she could read in his expression — a tenderness, and love, which it had pained her to admit had been no longer evident in their relationship since the earliest days of their marriage. He was attentive, solicitous towards her, as he had been in those now seemingly distant days of their courtship. Most significantly, that night in bed, he did not make his usual hasty move towards her in the darkness, but held her, with gentle awkwardness, as though she were some priceless and fragile object, in his arms, kissed her softly on her brow.

'I can't tell you how happy you've made

me, Rose,' he whispered, and his voice quivered with emotion.

Her own eyes moistened and she laid her head blissfully on his chest.

'That's all I want, Ned. To make you happy.'

Ten days later that new, fragile happiness had dissolved, vanished in the painful attestation of her loss, to which she awoke in the misty autumn dawn. She called in Dr Ealey — Ned was of course away in London — and submitted to his examination. Alarmed, she overcame her reticence to talk frankly with him

'My mother, I think, had similar problems. Could it be — is it possible there's something inherent — that I take after her?'

The doctor was bluffly reassuring.

'Stay in bed for a few days. Pamper yourself. Then get up to town. A change of scenery will do the world of good. Tell your husband it's doctor's orders. And don't worry. It's very early days yet, Miss Rose. How long since you married? Eight months or so? Plenty of time for raising a brood of little ones!'

It was the look on Ned's face when he came home a day later that hurt Rose most about the whole sad affair. It was an expression compounded of dismay and a

331

pale, inward rage — and also something closely akin to those regards of contempt and disgust she had observed in those intimate moments when she had tried to show some physical affection in the privacy of their bed. It marked a watershed in their relationship, for there was no hiding his bitter displeasure. He made no attempt to do so, and failed to show any anxiety about her health. He questioned her incisively about what she had done, what she had eaten.

'You weren't out riding again, were you?'

Struggling to mask her own disquiet, she gave him the details of Dr Ealey's visit, repeated his encouraging words to her. Ned frowned, his face set in a look of scorn.

'Doctor's orders, indeed! Yes. You shall come up to London, and damned quick! I'll have you to see someone reputable, a Harley Street man. Not some buffoon of a country quack!'

He was as good as his word, and within the week Rose had to endure yet another full examination, conducted behind screens, while her husband sat impatiently out of sight a few feet away, and able to overhear every intimate question and halting answer.

The men's deep tones rumbled on, while Rose, with the help of the nurse who had been in attendance, dressed once more. She was too agitated to take heed of what they were saying, but as she emerged, she heard the doctor say composedly;

'Well, she is of course of rather slight and delicate frame, the hips and pelvic area rather narrow . . . '

The colour of her embarrassment flooded her features, but she also experienced a choking, impotent rage. The words reminded her of one of the farm managers discussing the qualities of the breeding stock.

She was staying up in town, at the apartment belonging to the Strenshaugh estate. She had told Ned it would be a chance to see that things were well there, and the housekeeper fulfilling her duties. The real reason was that she wished to avoid meeting any of Ned's family after the trying events of the day, which she had no wish to discuss with anyone. They dined out, with a group of Ned's associates. It was as tedious as he had frequently described. The last straw, in a day which had been most distressing, was his packing her off in a cab, with a curt instruction that she should not wait up for him.

Though she was in bed, she was far from sleep. Her hair had been carefully combed out, but she had not tied it or covered it with a night-cap. It hung in twin black trails down

333

to her breasts. She was wearing one of her pretty, knitted bedjackets, over a nightgown of white silk, trimmed with lace, and a thin violet ribbon tied over the low-cut bosom. She was watching him closely, saw the frown, the quick curl of his lip before he looked away.

'Still up, my dear? I thought you would have been sleeping long since.' He gave a loud, theatrical yawn. 'In fact, I was thinking of sleeping in the single room to avoid disturbing you. However ... ' He sat and removed his coat and waistcoat, and shoes. Then he stood and drew on the heavy brocaded dressing-gown over shirt and trousers. He reached for his traveller's toilet-case. 'I shan't be long.' He stared pointedly at her. 'Isn't that a trifle thin for this weather? I should have thought you'd have brought something warmer.'

'I wanted to look pretty for you. I thought you would wish to begin again. Straight away. With your efforts to father a child.'

He started with shock at her unaccustomed directness. She saw the dull colour mount in his features, which closed over in coldness and distaste.

'That's an extremely coarse and unfitting remark!' He paused.

She stared at him, and did not lower her

334

gaze, though her heart beneath the silk was beating rapidly.

'And you think your *looking pretty* will make a difference, do you? What has flaunting yourself in silks got to do with it? There are plenty of women about who will do that sort of thing for a man, if he's a mind for it!'

She watched him go out, banging the door firmly shut behind him. Like your May Thompson! And she castigated herself for the unjust and wicked accusation that had popped into her furious mind.

29

As the old year ended, and 1904 began, Rose was forced to acknowledge that whatever she had imagined or hoped for from her marriage to Ned was doomed to failure. She reasoned that she could not take the entire blame for that failure, though the weight of her inadequacy continued to dog her.

'Why did you marry me, Ned?' she confronted him one day, with her new sharpness; that sharpness which always produced the same look of pained distaste on his part, as though she were displaying some embarrassing lack of good manners. 'You *said* you loved me. Was it simply to sire children? Why *me*?'

'I thought you were of good breeding. I respected your family, your traditions.' He did not go on, but his tone implied that he had been disappointed, too, in his hopes. Though it pained her to admit it, she feared that his answer contained a great deal of truth. He had married her for the name, for the connections with one of the scions of the old nobility. She had an inkling, unworldly as she was, how quickly and how much he had used it, to further the Lovatt commercial interests, to forge their empire ever wider. She learnt more from her father, who, with his wife, had become a regular visitor both to Strenshaugh and to their town houses. He spoke with nothing but admiration for Ned's seeming obsession with increasing his fortune and his power, not least because Walter Martingale himself had prospered greatly by it.

'Look here. When are you going to make me a grandfather, Rose? And give that man of yours a fine son and heir to take over the reins one day?'

But Rose was no longer the pitiful child who had been so terrified of the dominant figure.

'What if I fail in my duty, Papa? The way Mama did. What if I give him a girl? Wouldn't that be a terrible thing?'

In the spring, as part of the celebration of their first anniversary, Ned and Rose attended the opening of Richmond Park to the public by the king on 29 March. It was a grey and blustery day, but that did not deter a large crowd from turning out to cheer the ailing monarch. 'I have something to show you,' Ned declared. 'A present to mark the anniversary.'

The 'present' was waiting in the drive of the Lovatt mansion. It was a gleaming black horseless carriage, or motor car, as everyone was calling them nowadays. The hood was folded back, to show the high, leather seats.

'I've been talking to Mr Royce,' Ned told her proudly. 'He's going into production soon. Opening a factory, with a partner, Mr Rolls. Machines even better than this one. We'll have some investment in it, I think. This is how the future will be, Rose! Soon cities will be full of them!' He sounded so enthusiastic, and she tried hard to look pleased. It was good, that uncharitable inner voice told her, that he could sound genuinely enamoured of *something*, even if it was a fearsome, roaring, smelly object of metal and leather and rubber. He grabbed her arm, his other hand round her waist pushed her firmly towards the vehicle. 'Climb in, come on! We'll go for a spin!'

The next day, when Ned had departed as usual for the offices in the city, Rose was preparing to do some shopping when the butler came with an announcement that there was a telephone call for her.

'Mr Parr, madam. He wishes to speak to you personally. A matter of some importance, he said.'

An hour later, Rose was settled in his room, the glass of proffered sherry to hand. She knew at once from his manner that something untoward had occurred. Suddenly her heart began to pound at her ribs, and she felt the blood draining from her face.

'What is it? Is it Johnny? What's happened?'

He held up a hand. 'No, Mrs Lovatt, don't distress yourself. That is — I have received some correspondence from him. It's addressed to you.'

She had never seen the courteous, habitually imperturbable lawyer look so troubled. She saw he had an envelope in his hand, and she waited impatiently for him to pass it to her.

'Before you read it, I think I should tell you — confess, that I have been in touch. There are certain matters — pertaining to your husband, and . . . ' he hesitated, clearly in some distress. 'It's to do with finances. The managing of the estate. As you know, his present lordship signed power over to you, to act on his behalf. Made you legally responsible . . . '

'Yes, yes! For God's sake! What has happened, Mr Parr?'

The solicitor drew a deep breath. 'I have to tell you that there have been exchanges between your husband and his legal representatives about the taking over of the estate. Of placing responsibility for it in his hands,

transferring all matters pertaining to Strenshaugh over to the firm which represents him.
He wishes to have papers prepared, for you to
sign the authority over to him. He did not
wish you to be involved in the negotiations.
He simply wished to have the papers drawn
up, for you to sign.' Again a pause. 'I felt it
my duty to inform his lordship of what was
intended, and also that I did not think it wise.
Forgive me, Mrs Lovatt, but I felt I had no
choice.' He handed her the envelope.

She sat there, stunned, holding it. Ned had
planned all this, with never a word to her.
Planned to take over the entire Strenshaugh
wealth, with her connivance, when by every
moral right it was not hers to dispose of.

'You were quite right, Mr Parr,' she
murmured faintly. She roused herself to tear
open the envelope, and read its contents.

My dear Rosie,

*I swore I would never get in touch with
you and here I am breaking my promise,
same old me, eh? I suppose I should offer
you my best on your marriage, even though
it's a bit late for that now. You probably
won't like what I have to say but the
lawyers have been in touch and I feel I
ought to have my say. Ned Lovatt wants to
take over Strenshaugh. I told you you had*

more right to it than I had and that's still true, Rosie, so all I will say is be careful, think about what you are doing and take some advice. Not from me, God no! But from Parr and Kemp and the others who have looked after the family for so long. I guess Ned Lovatt is a good businessman. You know I don't rate him very highly but you made your choice. So all I say is if you think it's right, and I suppose you must do, he is your husband, when all is said and done, go ahead. Just don't be too quick to make up your mind. You're far too good for this wicked world, Rosie, I always knew it.

Don't worry about me, I am doing more than all right out here. In fact, if I'm not careful I could end up being rich myself. One of these days I'll send you some fine ivory or maybe a lion skin. You can put it up in place of that Venus picture in the library — I'll wager you've had it taken down long since!

Yours as ever,

Johnny.

In spite of her distress, the corners of her mouth twitched in an involuntary smile as she read his last sentence. If he had said the same thing to her little more than a year ago, she would have been puce with righteous indignation. But so many things had changed. And none more so than her attitude towards her husband. She could scarcely believe even now that he could have been capable of planning such a thing, and of using her like the naïve fool he clearly thought her. No wonder poor Mr Parr had been so embarrassed. It hurt her to think that he could not have come directly to her when Ned began his nefarious scheming. But then, he probably thought that her loyalty must lie with her husband, come what may. And doubtless that was how Ned would see it, in his supreme selfishness, and see any hesitation on her part to fall in with him as a dereliction of duty as serious as her failure to provide him with a son.

Trying to keep her hands steady, she slipped the sheet back inside its envelope. She cleared her throat.

'You were right to get in touch with his lordship, Mr Parr. And to inform me. I will have to discuss things with my husband.' But when she glanced up ashamedly at him, she could see from the troubled expression there was more. He gazed at her compassionately. Once again, there was that reluctance to proceed, which was far from his normally assured manner. She waited with a hollow sickness inside.

'There is another matter. Of the greatest delicacy. Perhaps when you hear it, you will be inclined to go ahead and remove all your affairs from our competence. I can only say that I have always served your grandfather with the utmost faithfulness. And the firm has looked after the interests of the Strenshaugh family for generations.' She nodded, waited breathlessly for him to continue. His reluctance was even more in evidence. 'I've had occasion to look into the charitable trust. The one initiated by Mr Lovatt. There were some discrepancies, some things to check.'

She gasped. Spying! He had been spying on Ned! Why? Why on earth . . . ? Her stomach churned, her lips moved. It was all she could do to stifle the cry of horrified protest that she could feel rising within her.

'Some of the payments. In particular there was one — the young woman you expressed an interest in. The girl you wrote to. May Thompson. You gave a reference . . . it was not taken up. Or, rather, the post she claims to have secured, the expenses paid to her . . . there is no such post, Miss Rose.' In his heightened emotion, he seemed unaware that he had forgotten her married title — or, perhaps, unconsciously he believed it to be worthless. 'I had someone make some discreet further enquiries. The young woman has not mended her ways. She continues to pursue her — profession.'

'But my husband has been deceived, too!' Rose blurted. Her dark eyes flashed in tearful appeal. 'It must be so! I'll inform him at once! I'm sure he has no idea how he has been deceived!'

'There are others — other names of those who have been helped, to whom sums of money have been regularly paid.' He shook his head. 'They have no positions in service. They continue to ply their trade.'

Even as she once again cried out Ned's innocence, somehow she knew, even though her heart refused to accept it, that it was impossible. She knew by his very nature, by his dedication to the pursuit of business, to all matters connected with money, that he could not have been duped so easily. Frantically, her brain searched around for an explanation which would exonerate him.

The solicitor gazed at her with a deep and genuine grief. He could not for the life of him disclose to her the rest of his findings — that the investigation by the hired agent had proved that Ned Lovatt was May Thompson's most regular client, and had been so since before his marriage — and after.

The tears glistened in Rose's eyes as she stared up at him.

'Please! You can't think that Ned — I'm sure he knows nothing.'

He could not offer the confirmation she so desperately needed.

'I think you need to discuss it with your husband — ma'am.' His belated acknowledgement of her married status had a morbid ring to it. Her head swam, and for a brief moment she felt she might swoon. She stared down at the letter she still held, its blurred image quivering visibly in her grip. Blast you, Johnny. You were right, all along.

30

'It shouldn't be long now, madam. She should be here any minute.' Mr Macdonald, the private investigating agent, who had done such useful work for Mr Parr, strove to inject the right note of confidence in his voice. He was certainly a great deal calmer than she herself was, Rose acknowledged. She was beginning to regret the untypical boldness, born of her humiliation and anger at being taken for such a gullible little fool by her husband, that made her ascertain the name of Mr Macdonald from the solicitor and employ him for her own private spying.

He leaned forward from his seat on the opposite bench of the hansom cab, so that his unremarkable face, with its drooping, tobacco-stained moustache, almost brushed against the veil which hid her own features. They both peered through the narrow slit in the cab's blinds at the dull, respectable façade of the building across the street. It might well have been any one of the many gentleman's clubs around the city, a fact reinforced by the steady coming and going of the well-dressed male figures, sometimes singly, sometimes in laughing groups, up and down its well-kept steps. Yet the detective had assured her this was one of the most profitable brothels in all of London, known simply as Mrs Moss's.

'The girls aren't generally allowed to use the front entrance,' Mr Macdonald murmured. 'Leastways, not when they're on their own. But Miss Lovejoy is different. She'll come across to the cab. I told her we'd be waiting here.'

Lovejoy! A name as evocative of her profession as Baker, Miller, or Cooper, Rose reflected, and no doubt chosen with tongue firmly in cheek. But at least, through the good and devious offices of Mr Macdonald, the black girl had agreed to talk with her. Rose was bound tight, with nervousness and apprehension. As though to highlight her disquiet, the door behind them opened, and she started as the cabby thrust his upper body into the interior. His cap was pulled down low on his brow and he wore a woollen muffler tied close about his neck, over his coat, though the April evening carried the new warmth of spring.

' 'Ere! How much longer we gonna be stuck 'ere? Not the best sort of place to be hanging about, outside Mrs Moss's.' He frowned, as he nodded at Rose. 'And not the sort of a place a young woman like yourself should be hanging around!' he added sternly, with a disapproving look at Mr Macdonald. 'Unless she's not all she should be!'

Rose was glad of the dark veil pulled down over the front of her hat, to hide the warm blush she could feel flooding her face. Yet, under her shame, there was a girlish kind of outraged excitement that he should suspect her of being a disreputable sort, in spite of her fashionable clothing.

'You're getting paid, aren't you?' the detective answered roundly. 'That's all that should be worrying you! We're just awaiting another passenger. If you'll excuse us!' he ended, sarcastically. The cabby muttered, and withdrew to his lofty perch once more. 'Blooming cheek!' Mr Macdonald huffed. 'They're getting as bad as the miners and the dockers! Bunch of rabble-rousers! It's these new motor cabs that's putting them up in arms! You remember the fuss they made about those electric carriages a few years ago, ma'am? Played merry hell — pardon me, ma'am — till they were taken off the roads. Now they're getting all uppity over these motor cars! Talking of going on strike, would you believe?'

Another figure appeared at the door. Rose stared at the brightly fashionable coat, nipped at the waist to emphasize the slimness of its wearer, the saucily tilted hat, with its cockade and wisp of gathered veil.

'Mrs Lovatt?' Lucy enquired coolly, while Mr Macdonald scrambled across and stepped down off the high step. He put his hand on her elbow, assisting her into the vehicle, which swayed slightly. He made to climb aboard after her, and she turned. 'I want to talk to her alone,' Lucy said firmly.

'Oh, no, I can't allow that. This young lady — '

'What I've got to say is for her ears only! I don't want you ready to bear witness to all and sundry afterwards! All right?'

Mr Macdonald's face grew red.

'That's not what we agreed at all. You can't expect Mrs Lovatt to go unescorted — '

'Right then!' Lucy gathered her skirts and ducked to climb down from the vehicle again. 'Sorry to have wasted your time, ma'am.'

'Wait!' Rose leaned out, looked appealingly at the detective. 'I'll be all right. I'll telephone you tomorrow, Mr Macdonald. And thank you for all your help.' He gazed at her uncertainly, and she smiled and nodded in polite dismissal. 'Just drive around, will you?' she said towards the frowning cabby. 'Anywhere!' she snapped, as he opened his mouth, in query or protest. The cab swung into motion, leaving Mr Macdonald standing on the busy pavement.

Lucy sat opposite Rose, their knees almost touching, as the cab moved slowly through the traffic. The dark girl waited silently, her face impassive. Rose lifted her veil, and tried to look composed, while her heart raced with her emotion. There was an awkward silence. She cleared her throat.

'Thank you for agreeing to talk to me, Miss — er — Lovejoy.' She felt her face grow warm as she pronounced the ridiculous name.

The white teeth showed prominently as Lucy smiled.

'Call me Lucy, Mrs Lovatt. Everyone does.'

'Right. It's rather delicate. I think you know — Mr Macdonald has told you something . . . ?'

Lucy nodded. 'I'm no nark, don't get me wrong. That's why I don't want him listening in to us.' She nodded back towards the place where they had left the detective. 'I already told him I won't say anything official, and I won't go to court for you. That's understood, yes?' Rose blushed visibly, as she gave her hasty reassurance. 'You've got to give me your word you won't tell a soul about our chat. You mention my name, to *anyone*, and I'll deny everything. You understand?' She leaned close, and put her gloved hand on Rose's knee. Through the thickness of her clothing,

Rose felt the pressure of the fingers. 'Especially not to your old man. He mustn't get to know you've talked to me. Right?'

For an instant, Rose was bewildered, then realized that her 'old man' was Ned.

'Of course. I understand. It's just for myself, I swear.' Now her face burned, and her shame was plain to see. 'I have to know — the truth,' she murmured, and her voice shook. She looked appealingly at the striking figure.

Lucy nodded. 'Fair enough. The 'tec was asking about the girls. About May, in particular. I know her well enough. And the others. She's still a tart. So's the others. Same as me.' She gazed challengingly at Rose, who lowered her eyes. 'They've not seen the light, I'm afraid.' Rose's body prickled with heat at the scorn in the voice. The truth, which she already knew, settled with sick heaviness inside her. 'But I guess you already knew that, didn't you?' She waited. Rose nodded, swallowed hard. There was another, even longer, pause.

'I want — I have to know.' Her voice was a faint whisper. 'My husband. Does he know? Does he still . . . does he see these girls? This May?'

For the first time, Lucy appeared to lose something of her calm manner.

'I told you! I'm no nark! I was asked about the girls! This fiddle they've been on with the money! That's all!' She glared at Rose, obviously uncomfortable. 'Why don't you just come out and ask him yourself?' Her mouth curved contemptuously. 'Or get your detective friend to snoop about for you!'

Rose felt the scorn in Lucy's voice. It caught her on the raw, for she had been feeling more than a little ashamed of her action in employing Mr Macdonald to spy for her. She stared desolately at her.

'I think you have, really. Already answered, I mean.' Suddenly, the tears welled up, she felt her throat closing, and her shoulders heaved. To her horror, she began to sob, totally unable to hold back the tide of grief, which swamped her.

For a few seconds, Lucy sat, staring at the woebegone figure, then she moved. She seized hold of the thin wrists, shook them.

'Come on, don't take on so!' she urged. Rose gave a louder wail, began to sob more abandonedly, and Lucy moved quickly to sit beside her. She slipped an arm across the quaking shoulders, drew the head down to her breast, and held the weeping girl close in her embrace. 'There there, miss. Come on now.' She dug into her pocket, pulled out a dainty lace handkerchief and gave it to Rose.

'Dry your eyes. Come on now. It's not the end of the world, believe me!'

Gradually, Rose's crying fit grew less violent, and she fought to control it.

'I'm sorry!' she said at last, easing herself from Lucy's hold.

'Listen!' Lucy told her, still holding Rose's hand in hers. 'Practically all our tricks — the men who come to Mrs Moss's — are family men. Married. There's hundreds of them, all cheaters.'

Rose stared at her. 'Why?' she asked forlornly. 'What is it . . . ?' She felt the colour stealing up into her face once more, as she thought of Ned's coldness, his brute force in the bedroom. 'It's not — I've never denied him — his rights as a husband!'

Lucy's smile was hard, glinting like steel, as she thought of all the bizarre episodes she had taken part in, in private and in public.

'Maybe they're afraid to show their women what they're really like. They want more than their rights, my dear, believe me! I could tell you things . . . ' She shook her head, and compressed her lips as though to prevent herself from continuing.

Rose lifted her tear-stained face, looked directly at the dark girl.

'You knew Johnny, didn't you?' she asked, with shocking simplicity. 'Lord Strenshaugh?'

Lucy stiffened, taken aback by the younger woman's candour. There was an instant of painful silence, then she nodded.

'I did. And a fine young chap he was! Worth ten of the lot of them!' The dark eyes shone, she seemed to fling her answer like a challenge in Rose's tragic face. 'And I'll tell you something that maybe I shouldn't. He thought a hell of a lot of you! He left England because of you!'

'But it wasn't just — it wasn't just up here, in town!' Rose cried out. 'There was trouble, back — my maid . . . '

Lucy nodded impatiently, waved a hand, as though conceding a point of little importance.

'Someone wrote to you, told you about me and Johnny, didn't they?' she said levelly. 'And I bet I know who. And so do you, Mrs Lovatt. Someone pretty close to you.'

Rose leaned back wearily, against the hard rear board above the cushioned seat. She nodded tiredly.

*   *   *

Rose was sick, physically, when she returned to the apartment. She realized that her nerves were stretched almost to breaking-point by the events of the past few days, and by her own actions to discover the truth. Her courage failed all at once. When Ned returned, expecting her to attend a dinner with some of his associates, she cried off. It was easy to convince him of her illness.

'You *do* look a little peaky. Perhaps you've been overdoing it?' The question in his tone, the unexpressed hope she detected, made her even sicker. No! I'm not carrying your child, Ned! she wanted to scream at him. And I pray I never will! But she said nothing, longing only to be free of his presence, afraid now that she might give away her true feeling of revulsion, anxious only to escape him. She was asleep when he returned, having dosed herself with an analgesic mixture. He did not disturb her. She was still in bed when he looked in on her the next morning. She told him she would go back to Strenshaugh, and see him there at the weekend.

'I might leave it until Saturday to come down,' he said. 'Might have some late business to see to on Friday.'

When he had left, she cursed herself for her cowardice. What had she to be afraid of? He was a liar, an embezzler, and a fornicator! She had every right on her side. Yet, with each hour that passed, her insides churned, she felt sick and afraid, as though she were the guilty one, for searching out the truth. By the time the Saturday came, her nerves and courage were in tatters.

'You really do look unwell, my love. Should we call in that quack, Ealey, for you?' He paused unmistakably. 'Is everything regular?' he asked heavily, with that knowing, hopeful expression that made her burn for shame, and writhe with secret, savage hate.

'If you mean my monthly, yes, I believe so.'

The shock on his face was deeply satisfying to her, as he exclaimed her name in outraged protest. Yet still, when she could no longer endure her own cravenness and told him she had something important to discuss with him, her heart throbbed fiercely, her limbs shook, and her tongue seemed to swell and fill her mouth. She blurted out the truth like a guilty schoolgirl, her face scarlet and her voice quavering.

'I know about the money! About May Thompson and the others! About Mrs Moss's!'

In that one thunderstruck instant, the truth of his guilt was emblazoned on him, stamped indelibly on his features and in his very stance. Twin spots of vivid colour came up on his cheeks, and his handsome face, recovering from his shock, was suffused with hate. He tried to bluster it out. Rose gave no details of her sources of information, simply reiterated her charges, struggling to keep from breaking down into floods of tears, and only partially succeeding.

'You played me false from the beginning! That's how you won me. You used it — the notion of helping those girls — those prostitutes! To make me — admire you all the more! And all the while . . . ' she shook her head, losing momentarily the battle against her grief. 'You even tried to blacken Johnny's character to me!' He gave another start of surprise as she held up the notes, then crumpled them and flung them to the floor at his feet, wishing fervently that she had done so when she had first received them, all those months ago.

'I don't know what you mean!' He glanced down at the pieces of paper, made no attempt to retrieve them.

She shook her head again, choked with disgust.

'Why have you done this to me? Have I denied you anything? Anything I have? In the bedroom — I've tried — tried to give you the son you want so much. Denied you nothing! You even made me feel as though *I* was the intemperate one, wanting more — and all this time you've been running to these harlots. Coming from them to our bed. God! You — you are like a beast . . . '.

357

He glared at her, then his face seemed to set like stone. He drew himself up, gathering his shattered dignity.

'You shouldn't even speak of such things. You have no idea how to behave. Yes, I use those girls. Men do, Rose! Men have needs, about which you know — should know — nothing. It is in our nature. These desires have to be satisfied — '

'And what of me? What if *I* have needs, too? Desires, like yours? Isn't it perfectly possible that I might feel those things, need that relief of — '

'Then, Rose, it means you are a harlot! A strumpet, a whore!' She gaped at him, her jaw literally agape, stunned at his superb effrontery. 'Decent women don't have those excesses. That's why London is full of places like Mrs Moss's, why those fallen girls are there on every street corner after dark. Perhaps you've missed your calling. Perhaps that's why you fail as a wife — and a mother!'

She gave a cry of rage, sprang up and came at him, aquiver with revulsion now.

'You filthy hypocrite! I'll tell the whole world about you! I'm leaving you!' She raised her arm, to strike at that handsome, hateful face, with its implacable superiority even after the last fateful minutes.

He caught her wrist, his grip like iron,

twisted her arm, swinging her round. With his free hand he slapped her hard across her cheek, the blow echoing, its stinging heat spreading in a scarlet brand. He flung her down, so that she fell sprawling, and lay at his feet, staring up through the haze of pain and tears, disbelievingly.

'Leaving me because I've found comfort in a doxy's arms? And you're going to make it public? You'll be the laughing-stock of every newspaper and magazine in the land, and beyond. Just as you were when Master Johnny tupped your maid under your very nose, you stupid little fool!'

31

'Look at that, man. Isn't that a sight?' Willy spoke softly, almost reverently. Johnny stared in the direction in which he was pointing. The early morning sun had that fresh sparkle that made one's head sing, up at this altitude. The undulating bush of the Kikuyu escarpment rolled before them like a gentle, sandy sea, dotted with clumps of low scrub, and the teeming herds of game. And there, as a background, appearing like a mirage above a trailing level of white mist, which was thinning and parting all the while, the summit of Mount Kenya reared like a jagged, broken tooth, the snowcaps glistening like diamonds in the sunlight.

They heard their boys muttering a dirge, their voices low, and full of awe. The mountain was considered sacred to all the Kikuyu, and even Daudi, the superior Somali gun bearer, fell silent with respect. Johnny and Willy were out early to shoot for the pot. They could see the thin smoke of the morning fires rising behind them, beside the clump of umbrella thorns where they had pitched camp. They stared their fill, for the cloud would soon descend and cover the summit again. Only rare glimpses were vouchsafed of the 'face of God'.

It was the summer of 1904. The long rains had come blessedly on time and in plenty at the beginning of March, and the handful of settlers to the north of the railway had got their crops down and their early harvests in. It was largely thanks to Rosa's efforts back in Nairobi that they had found this new route and source of business. She had given up her own line of work providing for the workers in Nairobi, and had come in with them.

'There'll be more and more families coming out,' she had predicted confidently. 'We have to be ready for them. And the native shambas will have plenty of maize ready, too. We'll need more wagons, more teams. You won't be able to carry it all out on mule-back.'

Johnny had not been convinced. Settlers were still few and far between. Disease, threatening both animals and humans, was still rife. A serious outbreak of plague had occurred at the lake port of Kisumu.

'You're not going back to Nyanza until we hear it's clear!' Rosa had decreed. Johnny shrugged nonchalantly. He believed the official warnings about the health hazards facing the whites were a load of nonsense.

The rays of the sun, falling vertically in this latitude, and at this height above sea level, could be extremely dangerous, the pundits declared. Never remove your hat or helmet, except in the shade. Flannel cummerbunds were swathed around the waist, to protect liver and spleen from the harmful rays; clothing, both male and female, was lined with red, which made one sweat most uncomfortably as soon as the temperature rose.

Johnny would invariably remove his hat in the blazing sun, grinning at Willy's scandalized shouts, and he refused to wrap his sweating body in the obligatory band of cloth the experts advocated.

'That's why your brain is addled!' de Voss often remarked.

Willy turned now, lining up his rifle on a grazing Tommy. A group of the dainty, light-coloured gazelles were feeding unconcernedly, though the men were in full view, until the rifle jerked, and the report echoed in the shimmering air. The victim went down, brushed out of life in a flurry of sticklike limbs, while its companions took off like a shoal of startled fish, darting wildly away, for only a short distance, before they stopped and bent their heads to the short grass once more. One of the boys swung the antelope up by its legs, draped it like a fur around his shoulders, and turned back for the camp. Willy broke his rifle, shook out the shell, and the two white men began to stroll side by side, heading for the small table, with its pristine white cloth, set out for breakfast outside the tent.

'Things have changed since last year.' Johnny glanced at the ordered encampment. 'We're bloody civilized now!' It sounded like the criticism it was meant to be. Willy merely grunted. 'Bloody potatoes!' the grumbling voice continued scornfully. 'We should be over in Uganda, going after tuskers! Not toting bloody sacks of potatoes back to the railway!'

'That's where the steady money lies,' Willy replied, loyally repeating Rosa's argument. 'How much ivory could we bring out? Every *shenzi* in the territory is down there, anyhow. We — '

A sudden outcry made them look up in alarm. '*Simba*! Lion!' They heard the cry at the same time as they heard the agonized shriek of one of the pack-animals from the roped-off lines where they were tethered. Willy set off at a lumbering run, and Johnny ducked inside the tent, grabbed his heavy gun and as many shells as he could stuff into his pocket before he ran after his partner.

The porters were yelling, and above their uproar could be heard the snarl of the lioness, who was trying to drag clear the carcass of a mule, from which the blood was still pumping. She was crouching low, her shoulders hugely bunched with her efforts, half-hidden by the body of the animal she had killed. Willy loosed off a shot, which furrowed across the back of her neck, spinning her round. She yelped and coughed in agony, squirmed away and vanished with a flick of her tufted tail.

There was not a lot of cover, and Willy ran through the terrified, plunging mules, incensed by this audacious daylight raid, and the death of the mule. Why does he get so upset over one bloody animal? thought Johnny irritably. Damned Boer penny-pincher!

'Be careful!' he called out, knowing that his advice was needless. Willy was an experienced bush hand. He wouldn't do anything outright stupid, not against a wounded *simba*.

There was one deep roar, and a young male, his mane almost black, exploded from Willy's right, from the area of the stores tent and the parked wagons. He was on to Willy before the Dutchman could swing his rifle fully round, and he went down under the great leap of the beast, its claws raking him to

364

the earth, the tawny, lashing body smothering him.

Johnny raced up screaming, and fired from almost point-blank range, blowing a hole in the side of the lion and bowling him over sideways. The second barrel exploded almost at once, and shattered the massive face as the jaw gaped in its death growl.

Willy was lying face down, an arm flung over the back of his neck, to protect it from the fatal bite. The forearm was laid open to the bone, in two long furrows, where the teeth had sunk in. The khaki shirt was ripped almost clear of the broad back, the thick undervest black with blood which flowed from the great gashes made by the lion's claws as they had swiped him down.

Willy's eyes fluttered, he moaned when Johnny cautiously rolled him on to his side. He plucked carefully at the fragments of the shirt, peeling them from the bloody flesh.

'You bloody Dutchman!' he panted, his eyes stinging. Willy groaned again, his eyes were closed.

'He still alive, bwana!' Daudi said, grinning.

Johnny stared up at him sombrely. He knew that, although Willy had survived the attack the odds were stacked against him. He could smell the fetid beast stretched out in death a few yards away, and knew that the danger from the wounds turning poisoned were very grave. In a day or two, Willy could be dead unless he could get back for some proper treatment and the life saving drugs he needed.

They made a litter and Johnny took four of the strongest boys as bearers. He had cleaned and bound the wounds as best he could, bathing them liberally with gin, wincing at the semi-conscious de Voss's screams and curses, and dabbing on the gunpowder he took from the cartridges, an emergency measure he remembered from his youth with Capitano and his men. He left Daudi, and the wizened headman, Wagombi, in charge of the wagon train, and pressed on southwards, driving the natives to their utmost, taking his turn at one corner of the litter with the rest of them, so that each man could be rested in turn.

Even though they pressed on through the dangers of darkness with the aid of lanterns, they were forced to take several short halts. While Johnny raised Willy's head and poured water into the parched lips, he noted with growing dread the unhealthy colour, the burning skin, and the crazed, disconnected ravings.

'You'll be all right now, my love! I've killed the bastard! You're free of him now, my love!

366

Come! Come! We've got to get out of here! Get out of the country! They'll never let us rest if we don't!' At one point, his eyes opened wide, suddenly clear of the delirium which had gripped him. He clutched feebly at Johnny's hand. 'Look after her, Johnny! She's a good woman. Too good for you, you young bastard!' His head fell back, the fingers loosened their grip as the hand dropped uselessly to his side.

★　★　★

It was the doctor's care, as well as the new drugs, which pulled Willy through, eventually, though it was acknowledged that, if it had not been for Johnny's immediate tending of the wounds and that mad dash through the rough country back to Nairobi, the Boer would not have survived. As it was, he came close enough to death. The blood poisoning raged for days, weakening him further after the loss of blood, but, slowly, with the best of medical care, and Rosa's devoted nursing, he made a recovery. It was three months before he could claim to be fully fit. His body was permanently scarred, and his right arm had a withered look now. He could not straighten it properly. Though he worked desperately to restore it to its former strength, he finally had to face the bitter truth that he was physically impaired. Managing a team, shooting to full effect, would never be possible again.

'Our business is growing too big, anyway!' Johnny argued. 'We've got to take on more men. A lot more. We need to manage things — Rosa needs help here. It's time you settled down. Became respectable.'

During the long weeks of Willy's illness and convalescence, Johnny and Rosa had become even closer, though not in the way he had envisaged and dreamed of disturbingly during many a long night in the bush.

'You saved his life, Johnny,' she said simply. 'Just as he once saved mine, and risked his own for me. I'll always love you for that.' There was a painful pause, and her great dark eyes fixed solemnly on him. 'I am prepared to show my gratitude. In any way you want. Like you, my body even desires it. But I love you as a friend. My love for him is deep, in my soul. Just as you love your English Rose.'

For a second he was white hot with rage and frustration. It passed like a bolt through him, left him smiling with sad wisdom.

'We are friends, Rosa. Always friends.' Gently, he kissed her brow and stepped away.

'I'm leaving, for a long while,' he told both of them some weeks later. 'I'll head west, with Lawford. I'll stay with him until I've made sure he's all right. But from what I've seen of him he'll be fine. Then I'm going to head on, to shoot some tuskers. I'll send the ivory back on the train. This whole place is changing. I've got to do it before the missionaries are everywhere, with their Bible-thumping and their bicycles! You two make a good team. I know I don't need to worry about things back here.'

Willy reached out, slipped his arm around Rosa's waist, and held her to his side.

'You *are* coming back, yah? I was counting on you to be my best man.' Johnny's eyebrows shot up, and he looked at Rosa questioningly. She blushed a little, and nodded. 'But we can't wait for ever.' He held up his right arm. 'Don't get chewed up, eh? God be with you!'

'Stay well!'

It was over a month later, when Rosa was finishing off some work in the front room of the modest bungalow Johnny had purchased. They had just received a cable telling them that he was leaving the caravan in charge of their new English employee, and heading over to Uganda, with only the faithful Daudi for company. 'Bleddy idiot!' Willy had said, with more than a little wistful envy in his tone. The short rains had come to Nairobi, and the street outside was churned to liquid mud, though the late-afternoon sun had emerged to make the roadway steam as the low cloud lifted.

There was the noise of a vehicle pulling up outside. As Rosa turned from the papers she was returning to the safe, she saw a shadow in the doorway, outlined against the blinding sun. A slim woman, in a dark, travel-stained costume, complete with feathered hat and veil, came into the room. She lifted the veil. Rosa saw her stop short, saw the look of surprise and dismay on the young, pale features. One of the rickshaws from the station stood outside, and behind it another, piled high with trunks and cases. The boys grinned in from the wooden sidewalk.

The girl's voice was soft. It contained the weariness apparent on her lovely, but clearly worn out face.

'Oh! I'm sorry — I was — I'm looking for Lord — I mean, Mr Able. They said . . . the sign . . . ' Her head moved slightly, towards the wooden sign hanging outside, which proclaimed, ABLE & DE VOSS, TRANS-PORT SERVICE. 'I've just come from the train. There was a delay, down the line.'

Rosa was staring at her closely now, and she advanced towards her.

'I'm afraid he's not here, miss. He's been away — he won't be back for some weeks.

He's somewhere over the border, in Uganda. Can I help?'

The girl's face was drained of colour. Her brown eyes looked huge and vulnerable. 'I — I've come, from England. I should have written.' She crumpled, the eyes filled with tears.

'You — you're his English Rose!' Rosa exclaimed, her own face mirroring her dawning realization. The stranger looked startled at this exotic description. Then she nodded, burst into a fit of abandoned sobbing and half-fell into Rosa's encompassing arms.

32

Rose felt as though some invisible curtain cut her off from the reality of what was happening around her. This is Johnny's lover, her numbed brain registered. This exotic, full-bodied creature is his. The stranger led her through the busy streets, responding to the endless greetings called out to her as she led the bemused Rose along, her arm about her waist. In the privacy of another bungalow, comfortably furnished as a home, she led her through to a bedroom, and a high, old-fashioned bed, which took up most of the limited space.

There was clear evidence of a man's living presence: the guns in the rack against the wall in the living-room, the pipe and tobacco-bowl on the table, the slippers by the wooden rocking-chair, the folded nightshirt on the covers of the bed. Johnny's? Rose's head swam. She thought she might faint. She looked around, sank on to the edge of the wooden chair behind the door. Rosa stood over her, put her hand on her shoulder, and shook her.

'Hey! Come on! I live with the other one!

Willy de Voss!' She grinned down at the bewildered figure.

Rose felt weak with relief. Her lips trembled in a smile, while the tears started again from her grimed cheeks. She could feel what was left of her strength and courage draining from her. It seemed that her nerves had been tightening for weeks, from the moment she had escaped from Strenshaugh, and embarked on the steamship for the long voyage out to Mombasa, and for the day- and night-long train journey, which had brought her here.

'You're done in, you poor thing! And all trussed and corseted, I'll warrant, like all you European ladies. Let's get you free of all these clothes.'

Rose stood obediently, too tired to argue, or even to feel embarrassed, as this stranger undressed her, tugging at the laces of the stays, stripping the garments from her aching body. She felt like a child again, especially when she compared her modest figure with the ripe beauty of the woman who had taken charge of her. Rosa wrapped her in a deliciously cool, fragrant dressing-gown of embroidered silk. At her call, an African girl entered, to carry out Rosa's commands. A while later, Rose was relaxing at last, in the soothing warmth of a tin bath, filled with fragrant suds, in the small, bare bathroom at the rear of the building. Rosa tended to her personally, rolling up the sleeves of her blouse and covering her skirt with a pinafore of sacking. She knelt, with a pitcher of fresh, tepid water, and helped to wash Rose's long, streaming black hair.

Rosa swiftly filled in Johnny's history of the past three years, since he had first arrived in Nairobi.

'I knew from the first.'

While Rose sat with knees drawn up in the small bathtub, Rosa took the long strands of dark hair and carefully rubbed them in the towel to dry them.

'I knew that he was in love with someone he had left behind. Then came news of your wedding. He got drunk for a day and a night. I could see then how he really felt.'

Rose gazed at her, her own love and longing clear in her eyes.

'I didn't write. I was afraid he might not — he wouldn't want to see me.' The bath and Rosa's warm friendship revived her more than the food and drink she ate a little later. When Willy came in, he gaped at her, then huffed and puffed with red-faced delight, his breath flavoured with the beer he had been supping at Storr's hotel.

'This is wonderful!' he exulted. 'We must

send a cable to Kisumu. They must get a message across the lake. Someone must find him. I'll go myself to bring him back!'

Tactfully, Rosa enquired about the circumstances which had brought Rose to Africa. The girl blushed, and as Rosa quickly tried to apologize for her own indiscretion, held up a detaining hand.

'No! It will be out soon enough, I should think, even here! I have left my husband. He proved — unfaithful, over many things. A liar — and a hypocrite!' In spite of her shyness, the dark eyes took on a defiant, proud expression, beneath which lurked a hint of mischievous pleasure at her own daring. It made her even more youthfully appealing to her two new friends.

'I'm a disgraced woman! I've run away! Deserted my husband! Left him to file for divorce, if he wishes! There's a scandal back home, with me running off to — to find Johnny. Everyone will sympathize with him. He will be seen as the aggrieved party, in spite of . . . all the things he has done to destroy the marriage.' The dark hair, unbound, still damp from its washing, hung in rich waves down her shoulders. 'And I don't care! I don't give a damn!' she concluded roundly, and giggled with Rosa, while Willy strove not to look shocked at her language.

When he reiterated the need to try to get in touch with Johnny and cursed the young fool for going so far astray, Rose took a deep breath.

'I'd like to go to him myself,' she said. 'I think it's only right — that I should go to him, wherever he is. That's how I'd like it to be.'

Willy began his shocked objection to such foolhardiness, only to be interrupted in mid-spate by Rosa.

'She can do it, my love! It's important. She can take the train to Kisumu, then the steamer across the lake, to Port Bell, or further south. You said Johnny will be somewhere near the Mara. We've got some good men who will look after her. Come on, Willy! Where is your romance? She has to do it, don't you see?'

He looked shocked, still.

'If anything happens — it's wild out there — '

'It's fate!' Rosa countered strongly. 'She's here, isn't she? It brought her here. It will reunite them. Have faith, you old Boer!' Her hands dug into his good left arm, urging him on, and at last he nodded. Rose gave a cry of delight, and kissed his red cheek, then hugged Rosa to her.

'Bless you both! Now it's up to him!'

She glanced round at the fringes of the dark water, where the tall grass formed a substantial screen. She wanted to make sure that none of the boys was lurking within sight. Her mouth twitched in a private little smile. As long as she couldn't see them, she told herself, it didn't really matter if they were peeking at her at her ablutions. As long as the loyal Juma was stationed handily with his gun, to protect her from any of the wild beasts that were liable to appear. It had happened on several occasions, though she had rapidly learned that the creatures of the bush were generally as eager to keep out of their way as they were to avoid them. Anyway, she was becoming quite wild and *shenzi* herself, she acknowledged. If anyone had told her months since that she would be trekking through some of the least tamed country on the surface of the earth, and sleeping by the side of six black men, with only a small canvas tent for privacy, and the nearest convenient thorn bush or anthill as a privy, she would have thought them quite mad.

She was wearing only her white lace bodice, and a plain white half-petticoat. She slipped off the bodice, covering her breasts with her folded arms in instinctive modesty as she stepped carefully into the warm, turgid water, feeling the sand ooze up between her toes. Gingerly, she lowered herself in the shallows, and sighed with bliss at the feel of the cool flow of water over her body. She moved her hands, splashed it over her torso, bent and wet her face, tasting its brackishness. The pocked surface of the narrow margin of sand, the sprinkling of dung, indicated how the inhabitants of this wilderness used the lake. But she had learned not to be fastidious in the two weeks of her adventure into this new territory. The first week of her *safari* had been taken up with the train-ride to Kisumu, a night spent in a quite reasonable hotel, before the day and night's journey across Lake Victoria on the steamer. One of the most truly unnerving experiences had occurred when she had been dozing under the awning on the deck of the small ship, and was suddenly wakened to a living nightmare. The air was dark, and she was choking, literally, in a cloud of insects — flies that were like thick smoke, clogging her eyes, her nose, her lips, covering every part of her skin. She had fled, choking and spitting, to her tiny cabin, which, though thickly infested, was a little clearer than on the open deck. Shivering, and still coughing, she had stripped off her few light clothes and rolled herself in the thin gauze of the mosquito netting, threshing on the mattress of her narrow bunk until they were finally clear of the dreaded lake flies.

She was still some days away from the end of her quest, for she knew Johnny was at a distance from the lake, on the plains around the River Mara, where the elephant he was hunting were abundant. Though why he should have chosen to bury himself so far from any civilization was incomprehensible to her. The whole country, the whole continent, was alive with wild animals. She had seen hundreds of them, from the very first day of the train-ride up from the coast at Mombasa, and each night in this strange land, as she lay by the fire with the native servants, wrapped in her blanket and fully clothed, or in her tent, the darkness was full of their roars and bellows and strange chirrups.

At times she had regretted her foolhardiness in rejecting Willy's sensible advice to wait for Johnny to turn up in Nairobi. But her biggest fear now was missing him altogether in this vast, untamed land, for she was longing for him, with every heartbeat and every fibre of her body — and her soul.

A twig snapped, there was a faint rustling which her newly sensitive ears detected. She stiffened, rose out of the water, to stand staring at the tall fronds. Naked, except for the garment which clung to her loins, she crossed her arms over her breasts.

'Juma!' she called out shrilly. 'Are you there? *Mzuri sana?* Everything all right?'

'*Mzuri, memsa'ab!*' came the reassuring reply.

She dipped her head close to the water, crouched again, and quickly washed her hair, then lay back, letting it float on the water to rinse away the soap. She waded on to the sandy strip, picked up her towel and began to rub vigorously at her hair. She screamed as a pair of strong arms clamped like iron bands round her waist, and lifted her high off her feet. A man, not an animal, was her attacker. She fought free of the towel, opened her mouth to scream again for Juma, and found herself staring, through the clinging strands of her wet hair, at Johnny's brown, beautiful, smiling face.

Before she could close her mouth, his lips descended, sealed themselves against hers, and her wet, bare flesh was plastered against the rough clothing as he crushed her to him in a dizzying rapture.

'A naked nymph!' he murmured, when their kiss ended. He still held her close to him. 'This must be my lucky day!'

'Where? How?' But her questions were cut

off, lost in the second kiss, as passionate and as lengthy as the first.

'I don't ever want to let you go again!' he breathed, and kept his tight hold of her as witness to his words.

She was crying, then blushing at the feel of her naked body laid against him, but she whispered, 'I don't ever *want* you to let me go!'

It was a long while before they did release each other. Still she blushed, as she bent and retrieved the short bodice, slipped it on and fastened the hooks over her breasts. The petticoat was still wrinkled, clinging to her form with its wetness. Her feet were caked with sand. She stared at him, held his hand as his arm slid around her bare waist.

'I don't know if I'm dreaming. How did you get here, Johnny? I wanted to come to you! To surprise you!'

Quickly he explained how Willy's responsible conscience had got the better of him. He had dispatched a cable via the railway network to the railhead, then on to the district commissioner's office at Hoima Bay. The message had been brought eventually to Johnny, who then set about locating the whereabouts of the young white memsa'ab who was braving the perils of the bush with only a few native bearers for company.

'You weren't difficult to find,' he told her. 'The whole countryside is talking about you, you wanton hussy!'

'I am!' She gazed at him, and he saw all the love, the vulnerability in her gaze, that made his heart ache for her. 'I left Ned. Just ran out on him. Told him I was coming to you — if you'd have me! Told him he could divorce me. That I didn't give a damn what people would say or think.' Despite her show of bravado, her voice quavered a little. 'And if he didn't divorce me, that I'd be your mistress. If you'd have me!' she repeated. Her eyes filled with tears.

'I love you, Rose. I always have. And I'm sorry for all the pain I've caused you. And for these three long, wasted years.'

They could scarcely bear not to be touching one another. In the evening, they walked back down to the lake, to the spot where they had met. She kept her eyes firmly on his as he undressed her, removing the few scraps of clothing she wore, then shed his own garments and drew her into him. He entered her slowly, moved slowly, and slowly they became one, and she wept with the new rapture of their union, and, at last, for an endless few minutes, she was lost in the thrill of a fulfilment she had been forced to believe hitherto could not exist.

Afterwards, clothed, they lay together in each other's arms, and watched the first stars show in the vast expanse of sky, while around them the varied night sounds of the bush rose in chorus.

'Hold me close. I'm not afraid with you.' She reached up, laid her hand softly along the line of his jaw. Her great, dark eyes filled suddenly with tears. 'I wanted you to be the first. The only one,' she whispered.

His finger crooked under her chin, lifting her mouth to his. His lips lay gently on hers.

'I am. And you're the first for me. Our first and only love. The one we've been waiting for. Always.'

THE END

We do hope that you have enjoyed reading this large print book.

Did you know that all of our titles are available for purchase?

We publish a wide range of high quality large print books including:
**Romances, Mysteries, Classics
General Fiction
Non Fiction and Westerns**

Special interest titles available in large print are:
**The Little Oxford Dictionary
Music Book
Song Book
Hymn Book
Service Book**

Also available from us courtesy of Oxford University Press:
**Young Readers' Dictionary
(large print edition)
Young Readers' Thesaurus
(large print edition)**

For further information or a free brochure, please contact us at:
**Ulverscroft Large Print Books Ltd.,
The Green, Bradgate Road, Anstey,
Leicester, LE7 7FU, England.
Tel:** (00 44) **0116 236 4325
Fax:** (00 44) **0116 234 0205**

ALL MANNER OF THINGS

C. W. Reed

Just before his departure for the desert campaign, newly commissioned John Wright marries his college sweetheart, Jenny. Their already fragile union, daily threatened by the London Blitz, is shaken by his long absence, leaving Jenny vulnerable as she enters the exciting world of Bletchley Park. John's brother, Teddy, becomes a POW after Dunkirk. His estranged but loyal wife, Marian, left at home with their little daughter, must also confront a lonely future. These enforced absences take their toll on both Jenny and Marian and their fidelity is cruelly tested. The boys' mother, May, widowed in the First World War, prays that tragedy will not rob her of those she loves for a second time.